The
MOTHER

Also by Jaime Raven

The Madam
The Alibi

The
MOTHER

JAIME RAVEN

avon.

AVON

A division of HarperCollins*Publishers*
1 London Bridge Street,
London SE1 9GF

www.harpercollins.co.uk

A Paperback Original 2017
2

First published in Great Britain by
HarperCollins*Publishers* 2017

A catalogue record for this book is
available from the British Library

ISBN-13: 978-0-00-825346-2

Set in Minion by Palimpsest Book Production Limited, Falkirk, Stirlingshire
Printed and bound by CPI Group (UK) Ltd, Croydon CR0 4YY

MIX
Paper from
responsible sources
FSC C007454

This one is dedicated to my agent Leslie Gardner, whose help and guidance is very much appreciated

1

Sarah

I was attending the morning briefing when I received the text message that was going to bring my world crashing down.

I heard the ping as it arrived on my phone, but I decided it would be impolite to check it straight away because DCI Dave Brennan was in full flight. He wanted us to know that there was a lot going on and that we should prepare ourselves for a busy week ahead.

'As you all know there was a near-fatal stabbing last night in Peckham,' he said. 'And in the early hours of this morning a warehouse was turned over in Camberwell. A security guard was badly beaten and goods worth a hundred grand were stolen. All this on top of a caseload that already has us stretched to the limit.'

It wasn't such an unusual start to a Monday morning, certainly not in this part of South London, which had been a crime hotspot long before I joined the CID team. That was four years ago, and in that time I'd come to realise that the job was never going to get any easier.

London's population was growing at an alarming rate and so were the number of criminal gangs. Yet at the same time cutbacks in manpower and resources were continuing to put pressure on the force. We were trying to control things from a position of weakness, and reckless politicians were content to let it happen.

'I've managed to beef up the overtime budget,' Brennan said. 'That means you should all expect to work longer hours, at least until we get a handle on things. And it goes without saying that I'll be turning down any requests for time off. So don't even think about booking any last-minute holidays.'

Chance would be a fine thing, I thought. I hadn't had a holiday since before Molly was born, when Adam and I spent a week in Spain. The aim of that sojourn had been to try to get our marriage back on track. But it had been a total disaster. We ended up screaming at each other during a drinking session on our hotel balcony and that was when he confessed to an affair and I told him that I wanted a divorce. A month later I discovered I was pregnant with his child and six months later we were both single again.

'I want you to assist on the stabbing, DI Mason,' Brennan said, looking at me with those bulbous eyes of his. 'The victim's undergone surgery on a punctured lung at King's College Hospital. He should be about ready to make a statement, so let's find out what he remembers.'

'I'll get right on it, guv,' I said.

Brennan was a tall, gruff Irishman who commanded the loyalty and respect of his team. He was in his mid-fifties, and I was one of his biggest fans, partly because he'd seen fit to promote me to detective inspector on my return from maternity leave. It was something I'd welcomed at the time, but the extra work and responsibility often conflicted with my role as a single mother.

2

More than once I'd considered switching to a desk job with regular hours and less stress. But I hadn't, mainly because I loved being a front-line copper despite the drawbacks.

'There's something else you all need to be aware of,' Brennan was saying. 'It's about my forthcoming retirement. For reasons I won't go into, I've had to bring it forward. So now I'll be bowing out at the end of September. That's four months from now.'

This didn't come as a great surprise to anyone. We all knew that Brennan's wife was suffering from early onset dementia and that she needed him to look after her. Nevertheless, it prompted a strong reaction.

'We'll miss you, boss,' one detective said.

'Hope we'll all get invites to the leaving bash,' said another.

Everyone else either rushed towards the front of the room to shake Brennan's hand or made a sound to express their disappointment.

I decided to hold back so that I could take the opportunity to see who had sent me a text message, just in case it was important. There were two messages in the inbox. The first had come in half an hour ago and I hadn't noticed. It was nothing important, just notification of my latest electricity bill.

But the second message made me frown. It was from a private number and there was a photograph attached. The photograph showed my Molly sitting on a sofa with a cuddly toy on her lap that I hadn't seen before.

The text below it was short and sweet and it caused my stomach to twist in an anxious knot.

Thought you might like to see your daughter settling into her new home.

*   *   *

The message totally threw me.

As usual, my fifteen-month-old daughter was supposed to be spending the day with her grandparents. But the picture had not been taken at their house in Streatham.

The white leather sofa that Molly was sitting on was unfamiliar to me. And so too was the room she was in. I was absolutely certain that I'd never set foot in it before. I didn't recognise the red cushions either side of Molly, or the framed print on the wall behind her. It looked like a sailboat on water.

I used my finger and thumb to expand the image and saw what appeared to be a startled look on Molly's face. She was staring directly into the camera, her large brown eyes wide as saucers.

I didn't doubt that the picture had been taken this morning. She was wearing the same pale green dress she'd had on when I'd dropped her off at my parents' house before coming to the office. And her shiny fair hair was just as it had been then, swept away from her face and held in place at the back with a grip, the fringe hanging down across her forehead.

Was this someone's idea of a joke? I wondered. And if so who? It certainly wouldn't be my parents, and I couldn't think of anyone else who'd think it was funny.

Panic churned in my belly as I looked again at the photograph and thought back to what Mum had said about her plans for the day. She was going to take Molly to the park this morning because the weather was set to be warm and sunny. My father was spending a few hours at his allotment and they were going to meet up later and have lunch together in a pub garden.

I looked at my watch. It was just after ten-fifteen, about the time I would have expected Molly to be enjoying herself on the park swings and slide and roundabout. But the photo suggested she was somewhere else.

4

Thought you might like to see your daughter settling into her new home.

What the hell did that mean? Molly's home was in Dulwich where she lived with me. So why had she been photographed sitting in what appeared to be a stranger's house?

I tapped out a short reply to the message – *Who are you?* – but three seconds after I sent it I got a message back: *The recipient you're sending to has chosen not to receive messages.*

I needed to halt the rising sense of alarm so I speed-dialled my mother's mobile number. But after a couple of rings it went to voicemail. I then rang my parents' landline. My heart leapt when no one answered.

I would have called my father next but he didn't have a phone of his own. He'd always insisted that he didn't need one.

The ball of anxiety grew in my chest as my eyes were drawn back to the photograph. I wanted desperately to believe that it was nothing more than a misguided prank and that Molly was perfectly safe. But surely if there was an innocent explanation then my mother would have answered the phone. Did that mean she was in trouble? Was Molly still with her?

'Oh, Jesus.'

The words tumbled out of my mouth and fear flooded through me like acid. I had to find out what was going on and I needed to be reassured that Molly was OK.

I took a moment to get my thoughts together, then dashed towards the front of the room to where my boss stood surrounded by a small bunch of detectives. I forced my way between them and seized Brennan's attention by addressing him in a voice that was charged with emotion.

'You'll have to get someone else to visit the hospital,' I said. 'I need to leave right away.'

5

He arched his brow at me. 'Bloody hell, Sarah. Whatever's happened? You look like you've seen a ghost.'

I took a deep, faltering breath. 'It's my daughter. I have to find out if she's all right.'

'Well I'm sure she's fine,' he said with a hesitant smile. 'Why wouldn't she be?'

I held my phone up in front of his face.

'Because someone just sent this photo to me,' I said. 'I've got a really bad feeling about it.'

2

Sarah

Brennan took the phone from me and squinted at the photo. Then as my fellow detectives fell silent he read the text message out loud.

'I have no idea who sent it,' I said. 'It's from a blocked number. And I don't recognise the room Molly's in.'

Brennan lifted his eyes and pursed his lips. 'You usually leave her with your parents, don't you?'

I nodded. 'That's why this is so weird. I dropped her off earlier and Mum was going to take her to the park.'

'And have you tried calling your mother?'

'Of course, but there's no answer on her mobile or on my parents' home phone.'

I explained that my father didn't have a mobile and that nothing like this had ever happened before.

'Well you shouldn't jump to conclusions,' Brennan said. 'We'll help you get to the bottom of it. First thing to do is run a check on your phone to see if we can unblock the number of the caller.'

'That'll take time,' I said shakily. 'I can't hang around. I have to go to the park and then to Mum and Dad's.'

'I quite understand, Sarah. In fact, I'll come with you while your colleagues make inquiries.'

Brennan assigned two of the other detectives to the task and told another to go to the hospital to interview the stab victim in my place. Then he got me to forward the message and the photo to the office manager's phone so that he could arrange for it to be checked out.

'Try not to worry,' he said, turning back to me. 'I'm guessing this is some unfortunate misunderstanding or someone's pathetic attempt at humour.'

The trouble was he didn't sound convinced of that, and the knowing looks he gave the others sent a wave of adrenaline crashing through my bloodstream.

Brennan drove and I sat in the passenger seat of the pool car. The park was only a few miles from the police station in Wandsworth, and that was going to be our first stop.

It was within walking distance of my parents' house and where my mother usually took Molly. If they weren't there, then we'd go straight to the house.

I prayed silently to myself that I was overreacting, but it was impossible not to dwell on the worst-case scenario – that my daughter had been abducted.

It was every parent's nightmare, and I'd had first-hand experience of the devastating consequences of such an event. During my time on the force I'd investigated seven cases where children had been kidnapped by strangers. Only four of them had been found safe and well. Two were still missing, and one six-year-old girl had been brutally raped and murdered.

But in none of those cases had the abductor sent a photograph of the child to the mother. And I hadn't heard of it happening before. That at least gave me reason to believe that this might not be a straightforward snatch; that perhaps it was indeed some pathetic prank.

'Try calling your mother again,' Brennan said, as he steered the car along side streets in order to avoid the worst of the South London traffic.

I tried but it rang out and went to voicemail. I'd already left a message for her to call me and it wasn't like my mother not to respond asap. I left another just the same and this time I told her I was desperately worried.

'Please get back to me straight away, Mum. It's urgent. I need to know that Molly is OK.'

I rang my parents' landline again but still there was no answer.

My heart was in my throat as I hung up. I gulped down a breath and squeezed my eyes shut.

Oh God, please don't let my worst fear be realised.

I opened my eyes and looked again at the photograph of Molly on the sofa. My beautiful little girl clutching a beige teddy bear that I didn't recognise. I wanted to believe that my parents had bought it for her, but I doubted it. Molly had plenty of cuddly animals both at home and at her grandparents', and I had always discouraged them from spoiling her with too many toys.

So who had got it for her? And who had sent me a picture of my daughter claiming she was settling into her *new home*? What the fuck did it mean?

'Are you sure you have no idea where the photo was taken?' Brennan asked me.

'I'm positive,' I said.

9

'Then it could be the home of someone your mother knows. Maybe she went there instead of to the park.'

'I've thought about that,' I said. 'But it doesn't explain the creepy message or why the photo was sent.'

'What about your ex-husband? Could he have taken Molly?'

My body stiffened. I hadn't given any thought to Adam, but that was partly because I knew he wouldn't dream of scaring me like this. Sure, we were divorced, but we made every effort to get along for Molly's sake. He saw her every week as part of the custody arrangement, and as a copper himself he would know better than to do something that would cause such alarm.

I said as much to Brennan and added that I'd been to Adam's flat in Mitcham and he did not have a white leather sofa like the one in the photo.

'Perhaps you should call him anyway,' Brennan said. 'I'm sure he'd want to know what's happening.'

'I will, but not yet,' I said. 'I don't want to worry him unnecessarily if Molly's at the park or at home with Mum.'

It was a big *if* and with every passing second I was becoming more worried.

Why hadn't my mother called me back? Why hadn't I received another message from whoever had sent the first one?

What was I going to do if we couldn't find Molly?

We reached the park fifteen minutes after leaving the station. It wasn't much more than a small patch of greenery surrounded by flats and houses.

There was a children's playground in the centre and as we pulled into the kerb I could see that it was busy. But then it usually was on a day like today with the sun beating down and not a cloud in the sky.

I jumped out of the car even before Brennan had switched off the engine. As I ran across the grass I stared intently at the playground in the hope of spotting my grey-haired mother.

But as I drew close it became evident that she wasn't there, and I felt the panic swell up inside me.

I counted eight mums, two dads and about fifteen pre-school kids. But my own mother and daughter were not among them.

I walked around the playground and looked beyond it towards the surrounding roads, but there was no sign of them.

When Brennan caught up with me he was out of breath and struggled to speak.

'Don't assume the worst,' he told me. 'Maybe they've been here but are now on their way back to your parents' place.'

'We've got to go there,' I said.

'Is it far from here?'

I pointed. 'About half a mile in that direction.'

'Come on then.'

As we hurried back across the field towards the car, Brennan took out his phone and made a call that I assumed was to the station. But I couldn't hear what he was saying because my head was filled with the sound of my own heart banging against my chest.

I couldn't believe that this was happening. The day had started off so well. Molly, bless her, had been on her best behaviour this morning, as excited as ever at the prospect of spending time with her grandparents.

I felt tears well up in my eyes as I thought back to when I'd dropped her off. My dad had picked her up in his arms and got her to wave goodbye and blow me a kiss.

She was so sweet, the sweetest little girl. The centre of my world. I couldn't bear the thought that she might be in danger. Or that

11

I might never see her again. The prospect filled me with a cold, hard dread that settled in my stomach like a heavy rock.

'You need to stay calm, Sarah,' Brennan said, when we were back in the car.

'That's easy for you to say, guv,' I replied. 'I just don't understand what's going on. The photo, the message, the fact that my mother won't answer her phone.'

He left it a beat and said, 'I've just called the office and told them to circulate the photo and alert uniform. Just to be on the safe side.'

It should have reassured me but it didn't. Instead his words brought a sob to the surface and I had to force myself not to burst out crying.

'Take this,' Brennan said, handing me a handkerchief he produced from the inside pocket of his suit jacket.

I lowered the visor and looked at myself in the mirror. The face that stared back at me was pale and gaunt. I suddenly looked much older than my 32 years.

Tears sparkled in my eyes and my short brown hair was dishevelled from where I'd been raking my hands through it.

I dabbed at my eyes with the hanky and then used it to blow my nose.

'You need to tell me where to go,' Brennan said.

I cleared my throat and told him to take a left at the next junction and then the first right after that. He didn't respond, just concentrated on the road ahead.

'Thank you for coming here with me,' I said. 'I'm grateful.'

'You don't need to be,' he said. 'I couldn't let you do this by yourself. I can imagine what you must be going through.'

Brennan, who had a grandson a similar age, had met Molly a couple of times when I'd taken her into the station. He had always been understanding of the problems faced by single mothers in the department and I'd come to view him almost as a father figure as well as my boss.

Right now I was so glad he was with me. I knew he would do whatever he could to help me find my daughter.

'It's the house up there on the left behind the privet hedge,' I said.

My childhood home was a semi-detached pre-war property in a quiet, tree-lined street. My father's ageing Mondeo wasn't parked out front so I took that to mean that he was still at his allotment.

'Have you got a key?' Brennan asked.

I nodded and extracted my keys from my shoulder bag.

A short paved pathway led up to the front door and as I approached it my emotions were spinning. I didn't bother to ring the bell, and my hand shook as I fumbled to insert the key in the lock.

As soon as the door was open I called out and stepped inside. But my heart sank when there was no response.

'They might be in the back garden,' Brennan said as he followed me in.

I hurried along the hallway and threw open the door to the kitchen, hoping to see or hear Molly.

Instead I was confronted by a sight that caused my stomach to give a sickening lurch.

3

Sarah

My mother was tied to one of the kitchen chairs and a red silk scarf had been wrapped around her face to gag her.

Her chin was resting on her chest and she appeared to be unconscious. But when I let out a muffled scream her head jolted up and she looked at me through eyes that struggled to focus.

For a moment I just stood there in shock, unable to move, unable to take in what I was seeing. All my police instincts, training and experience deserted me. It was left to Brennan to rush forward and remove the scarf from around my mother's head.

'I recognise that smell,' he said as he put the scarf against his nose and sniffed it. 'It's chloroform.'

My mother gasped and spluttered and then went into a coughing fit.

'You're going to be OK, Mrs Mason,' Brennan said as he started to untie her hands that were secured behind her back with a length of plastic cable. 'We've got you now. You're safe.'

I came out of my trance-like state and ran forward to my mother. She was shaking and dribbling and having great difficulty breathing properly. But at least she was alive and looked as though she hadn't been physically harmed.

'Where's Molly, Mum?' I said as calmly as I could. 'Where is my baby?'

She tried to speak but the words got stuck in her throat.

I rested a hand on her shoulder, crouched down so that we were face to face.

'Mum, please. Where's Molly?'

Her eyes grew wide and confusion pulled at her features. Then she shook her head and her lips trembled.

'I . . . d-don't know,' she managed. 'She was in the high chair when the doorbell rang.'

That was when I noticed the high chair for the first time, on the other side of the room next to the back door that stood open. There was a plastic bowl on the tray, along with Molly's familiar spill-proof beaker.

'Did you go and answer the door, Mrs Mason?' Brennan asked her. 'Is that what you did?'

I turned back to my mother. She nodded and closed her eyes, and I could tell she was trying to cast her mind back to what had happened.

'A man,' she said, her tone frantic. 'He was wearing a hood, like a balaclava. He forced himself in and grabbed me. Then he put something over my face.'

My mother lost it then and started to cry, great heaving sobs that racked her frail body.

She was almost seventy, and seeing her like this, I felt the urge to comfort her, but a more powerful impulse seized me and I jumped up suddenly and went in search of Molly, praying that she was still here and hadn't been taken away.

I ran out into the garden first, but it was empty except for the

15

cat from next door that was lying on the lawn like it didn't have a care in the world.

Then I dashed back into the house and through the kitchen, passing Brennan who was standing next to my mother while talking anxiously into his phone.

I checked the living room and ground floor toilet, then hurried upstairs in the hope of finding my daughter in one of the three bedrooms. I called out her name, told her that Mummy had come to get her. But there was a resounding silence. She wasn't there. She was gone.

A new wave of terror roared through my body as I ran back downstairs. Now it was confirmed. My daughter had been abducted and I had no idea by whom. The nightmare that had loomed over me since I opened up the photograph on my phone had turned into a horrific reality.

The temptation to collapse in a tearful heap was almost over-whelming, but I told myself that I had to hold it together. For my sake and for Molly's.

My mother was still on the chair in the kitchen and Brennan was trying to coax more information out of her. When she saw me she reached for my hand and said, 'There was nothing I could do. It happened so – so quickly.'

'Who could it have been, Mum?' I said. 'Do you have any idea?'

She shook her head. 'I didn't see his face. He knocked me out and when I woke up I was tied to this chair.'

I reached out and put an arm around her shoulders.

'I'm so sorry, Sarah,' she sobbed. 'I really couldn't . . .'

'It's not your fault, Mum,' I said, choking back tears. 'We'll get her back. I promise.'

I heard a siren and the sound of it caused my heart to flip.

'Your father needs to be told, Sarah,' my mother said. 'He's still at the allotment. He thinks we'll be meeting him at the pub.'

'I'll see to it, Mum,' I said. 'Don't worry.'

I straightened up and looked at Brennan who told me that he had raised the alarm and that teams of officers were about to descend on the area.

'I've also summoned an ambulance,' he said. 'The paramedics will take care of your mother.'

His words registered, but only just, and they failed to provide any comfort. How could they? My precious daughter had been kidnapped. My mind was still reeling and I felt weighted down by a crushing despair.

I was on the verge of losing control so I lowered myself onto one of chairs around the kitchen table. There I sat, my head spinning, my stomach churning, as Brennan gently prised more information out of my mother.

She revealed that the man had rung the bell at just before nine – an hour or so after I had dropped Molly off. My father had just left the house to go to his allotment and she was giving Molly her breakfast before taking her to the park.

She remembered very little about her attacker. His face had been covered and he'd been wearing what she thought was a dark T-shirt and jeans.

'He was average height but strong,' she said. 'I tried to struggle free when he attacked me but I couldn't.'

She started crying again and this time it set me off. I broke down in a flood of tears and heard myself calling Molly's name.

I was only vaguely aware of the commotion that suddenly ensued, and of being led out of the kitchen and along the hallway.

Raised voices, more people entering the house, some of them in uniform. Molly's face loomed large in my mind's eye, obscuring

17

much of what was going on around me. I wondered if I would ever hold her in my arms again. It was a sickening, painful thought and one that I never thought I would have to experience.

I'd witnessed the suffering of parents who had lost children, seen the agony in their eyes. But as a copper I had always been one step removed, professionally detached and oblivious to the real extent of their plight.

Now I had a different perspective. I was in that horrendous position myself. The grieving, desperate mother wondering why fate had delivered such a crushing blow.

'We're taking you next door,' Brennan was saying as we stepped outside, to be greeted by the flashing blue light on top of a police patrol car. 'This house is now a crime scene and the forensics team needs to get to work. Mrs Lloyd, the neighbour to the right, has kindly agreed to make some tea for you and your mother.'

'I don't want tea,' I wailed. 'I want Molly.'

'I'll do whatever it takes to find her, Sarah,' Brennan said. 'We all will. But look, I really think it's time that Molly's father was informed about what's happened. Do you want to call him or shall I?'

The prospect of breaking the news to Adam that his daughter had been abducted filled me with dread. I knew I couldn't do it, that as soon as I heard his voice I would fall apart.

'You ring him,' I said. 'Tell him to get here as soon as he can.'

4

Adam

The man in the dock at the Old Bailey looked as though he hadn't got a care in the world. Even when the judge instructed him to stand up and turn to the jury he didn't appear to be in the least bit anxious. He was facing the prospect of a long stretch behind bars, but from his expression you would never have guessed it.

'The bastard is cocksure that he's about to be acquitted,' Detective Inspector Adam Boyd whispered to his colleague who was sitting beside him in the courtroom. 'And I have a horrible feeling he could be right.'

The case against Victor Rosetti – a Romanian national – had been undermined during the past couple of days. One of the prosecution witnesses had disappeared before taking the stand, and the defence had managed to refute some of the forensic evidence, claiming it had been contaminated.

For the National Crime Agency, which was set up to fight organised crime in the UK, it would be a bitter blow if Rosetti did walk. As one of London's nastiest villains and drugs traffickers, the man deserved to be locked behind bars. But securing a conviction was always going to be a challenge for Adam and his team.

Rosetti had an army of foot soldiers working for him, along with some powerful contacts. Several senior police officers were also believed to be on his payroll.

Adam had managed to build a strong case against him before bringing a charge that related to the importation and distribution of cocaine. But Rosetti's defence had dismissed much of the evidence as circumstantial and had accused the police of 'fitting up' their client.

Things had gone from bad to worse two days ago when the prosecution's key witness – one of Rosetti's own drug couriers – slipped out of the safe house he was staying in. All attempts to trace him had failed, and Adam thought it likely that Rosetti's people had 'encouraged' him to vanish by threatening his family.

The jury foreman was now being asked if a verdict had been reached. The foreman said it had and passed a slip of paper to the clerk.

Adam stared with ill-disguised contempt at the man who was known as 'Rosetti the Cutter' because of his fondness for slicing up his enemies with a knife.

He was a short, heavyset man with a round face and shaved head. He'd been on the NCA's radar for a couple of years, but this was the closest they'd come to bringing him down and Adam wasn't sure they would get an opportunity like this again.

As the judge prepared to ask the jury foreman to announce the verdict, Adam felt his mobile phone vibrate with an incoming message. He ignored it, deciding that whatever it was it could wait. Right at this moment the only thing that mattered was seeing if this Romanian scumbag got what he deserved.

Adam felt his insides contract as he switched his gaze from Rosetti to the jury foreman, a thin-faced man with a scruffy beard.

'So do you find the defendant guilty or not guilty?' the judge asked him.

Adam bit his bottom lip and held his breath. The courtroom fell silent. The jury foreman spoke without hesitation.

'Not guilty, your honour,' he said.

Rosetti's reaction to the verdict was to grin broadly and punch the air with his fist.

It made Adam want to throw up. Although he'd seen this coming it was still a sickening blow.

He had to resist the urge to leap to his feet and berate the jury for being so stupid and to ask who among them had been nobbled. Instead he just sat there, gritting his teeth so hard his jaw ached.

Shouts of support came from the public gallery as Rosetti was led out of the dock.

'What a bloody disaster,' Adam said to himself, loud enough for those around him to hear.

He didn't move for several minutes, waiting for the courtroom to empty. He felt wrung out, the emotions thick in his throat.

At length, he threw out a long sigh and got to his feet. He needed some fresh air and a cigarette. And after that a stiff drink, or two, at the nearest boozer.

Outside, a few newspaper reporters and a TV camera crew had gathered on the street. But it could hardly have been described as a media frenzy. The case hadn't been as high-profile as some of the others that had been taking place at the same time. Victor Rosetti wasn't exactly a household name, and drugs trials had become so commonplace that they failed to attract much attention these days.

The Romanian stood on the pavement, flanked by two burly minders, as he answered the reporters' questions.

Adam's boss, DCI Mike Dunlop, stood to one side preparing to make a statement on behalf of the NCA, in which he would no doubt express profound disappointment.

Adam slipped away from Dunlop and the rest of the police team and crossed the road where he sparked up a fag and tried to suppress the rage that was bubbling up inside him.

He regarded what had just happened as a travesty of justice, and it was going to take him a while to get over it. The thought that Rosetti would now go away and continue to ply his illicit trade made his blood boil.

He watched as the bastard finished answering questions. Then a black Mercedes pulled up to the kerb and he climbed in with his minders. The reporters immediately turned their attention to Dunlop. The Mercedes then pulled away, but instead of driving straight off, it shot across the road and parked next to where Adam was standing.

The rear window was lowered and Rosetti's face appeared.

'Cheer up, Boyd,' he said. 'You win some, you lose some.'

Adam felt the bile rise in his throat. 'We may have lost the battle, scumbag,' he said. 'But not the war. It won't be long before I collar you for something you won't be able to wriggle out of.'

'Don't waste taxpayers' money,' Rosetti said. 'It will never happen. Besides, I should be the least of your worries.'

'What's that supposed to mean?'

Rosetti grinned, showing a set of yellow teeth. 'You'll find out soon enough – word is, you're in for a nasty surprise.'

Adam took a step forward, but Rosetti tapped the driver's shoulder and the Mercedes drove off, tyres squealing.

Adam stared after it, cursing under his breath. It wasn't the veiled threat that infuriated him – he'd received so many over the years that he no longer took them seriously. No, it was the fact that he knew that getting Rosetti into the dock again was going to be hellishly difficult, if not impossible.

He dropped what remained of his cigarette and ground it into the pavement with the heel of his shoe. Then just as he was about to cross back over the road he felt his phone vibrate again with another message.

This time he whipped it out of his pocket and saw that both messages had come from DCI Dave Brennan, who was asking him to call as a matter of urgency. Brennan was his ex-wife's boss and it was a long time since he'd heard from the guy.

Adam arched his brow and called the number. He had no idea, of course, that the bad day he was having was about to turn into his worst nightmare.

5

Sarah

I was in Mrs Loyd's back garden puffing on a cigarette while praying that my daughter hadn't been lost to me forever. But it was impossible to keep the negative thoughts at bay. They taunted me, each one a loud, desperate scream inside my head.

Two hours had passed since Brennan and I had arrived at my parents' house and a lot had happened in that time. My mother had been taken to hospital to be checked over, a police car had been dispatched to pick my father up from his allotment and take him there too, and I'd been sick twice – once on the kitchen floor and once in her downstairs toilet. Luckily I'd known my mother's neighbour Mrs Loyd for years and she told me not to worry, that she would clean it up.

I was still in a state of raw shock, only half aware of what was going on around me.

A PC was with me in the garden. Her name was Penny and we knew each other fairly well. She kept telling me that everything would be all right and I would soon be reunited with Molly. But, of course, she couldn't possibly know that and was just saying it to make me feel better.

But words alone were not going to relieve the emotional turmoil that was raging inside me. I needed to find my baby, to see her smile, hear her laugh, hold her in my arms.

I was clutching my mobile phone in my free hand, willing it to ring, for the kidnapper to make contact. If he called to demand a ransom then I'd willingly pay it, no matter how much it was. I'd move heaven and earth to get Molly back, sell my flat if need be, borrow the rest. That wouldn't be a problem. And I was sure to get all the help I needed from Adam and my parents.

The sun was beating down as I paced up and down the garden, Penny watching from the patio with her arms folded across her chest.

For some reason that made me angry. Why didn't she appear upset? Why was her face so expressionless? Didn't she realise how bad this was and how hard it was for me to keep from screaming?

But then it hit me. She was just being professional, doing her job. In the same way I'd done mine for years. Only this time the tables had turned on me and I was the victim, along with Molly and my mother. It was a new and terrifying experience.

Next door in my parents' garden several uniformed officers were carrying out a search. They were checking to see if there was any evidence to suggest that the kidnapper had taken Molly out the back way.

There was a small patch of woodland on the other side of the fence at the bottom of the garden. Beyond that was a road that wasn't overlooked by houses or flats. Brennan had already raised the possibility that the kidnapper had parked a car or van out there. He'd also told me in the last half hour that none of the neighbours had seen or heard anything.

Mrs Lloyd had been in her bathroom when the kidnapping took place and hadn't become aware of what had happened until the police called on her.

I wanted to do something, to join the search, put my police skills to good use, but right now I was in no fit state to be of any use. My body was numb, my mind in utter disarray, and I felt smothered by a dark blanket of despair.

When Brennan suddenly stepped out onto the patio, my stomach leapt. I assumed straight away that it was bad news.

'Don't panic,' he said quickly. 'There's been no change. I've come to tell you that Molly's father has arrived. If you pop back in I can update you both at the same time.'

My legs threatened to collapse under me as I walked towards the house, and I could feel a fresh batch of tears building behind my eyes.

When I entered the kitchen and saw Adam standing there next to Brennan, I totally lost control and broke down. Adam rushed over and put an arm around me, and I sobbed into his shoulder. We were used to seeing each other during his frequent visits to the flat to pick Molly up, but this was the first time we'd had physical contact since the divorce.

He spoke in a soothing voice, but I couldn't hear what he was saying. I was just glad he was there and the scent of him filled every intake of breath.

When I eventually stopped crying, Brennan handed me a tissue and I used it to dry my eyes. Then I stepped back out of Adam's embrace and looked up at him.

At six feet he was a good four inches taller than me and was wearing a dark suit and white open-neck shirt. His familiar face was sharp and angular, with high cheekbones and a thin nose. But his expression was totally unfamiliar, a mixture of fear and

26

incredulity. Sweat had gathered in the creases of his brow and his lips were drawn into a tight line.

'I've been told what's happened, Sarah,' he said, his voice barely above a whisper. 'I can't believe it. Why would anyone take Molly, for God's sake?'

I had a sudden, violent urge to vomit again. Brennan must have sensed it because he quickly pulled over a chair and told me to sit down.

Adam came and stood in front of me, placing a hand on my shoulder. I could feel the tension in his fingers.

He held out his other hand and said, 'Can I see the photo?'

Before I gave the phone to him I opened up the message.

'You should check that first,' I said.

He clamped his top lip between his teeth as he read the text.

'This is fucking insane,' he said. 'What kind of lunatic would pull a stunt like this?'

He took a shivering breath and exhaled, then tapped on the photo.

I watched the muscles in his neck tighten as he stared at it, his eyes narrowing to slits.

'Do you by any chance recognise that room?' Brennan asked him.

Adam's eyebrows knitted together, and for just a moment hope surged within me.

Please say yes, I wanted to cry out. *Please tell us you know who lives there and where it is.*

But after an agonising wait he shook his head and my insides shrivelled up.

'I've never seen it before,' he said. 'I'm absolutely sure of it.'

He continued to stare at the photo and I saw his eyes start to glisten with tears.

'The bloke who did this obviously knew that Molly would be with her grandmother,' Brennan said. 'It's likely he was watching the house and waiting for your father to leave before striking. That suggests he knew that you were all locked into a routine. And it also suggests that you might know him – or them – since it's quite possible he wasn't acting alone.'

It was something that hadn't occurred to me because my head was all over the place. But now the thought that Molly had fallen prey to more than one man sent my pulse racing.

'Can you think of anyone you know who'd be capable of this, Sarah?' Brennan said. 'Or someone you've seen around who was perhaps acting suspiciously?'

I narrowed my eyes, tried to focus, but it was hopeless.

'I can't,' I said.

'Well keep thinking,' Brennan said. 'Something might come to you.'

No one spoke for at least twenty seconds, and the silence threatened to become deafening. Finally Brennan said, 'You both need to know that we've had no success tracing the message. It must have come from an unregistered phone that's now switched off.'

Adam turned to face him. 'What time was Molly taken?'

'Well according to Mrs Mason the guy arrived here at just before nine.'

'And this message was received about an hour later?'

'Just over. We're checking all CCTV and road cameras within a half-mile radius. Unfortunately there aren't any in this street or in any of those around it.'

'What about the neighbours? Someone must have seen something.'

Brennan shrugged. 'We're still going door-to-door, but none

of those we've spoken to so far saw a man with a child around the time it happened.'

Adam twisted his lower jaw, considering. Unlike me he was still able to think like a police officer, despite the shock to his system. That was impressive. *My* brain was far too splintered, and I was struggling to focus on anything other than Molly's startled expression in the photograph.

'What about Sarah's mum?' Adam said. 'Has she been able to give you anything useful?'

'I'm afraid not,' Brennan said. 'I've sent officers to the hospital to get a formal statement from her, but the kidnapper was wearing a balaclava of some sort when she answered the door. The one thing she is certain of is that it was a man and not a woman. He grabbed her and put a scarf doused in chloroform against her face. She was unconscious in seconds then woke up tied to the chair and saw that Molly was gone.'

Brennan went on to say that a full-blown search of the immediate area was under way and that the photo of Molly on the sofa would shortly be sent to media outlets.

'Reporters and television crews will soon start to descend,' he said. 'It'll turn into a media circus outside for sure. So I suggest that you go home.'

'I don't want to go home,' I said. 'I have to be involved in this. I have to help find my daughter.'

'You know that's not going to be possible,' Brennan said. 'You've both got to step back and let us get on with it.'

This was something I was going to find hard to accept, but I knew we'd have no choice. We were the parents of the child who had been abducted. It meant we could not be involved in the investigation. We'd just have to sit it out and pray that our colleagues got a quick result. But it wasn't going to be easy.

'Come on, Sarah,' Adam said. 'I'll take you home. There's nothing we can do here anyway.'

Every nerve in my body was vibrating as I stood up. Despite my best efforts, my eyes began to fill with tears, but something in me resolved not to break down again.

'If there's a development, I'll be sure to let you know straight away,' Brennan told me.

He walked with us to the door and said that a number of officers, including someone from family liaison, would be sent to my place to be with us.

I knew the drill, of course. And I knew that the Met would commit a huge amount of resources to finding Molly, and to providing us with support. They would look after their own.

But what I didn't know was that the person who had taken my daughter would soon be making contact again.

And sending me another photograph.

6

Sarah

The drive to my duplex flat in Dulwich was akin to an out-of-body experience. It felt like I was looking down on someone who wasn't me.

Surely the real Sarah Mason was at work, investigating crimes, while her daughter was playing safely with her grandmother. It was inconceivable that she was actually in her ex-husband's car fearing that she would never see their daughter again.

The reality of the situation was almost too painful to face up to. But I knew I had to, and it was making me feel light-headed and dizzy.

I drew some comfort at least from Adam's presence. It meant the burden of despair could be shared between us.

My ex had many faults, but among his strong points was an ability to hold his nerve, even in the most perilous of situations. It was something I'd discovered when we'd worked together in Lewisham CID. He was always so sure of himself, always in control. It was what made him a better than average detective.

I turned to look at him and saw a face that was pinched and

solemn, and his hands were gripping the wheel so tight his knuckles were white.

'I never thought I could be this scared,' I said, my voice breaking. 'I can't stop wondering what's happened to our baby.'

'We have to stay positive,' Adam said. 'We've both dealt with other parents in this position and that's what we told them they should do.'

'But that was our job. This is our life. It's so different.'

'I know. But all the more reason to be strong and to keep telling ourselves that we'll get Molly back.'

'But I can't help thinking . . .'

My breath got caught in my throat, cutting off the words. I closed my eyes and tears pressed against the lids, burning as they fought to escape.

It was at this point that guilt reared its ugly head for the first time. I suddenly felt that I was to blame for what had happened because I hadn't been there for my daughter. Instead, I'd been content to palm her off on my mother so that I could continue pursuing a career as a police officer.

Now she was gone I had no choice but to accept some of the responsibility. I'd been selfish by opting to be a cop rather than a full-time mum.

And whatever happened in the coming hours and days, it was something for which I'd never be able to forgive myself.

My split-level flat was on the top floor of a four-storey, modern block off Lordship Lane, just a few hundred yards from Dulwich Park. It had two bedrooms, a balcony, and plenty of living space. The estate agent had described it as a '*luxury duplex penthouse*', which made it sound posher and grander than it actually was.

Adam and I had lived there during our three years of marriage, and it came to me as part of the divorce settlement. He kept the buy-to-let flat we owned in Mitcham, so in our case the division of assets had been fairly straightforward and uncontroversial.

Adam had been here numerous times during the last six months, after Molly had reached an age when he could take her on days out and for overnight stays at his place.

Despite the fact that he had fucked up our marriage I'd never made it difficult for him to have access to his daughter. He may have been a shit husband but he was a pretty good father. And that was why I knew that the pain he was feeling was just as acute as mine.

There were two police patrol cars already parked in front of my block when we arrived. That wasn't unexpected, but it did cause my stomach to fold in on itself. It was another unwelcome image, another gut-wrenching reminder that I wasn't about to wake up from a terrible nightmare.

Adam parked in one of the bays and we both climbed out. A woman in a grey trouser suit approached and I recognised her as Sergeant Rachel Palmer, from the family liaison team. She was tall, with dark, shoulder-length hair and a face that was conventionally pretty. She asked if it would be all right to come up to the flat and that other officers would stay downstairs to fend off the reporters and photographers when they started to turn up, as was inevitable.

I said it was fine and she introduced herself to Adam, who led the way into the block and up the stairs to the apartment.

Once inside, Palmer offered to make some tea while Adam and I went into the living room.

The first thing to seize my attention was the box of Molly's toys next to the sofa. The sight of it hit me for six and violent shudders racked my body.

'This should never have happened,' I said. 'It's my fault, all my fault.'

'Don't be silly,' Adam said. 'Of course it's not.'

'But if she had been with me she wouldn't have been taken.'

Adam guided me to the sofa. I was shaking convulsively and my heart felt like it was on fire.

'You need something to help you cope with the shock,' Adam said. 'Maybe I should call a doctor.'

I shook my head. 'It won't do any good. I just have to get a grip.' But I knew that was going to be a lot easier said than done.

He sat opposite me in the armchair, threw himself back against the cushion and stared up at the ceiling. His face was a portrait of anguish and disbelief, his mouth drawn in tight. The light had gone from his eyes and I could tell that he was also struggling to control his emotions.

'Thanks for bringing me home,' I said. 'Are you going to stay?'

He wiped his hands across his face and then looked at me.

'Of course I am,' he said. 'We might not be together anymore but that doesn't mean I'd let you go through this by yourself. Molly's our baby. We have to face this together.'

For a few minutes we sat in silence, tormented by our own dark thoughts. Then Palmer appeared and put a tray of teas on the coffee table.

She was about to speak when my phone pinged to indicate an incoming text message. It came as such a shock that I leapt to my feet and the phone fell from my lap onto the floor.

I felt a shiver of apprehension as I reached down for it. My hand shook as I opened up the message. I could feel Adam's and Palmer's eyes on me and the tension in the room was almost palpable.

The message appeared and I read it out loud.

34

It's me again. There are two attachments. The first is a photograph of your daughter having an afternoon nap in her new cot. The second is a document that you need to read.

Adam was suddenly at my side, holding my hand and turning the phone towards him so that he too could read the text.

'Check the photo first,' he said.

I opened it up and stared with a heavy heart at my baby lying fast asleep in a cot. She was on her back and wearing plain pink pyjamas that I hadn't seen before. Her eyes were closed and she was sucking on her thumb, just as she always did in her sleep.

I felt a wash of cold sweat and a sharp pain speared through my chest.

'At least she looks OK,' Adam said over my shoulder. 'She hasn't been harmed.'

That wasn't the point. She still wasn't safe. She was with a stranger and we had no idea what he planned to do with her. She would certainly be scared, and maybe he'd already hurt her in some way since the photo was taken.

'Check the document,' Adam said. 'Let's see what it says.'

But by now my hands were shaking so much I couldn't operate the phone, so Adam took it from me and opened up the document.

'Read it out,' Palmer told him. 'I need to hear this too.'

But Adam ignored her and read it to himself, and from the look on his face I knew it was bad.

I wasn't sure how long it took him to get through the message, or if he read it twice, but it felt like a lifetime. When he'd finished, the blood had retreated from his face and there was a look of feral rage in his eyes.

'What is it?' I said. 'What does it say?'

But he couldn't speak. He was shell-shocked. I went to grab the phone from him but Palmer beat me to it.

'Give it to me,' I demanded, my voice shrill, high-pitched. 'I want to see it.'

I moved towards her but Adam got between us.

'You need to prepare yourself, Sarah,' he said, holding my arms. 'This isn't good.'

I froze and felt a cold panic tighten in my chest.

We stared at each other and the haunted expression on his face was truly terrifying.

'However bad it is, I need to see it,' I said.

A moment later Palmer handed me the phone, and her face was stiff with shock. As soon as I started to read what the kidnapper had written I felt the darkness rise up inside me.

Sarah Mason . . . FYI I've taken your daughter as punishment for what you did to me. You'll never touch or speak to her again. But you will see her grow up. That will be my way of making sure that your suffering does not diminish over time. I'll send you photos and video clips on a regular basis. If I find out at any point that you've stopped looking at them, I'll take it out on Molly. She will also suffer if you or the police make any of the images public through newspapers or on the television. Remember – I don't love your child and I won't hesitate to hurt her – or even kill her – if you give me cause.

Yours . . . Molly's adoptive parent.

7

DCI Brennan

Detective Brennan arrived at Sarah's flat thirty minutes after she received the second text from the kidnapper. The message with the attached document was forwarded to him by her ex-husband, and having read it through twice he'd concluded that it was one of the most disturbing things he'd seen during three decades on the force, and that was going some.

Whoever was behind it had to be some kind of monster; a monster with a serious grudge against Sarah Mason.

Brennan wondered what she could possibly have done to make the perp want to inflict such a painful and bizarre form of 'punishment'. Did the perceived wrongdoing relate to an issue in her private life, or did it have something to do with her work as a police officer?

These were questions that would be central to the investigation, and it was crucial that they be answered quickly, so as not to waste time storming off in the wrong direction.

The life of an innocent child was at stake, and so too was the sanity of the child's mother.

As soon as Brennan saw Sarah sitting on her sofa he realised that the shock had numbed her senses. She was staring at the wall opposite, her eyes wide and unblinking, her body rigid as a fence post. Her cheeks were streaked with mascara and her hands were clasped together in an anxious knot in her lap. She didn't even turn towards him as he entered the living room, and he didn't want to imagine what terrible thoughts were rushing through her mind.

His heart went out to her, and for a few moments he was lost for words. Sarah Mason wasn't just another victim of crime. She was a valued member of his close-knit team and as such he felt protective towards her.

She was one of his brightest detectives, and she had never let him down, not even during those dark days after she split from her husband and discovered she was pregnant. She'd coped then with a quiet dignity, revealing an inner strength that had so impressed him he'd decided to promote her to detective inspector.

But getting divorced and giving birth were nothing compared with the terrifying ordeal that now confronted her.

Brennan had a flashback to the first time he saw her with Molly. She'd brought her into the office two months after she was born. Sarah had been so happy and proud and had clearly been ecstatic about being a mother.

The last time he saw Molly was at the staff children's party at Christmas. He'd gone along with his own grandson who was just a few months older than Molly. Seeing the children now in his mind's eye gave rise to a deep sense of foreboding that he tried desperately to keep out of his voice when he finally spoke.

'I want you to know that the whole of the Met is on high alert, Sarah,' he said. 'I spoke to the Commissioner himself on the way here. He wants us to throw everything we've got into finding your daughter.'

She turned her head then and looked up at him. Her face was drawn and pallid and her eyes brimmed with bright, shiny tears. The fear and despair was coming off her in waves.

Brennan was about to reach forward and put a reassuring hand on her shoulder, but her ex-husband beat him to it. Adam Boyd moved swiftly from where he'd been perched on the arm of the sofa and sat beside her. He put an arm around her and pulled her close to him.

Brennan knew from what Sarah had told him that Adam was close to his daughter and saw her regularly. So he'd be in just as much pain as she was, even though he was doing a better job of not showing it. He'd met his fellow police officer a couple of times and he seemed nice enough, but his concern right now was for Sarah.

'We're working closely with the phone company,' Brennan said. 'With any luck we'll soon have a fix on who's behind this.'

But even as he said it he knew it was wishful thinking. The person who had taken Molly would make sure to cover his tracks. He'd know how to send a text message and an email that couldn't be traced. It wasn't rocket science, after all. The information on how to do it was freely available on the internet.

'Is my mum OK?' Sarah asked.

Brennan lowered himself onto the chair opposite her and nodded.

'Your father's with her at the hospital,' he said. 'There's nothing physically wrong with her but she's understandably shaken up and feeling guilty. She'll soon be discharged. I gather her sister lives in Balham and that's apparently where they'll be spending the night because their house is now an active crime scene.'

'Does she know about this latest message?'

'Not yet.'

Sarah closed her eyes and pulled a face as though reacting to a sharp pain. Then she started rocking herself back and forth, her breathing hard and rapid.

At this point the family liaison officer, Sergeant Rachel Palmer, explained to Brennan that she had spoken to a police doctor who had agreed to come to the flat and prescribe medication for Sarah.

'No one is putting me to sleep,' Sarah snapped. 'I have to stay awake in case there's another message or even a phone call.'

'But you need something to help with the shock,' Adam said. 'And it doesn't mean you can't stay awake.'

Brennan watched Adam rub his fingers across his scalp. The man's lean, sharp-edged features were tight with tension, the cheeks marked with a hint of stubble.

Brennan had already spoken to Adam's boss at the National Crime Agency to apprise him of the situation. DCI Mike Dunlop had described him as a solid detective and had offered to help with the investigation. Brennan was hoping he wouldn't have to take him up on the offer, but if the last message was anything to go by they might need all the help they could get.

'Sounds to me like their poor little mite has been snatched by some sick, twisted perv,' Dunlop had said. 'The fact that she's the daughter of two coppers will make it big bloody news.'

Brennan knew that only too well. A media firestorm was brewing for sure. And dealing with it was going to be far from straightforward, given what the kidnapper had threatened.

She will also suffer if you or the police make any of the images public through newspapers or on the television.

That was going to complicate matters no end. But from the kidnapper's standpoint it was a clever move as it would limit the impact of any public appeal.

'The note makes it clear that we can't air those photographs

40

of Molly that he's sent you,' Brennan said now. 'You'll therefore need to provide me with a couple of recent pictures of her that we can give to the media.'

'But how do we know he won't mind those being aired?' Sarah asked.

'Because I'm certain he would have told us if he did. He knows we'll have to put out pictures of Molly, but if we air the ones he's taken himself then there's a risk that something in them will be recognised – such as the room she's in or the sofa she's on. He's being cautious.'

'It makes sense, I suppose,' Adam said. 'Well I've got plenty of pictures on my phone.'

Brennan pulled at the knot of his tie and swallowed the saliva that had gathered in his throat. Then he said, 'Have you given any thought to who could be responsible for this?'

The question was directed at Adam, but it was Sarah who answered it.

'To do that I'd have to think beyond what's happened,' she said. 'And right now, I can't. All I can think about is Molly and what might be happening to her.'

'I appreciate that,' Brennan said. 'I really do. But you've got to try to focus, Sarah. Can you think of anyone who has a grudge against you? Anyone who believes you should be punished?'

She passed a hand over her face and shook her head.

'I really c-can't,' she sobbed. 'I wish I could.'

'So you haven't fallen out with anyone recently?'

'No I haven't.'

'Then that leads me to believe that this is to do with the job. Perhaps someone you put away is out to get revenge.'

Sarah grimaced. 'But it means there'll be scores of suspects going back years.'

Brennan nodded. 'We're going to have to trawl through all the cases you've been involved with.'

'Jesus, guv. That'll take forever and most of those guys are probably still banged up.'

'Well we shouldn't assume that the kidnapper is working alone,' Brennan said. 'He could have an accomplice.'

Adam leant forward, a frown cutting into his forehead. 'I just can't believe that this is the work of a pissed-off perp,' he said. 'You know yourself that it's very rare for the people who are put away to seek to get their own back against an arresting officer. They know they'll be a prime suspect if they do. And what this bastard is threatening to do with Molly is off the chart when it comes to risk. The longer he drags it out, the more chance of getting caught.'

It had already occurred to Brennan that the kidnapper might be bluffing about holding Molly in order to torment Sarah and prolong her agony. More likely he was planning to let her go or, God forbid, kill her after a few days. But Brennan was reluctant to explore this theory with Sarah and Adam because he didn't want to give oxygen to the thought that they would never see their daughter again.

At least if they believed that Molly's abductor was going to keep her alive they could cling to the hope that one day she'd be returned to them.

Brennan persevered with the questions for almost an hour, delicately probing Sarah in the hope of extracting some useful information from her. But she was too distressed to concentrate and broke down twice in a paroxysm of tears.

She struggled to hold her thoughts together and found it harder still to summon up names and faces from the past.

'There are so many,' she kept saying. 'For Christ's sake, I've been a copper for over ten years, so I'm bound to have lots of enemies, including all those buggers who claimed they were innocent. Maybe one of their friends or relatives is convinced they were and has decided to get back at me for it.'

'What about the perps?' Brennan asked, as he stood up and rolled his shoulders to take out some of the stiffness. 'Do you recall the names of any that threatened actual retribution against you?'

After thinking about it for a minute or so she remembered two offenders who had threatened her. One she collared seven years ago for smuggling hard drugs into the country from Turkey. His name was Frank Neilson, and after he was charged he told her that he would make her pay if he was eventually convicted. He was, and as far as Sarah knew he was still locked up in Belmarsh Prison.

The second man was a rapist named Edwin Sharp who attacked her with a hammer when she went to his home in Lewisham to arrest him. He said he would 'see to her' after he had served his sentence. That was five years ago and she had no idea if he'd been released.

'This is a good start,' Brennan said. 'I'm sure that other names will come to you and we can throw them into the mix as well.'

She was a strong woman, Brennan told himself. He just hoped she'd be able to get over the initial shock quickly. He needed her to focus her mind and help them identify the kidnapper.

The words of the kidnapper convinced Brennan that Sarah probably knew who the man was and that his name was buried deep in her subconscious. If so, then surely it was only a matter of time before she managed to dredge it up.

Brennan decided to leave just as the police doctor arrived at

43

the flat. He got to his feet and told Sarah and Adam that he wouldn't rest until Molly had been found.

'I know it won't be easy, but you both need to stay strong,' he said.

At that moment his phone rang. All eyes turned towards him expectantly and Sarah said, 'Answer it, guv. Please. It could be news.'

He slipped the phone from his pocket and took the call. It was indeed someone from the office with an update on the case and it made him catch his breath.

A man carrying a young child had been spotted just minutes after Molly was taken. The sighting took place close to the home of Sarah's parents in Streatham.

Even more significant was the fact that it was believed the pair had been captured on a street camera.

8

Sarah

Brennan had left the flat and so had the police doctor, who had stayed for barely fifteen minutes. He'd convinced me to take a sedative even though I wasn't keen, but it hadn't yet kicked in, so it still felt as though I was trapped in a silent scream.

My thoughts raced, my mind was in turmoil, and the fear was twisting in my gut like some caged animal.

I so wanted to believe that the nightmare would end soon and I'd be reunited with my baby. But although the sighting and potential CCTV footage was positive news, the note from the kidnapper stifled any sense of optimism. Every word burned into my soul with a fierce intensity.

It was hard to believe that someone could be so cruel. This wasn't an opportunistic abduction by a crazy woman who longed for a child of her own. Or an act perpetrated by a couple who didn't want to go through the rigmarole of an adoption. No, this was pre-meditated and well-planned by someone whose objective was to cause me unbearable pain.

I've taken your daughter as punishment for what you did to me.

You'll never touch her or speak to her again. But you will see her grow up. That will be my way of making sure that your suffering does not diminish over time.

Tears began to form in my eyes again and I struggled to hold them back. Who was this person and what terrible crime was he accusing me of committing against him? Sure, I had arrested lots of men during my police career, but I couldn't imagine that any of them would have cause to seek such a brutal revenge. Not even those whose names I'd given to Brennan.

So had the kidnapper picked me at random so that he could fulfil some psychopathic fantasy? These thoughts and a million others crowded my mind.

'Why don't you go and lie down,' Adam said. 'Your boss told us he'll call as soon as he's seen the footage from the street camera.'

'Lying down won't make me feel any better,' I said. 'I need to be ready to go to the station if it turns out that Molly has been sighted.'

It was a glimmer of hope that I wanted to cling to, despite the voice inside my head cautioning me against it. In all likelihood it was a different child who'd been spotted, a toddler being carried somewhere by his or her father. And even if it was Molly with the man who'd snatched her, it wouldn't necessarily be of much help – not unless he could be identified or they were seen getting into a car or entering a house.

Adam heaved himself up off the sofa and took off his jacket. The back of his shirt was soaked with sweat. He looked down at me, his face furrowed with worry, his jaw locked as he spoke.

'I need to make some calls,' he said. 'Let some people know what's going on.'

He told Sergeant Palmer that he was going into the kitchen and asked her to stay with me.

'Of course,' she said. 'And if there's anything either of you need then please just ask.'

As I watched Adam walk out of the room I drew in a sharp breath and felt my ribs smart.

I dreaded the thought that he would soon leave me and go back to his own flat. I wasn't sure I'd be able to cope on my own. The despair was growing inside me like a malignant tumour and the simple act of breathing had itself become a challenge.

Everywhere I looked there was something to remind me of Molly. Her box of toys, her pink cardigan, the bag packed with her nappies, her favourite *Shrek* DVD, a tiny white sock poking out from beneath the cabinet where she had probably stuffed it.

A sob welled up inside me and I swallowed it down. I couldn't allow myself to lose control. Molly needed me and I'd be next to useless if I became an emotional wreck.

'I'll find you, sweetheart,' I said under my breath. *'I promise I will find you.'*

I closed my eyes and pictured her beautiful little face. I could almost feel her bouncing on my knee and it made me smile. And then I heard her infectious laughter and for a blessed moment my mind carried me back in time – away from the unbearable agony of the present.

'She's absolutely gorgeous,' the midwife said as she delivered my baby into the world. 'Have you got a name for her yet?'

'Molly,' I said. 'After my late grandmother.'

'It suits her,' she said, wrapping the tearful little bundle of joy in a soft blanket. 'Here you are, my dear. Meet your new daughter.'

She gently placed Molly in my arms and the love poured straight

47

out of me. It was without doubt the most precious moment of my life, marred only by the fact that I wasn't sharing it with her father.

Oh, the cheeky sod had asked if he could be present at the birth, but I'd said no, just as I'd said no when he'd suggested we get back together on learning that I was pregnant. I didn't want to be with someone who didn't love me, and even though he said he did I didn't believe him. Things became strained between us just two years into the marriage, partly because he didn't want children immediately and I did. But finding out about his affair with a colleague in the NCA broke my heart and made me lose all respect for him.

It had been tempting to succumb to getting back together, of course. He told me that he wanted to, and even my parents had urged me to give him another chance. And perhaps I would have if I'd believed it could work out between us. But the damage had been done and I wasn't convinced I could ever trust him again.

Despite all that, I'd be forever grateful to him for giving me Molly, who was conceived the very last time we had sex. It was during our make-or-break holiday in Spain, just before the drink-fuelled bust-up that led to his confession of adultery.

It wasn't a mind-blowing experience for either of us, but especially not for me because I was trying to suppress all the anger and suspicions that had been building up for weeks.

He came inside me while I was lying face down on the bed and I didn't even bother to fake an orgasm. It was so very different from the lovemaking during those early months of the marriage when we couldn't keep our hands off each other and I never imagined that he would ever cheat on me.

It was hard at first, coming to terms with the end of the

relationship, especially after I learned that Adam continued to date the woman he'd had the affair with. Her name was Gemma and she was fifteen years younger than him. But Molly helped me through it. From the moment I discovered that she was inside my belly I knew that I didn't need anyone else. She was all that mattered. She was my future, my life – my saviour.

My eyes snapped open and I was back in the present. My throat quivered and I had to force myself to breathe.

It felt like everything around me had been leached of colour. My body shivered and my heart beat like a jack hammer.

Sergeant Palmer stood on the other side of the room looking through the front window. I wondered fleetingly what was going on outside. Had the press turned up or were curious neighbours gathering to try to find out what was going on?

My watch told me it was three p.m. So surely the news had broken by now.

It was a wretched thought that seven hours had passed since Molly was abducted. I had no idea what was happening to her and it was killing me. Was she being fed? Given drinks? Was her nappy being changed? Was she being spoken to or ignored? Was she upset and confused?

I grabbed my phone and brought up the latest picture of Molly asleep in the cot. The thumb in her mouth. The pink pyjamas. The off-white sheet she was lying on. I wondered if she was awake now and if so whether she was calling for her mummy.

Mummy!

It was one of the few words she knew, along with *cat, cuddle, bird, wow* and *no*.

I loved it when she tried to speak. It was so cute and funny, especially when she struggled to explain what it was she wanted.

49

These past few months she had got so much better at communicating. At the same time, she'd become more of a handful. Throwing tantrums, refusing to sit quietly in her buggy, fussing over her food, waking up most mornings around five a.m. But it was all part of growing up and I'd embraced it, as mothers do. Not because I had no choice, but because it made me happy and proud and . . .

You'll never touch or speak to her again. But you will see her grow up.

Oh God . . .

My blood turned cold at the prospect of never holding Molly in my arms again. Of never tucking her into her bed, of never wiping away her tears. And I couldn't even imagine how painful it would be to be forced to watch from a distance as she grew from a toddler into a little girl. It would destroy me knowing that someone else was bringing her up.

I'd already had a taste of what it was going to be like if he carried out his threat to keep her while sending me photos and video clips. The two pictures I'd already received – of Molly sitting on the sofa and sleeping in the cot – had opened up wounds in my heart that would never be healed.

Jesus, it was all too much. I hunched forward, dropping my face into my cupped hands.

Suddenly Sergeant Palmer was leaning over me, a hand on my shoulder, telling me that she wished there was more she could do. But there wasn't, not unless she could bring my daughter back to me.

I felt a sharp stab of fear and dread work its way under my ribs, and this was followed by a bolt of nausea that hit me hard.

And then the sound of my own voice, oddly unfamiliar.

'I think I'm going to be sick again.'

9

Adam

Adam stood in the kitchen, his back to the sink, his stomach in knots. The blood was pounding behind his eyes and his emotions were swimming.

He had already spoken to his boss. DCI Dunlop had offered up a bunch of well-meaning platitudes and had promised that the NCA would assist in the hunt for Molly.

'I've reassigned all of your casework,' he'd said. 'You just need to concentrate on getting your little girl back.'

Now Adam paused before making another call, distracted by the sound of Sarah crying in the living room. He shared her pain and was on the brink of breaking down himself. But he fought against it because he knew that tears would blur his thoughts and make him even more helpless than he was.

His beloved daughter had been viciously kidnapped and all he could do was wait and worry as the panic closed in around him.

Molly, tiny and helpless, was at the mercy of a ruthless predator who was on some monstrous mission. What the bastard was intending to do was beyond belief and unless he was caught there was no telling how long it would carry on. Days? Weeks? Months? There'd be no escape from the anguish, the sheer torture of seeing images of Molly and yet not knowing where she was or who she was with.

Adam felt a tightening in his chest, a sudden breathlessness, as his mind spiralled back to Saturday when he'd last been with his daughter.

Sarah had been expecting him to have her all day and into Sunday morning. But he'd told her he had to work in the afternoon and could only take her to the park for a few hours. It was a shameful lie because he had simply chosen not to reveal the truth.

Now he was consumed by a wretched guilt that was tearing him apart. How could he have been so selfish? So stupid? Molly loved being with him and he should have put her first, instead of going to that hotel in Windsor. He feared now that he would regret that decision for the rest of his life.

He wished now that he had taken some pictures of Molly in the park, but he hadn't bothered to. He'd been too preoccupied, thinking about what was going to happen in Windsor. Another ghastly mistake. Another thing to feel guilty about.

He should have made the most of the weekend with his daughter. She'd been full of life, laughing hysterically as she ran across the grass, her eyes filled with wonder as she fed the ducks and chased the pigeons. Now he had to accept that he might never get to take her to the park again, or give her piggy-backs, or rock her to sleep before putting her to bed.

He released a long breath and mashed the heels of his hands into his eye sockets. Every muscle in his body was taut, and his heart was pumping blood so fast it was making him dizzy.

He thought about what Sarah's mother had said, how the kidnapper had suddenly turned up at the house and attacked her. He tried to picture the scene as the man snatched Molly from her high chair and carried her out of the house. She must have been terrified, and he couldn't believe that she didn't scream and cry.

But where did he go from there and how did he manage to calm Molly down enough so that he could take the photo of her on the white sofa?

This and other questions were piling up in Adam's head.

Why was his daughter targeted?

What was the kidnapper's beef with Sarah that he felt justified in meting out such a cruel punishment?

Would he actually carry out the threat he had outlined in his text messages?

And what were the odds on the police finding him?

This last question reminded Adam that they still hadn't heard from Brennan. The DCI had left the flat over an hour ago, so surely he would know by now whether Molly and the kidnapper had been caught on a street camera.

Adam was about to call Brennan when his phone started to ring, making him jump. He looked at the caller ID and felt a shiver run through him. No way could he answer it, not with Sarah in the other room. She might suddenly burst into the kitchen to find out who was ringing, and overhear something he didn't want her to. So he pressed his thumb against the call-end button and released a thin whistle from between his teeth.

Then he quickly found Brennan's number and called him. The detective answered just as the kitchen door was pushed open and Sarah walked in, her eyes wide in anticipation.

Adam held up a hand to indicate that he was about to say something and spoke into the phone. 'This is Adam Boyd,' he said. 'We want to know if you've checked the CCTV footage yet.'

'Only just,' Brennan replied. 'As a matter of fact I was about to call you.'

'Is Molly on it?'

'She is, but sadly it's not that helpful.'

'Why not?'

'We see the kidnapper holding Molly, but his face isn't visible, and the sequence only lasts a few seconds. We're now pulling in footage from various other cameras in that area.'

'Shit.'

Sarah stepped towards him, anxious to know what he was being told. Behind her, Sergeant Palmer stood in the doorway, her lips pressed into a thin line.

'There's something else you need to know,' Brennan said. 'It's about the photo Sarah received of Molly sitting on a sofa.'

'What about it?' Adam said.

Brennan cleared his throat. 'As you know, the kidnapper threatened to make Molly suffer if any of the images he sends to Sarah are made public.'

'Yeah, so?'

'Well it pains me to have to tell you that there's been a cock-up.'

'What do you mean?' Adam said, a note of alarm in his voice.

'That first photo was released to the media before everyone got my message about holding it back. I'm so, so sorry, Adam.'

10

Sarah

Adam's face was ashen as he hung up his call.

'You won't believe this,' he said. 'They've given that photo of Molly on the sofa to the media.'

At first, the significance of this didn't register. But then I remembered the kidnapper's warning and gave a frightened gasp.

'He's not sure how it happened,' Adam said through clenched teeth. 'But it's a cock-up, and they're now having to contact news outlets to tell them not to run it.'

His words hit me like ice water and it was all I could do not to scream.

'Has he checked the street camera footage?' I said. 'What does it show?'

'Not much apparently. The guy is holding Molly but you can't see his face.'

'Shit.'

'Look, I'm going to the nick,' Adam said. 'I want to know how the fuck this happened and I want to see the camera footage for myself.'

'Then I'm coming with you,' I said.

Sergeant Palmer stepped further into the kitchen, shaking her head. 'I really don't think that's a good idea,' she said. 'You should both stay here. I'll talk to the gaffer about having the camera sequence sent over.'

But Adam wasn't going to be talked out of it. He nudged past her and into the hall and I followed him. I thought he would march straight up to the front door, but instead he went into the living room and switched on the television.

I stood just inside the room and watched the screen come to life. A drum was beating in my head and it felt like a large stone was crushing my chest. This latest development terrified me. The kidnapper had issued a specific threat.

She will also suffer if you or the police make any of the images public through newspapers or on the television.

I was pretty sure it wouldn't matter to him that it was a mistake by the police. But how would he react? Would he really take it out on Molly to show us that he meant what he said and that his threats shouldn't be ignored?

I started to think about all the ways he might hurt her, but then stopped myself because I suddenly felt as if my head would explode.

As Adam used the remote to switch between channels, I tried to concentrate on my breathing because I feared I might faint. But my lungs felt like they were squeezing shut and every breath made me shudder. I was also having to fight the effects of the sedative, which was starting to cloud my thoughts and slow me down.

Sergeant Palmer was behind me in the hallway, speaking into her phone. I assumed she was talking to Brennan, telling him that we were coming to the station. There was no way they could stop us, of course, and I didn't think they'd dare try. It was *our* daughter who'd been taken. *Our* daughter who now faced the wrath of the kidnapper because of *their* bloody mistake. I swore to myself that if and when I found out who was responsible they would feel the full force of my anger.

'Jesus Christ,' Adam exploded. 'They're running it.'

By *it* he meant the photograph of Molly on the white sofa, which suddenly filled the TV screen.

A choking sound rushed out of me and I felt the air lock in my chest. But I stifled a scream because I wanted to hear what the news reporter was saying.

'Fifteen-month-old Molly Mason was abducted this morning from her grandparents' home in Streatham. Her grandmother was attacked in the process by a masked man. Molly is the daughter of two Metropolitan police officers and a huge hunt is under way to find her. The BBC understands that this photograph was sent to her mother, but it's not yet been confirmed if a ransom is being demanded for her safe return. A Scotland Yard spokesman said further details would be released as and when they have them . . .'

The reporter's words chilled me to the bone. It didn't seem possible that he was talking about Adam and me, about Molly. It was always other people who featured in the news. Other people whose lives were shattered by terrible events. Never us.

Until now.

Molly's picture disappeared from the screen and the news reader started talking about a couple who had become Britain's biggest lottery winners. The abrupt change of subject prompted Adam to throw his hands up in the air.

'Talk about fucking insensitive,' he yelled. 'How can they go from bad to good news just like that? It's not right.'

I knew what he meant, but it was something we would have

57

to face up to. Other people's lives would go on as before, despite what was happening to us. It seemed so unfair, but that was the harsh reality.

Adam spun round and looked at me, his face grave, his eyes hard.

'Are you all right, Sarah?'

I nodded, but I wasn't all right. Not by a long shot. My stomach was now twisting and turning and I thought I might be sick again. I wondered if the kidnapper was watching the same news bulletin and if so whether he was taking out his anger over the airing of the photograph on Molly. It was a sickening thought.

'Why don't I go and see Brennan by myself,' he said. 'You stay here. Try to eat something. And maybe get your parents to come over.'

Food was the last thing on my mind even though I hadn't eaten since this morning when I'd had a bacon sandwich in the staff canteen.

'I want to find out what's going on as much as you do,' I said. 'If Mum and Dad are at Aunt Tessa's then they'll be OK. I can drop in on them later.'

'Well if you're sure, then let's go.'

Sergeant Palmer told us that if we were adamant about going to the station then she would take us.

'But be aware that there are some reporters downstairs and a TV camera crew,' she said.

I grabbed my bag and Adam picked up his jacket. Before leaving the flat I rushed into the bathroom and dry-retched into the sink, the bile burning my throat. Then I splashed water on my face and took a moment to stare at the stranger in the mirror. She wasn't a pretty sight. Her eyes were bloodshot and the skin beneath them was bruised and puffy. I wondered if she would ever again look like she did before today.

Adam was waiting for me at the open front door and I followed him out, dragging in ragged gulps of air as I did so. The sun had disappeared but the late afternoon was still bright, with ominous clouds gathering at the edges of the grey sky.

We hurried down the stairs and out the front, where a police car was parked next to the entrance.

A small crowd of people had gathered and some of them I recognised as neighbours. The others were reporters and photographers and they fired questions at us as we stepped towards the car.

'Have you heard from the kidnapper, Miss Mason?'

'Where are you going? Has there been a development?'

'Do you have a message for the man who's taken your daughter?'

Cameras flashed as we threw ourselves into the back of the car. Seconds later we were pulling away from the estate and the plaintive wail of the siren drowned out all other sounds. But it offered no comfort. Granted, having left the flat I was infused with a sense of purpose, but that in itself wouldn't change anything or bring to a halt the emotional roller coaster I was trapped on. Instinct told me that Adam and I were in for a long and tortuous ride.

He reached for my hand and I let him take it. We looked at each other for a moment, sharing the same horrible thoughts, our troubled past forgotten because we needed to work together for our daughter's sake.

'We'll get through this, Sarah. Then we'll . . .'

Adam stopped mid-sentence because the phone gripped tightly in my right hand pinged again with another incoming message.

'Do you want me to check it?' Adam said.

'I've got it,' I told him. This time I didn't drop it and managed to swipe the screen even though my body froze.

A second later I was staring at the third text from the kidnapper and a new wave of fear and terror washed over me. There were no photographs attached and this made me fear that he had already harmed my little girl.

You were warned about the images. Now your darling little girl is going to suffer the consequences.

11

DCI Brennan

The incident room was alive with the discordant sounds of phones ringing and detectives chatting.

Brennan could tell that his team were working flat out and would continue to do so throughout the night. Even off-duty officers had decided to come in on hearing that the victim of this particular crime was one of their own.

To them, Sarah was more than just a colleague; she was a friend in need of help. And help they would, although they all felt guilty because she'd already been so terribly let down.

The photo of Molly on the sofa had been released to media outlets before the kidnapper's second text message arrived on Sarah's phone. At that stage Brennan had only wanted it to be circulated within the Met, but his instruction was misinterpreted by an over-zealous press officer who made it available to those news organisations, including the BBC, who had a jump on the story.

The Beeb had agreed to take it off the air as soon as they were told it was a mistake to run it, but by then it was already too late. The kidnapper had seen it and had sent yet another threatening text to Sarah.

You were warned about the images. Now your darling little girl is going to suffer the consequences.

Sergeant Palmer had got Sarah to forward the message to him and even now, five minutes later, it was still causing wild, disturbing thoughts to flash through his mind.

Brennan decided to have another briefing. He wanted to get it out of the way before Sarah and Adam arrived.

'It's time for a team talk, everyone,' he said aloud, clapping his hands to get their attention as he walked to the front of the room.

He stood between a whiteboard and a television monitor on top of a stand. Pinned to the whiteboard were the two photos taken by the kidnapper. In themselves they weren't unusual; seemingly innocent pictures of a child sitting on a sofa and lying asleep in a cot. But it was what they didn't reveal that made them so sinister.

Where were they taken?

Who was behind the camera?

Was he doing this by himself or did he have an accomplice?

It was the job of Brennan and his team to seek out the answers, but they were making slow progress. And that worried him.

He said as much to the troops when he started to address them. He spoke slowly, his tone measured and calm.

'In view of this latest text from the kidnapper we need to raise our game,' he said. 'DI Mason's little girl has been taken by someone with an obvious grudge, and we have to assume that he's not making empty threats when he says he'll hurt her.'

He explained why the photo of Molly on the sofa had ended up on the BBC and several online news sites, and said he would make a point of speaking to the person or persons responsible.

'But so far we've managed to keep a lid on the reason the kidnapper has given for abducting Molly,' he went on. 'For now that stays within these walls and I'll come down hard on anyone who decides to leak it.'

He paused to let that sink in. He knew all twenty-five officers in the room, and on a run-of-the-mill case he'd have trusted them not to succumb to temptation. But this was no ordinary case, and the press were going to be offering big money for inside information.

Brennan waited about fifteen seconds before continuing. Then he pinned back his shoulders and said, 'Now I want those of you who were assigned specific tasks to provide updates. But first let me reiterate what I told you earlier – that we need to handle this case just like any other. I know we all have a personal stake because of DI Mason, but we can't allow that to cloud our judgement. We have to stay focused and we need to be objective. One serious mistake has already been made. We can't afford for there to be any more.'

Harsh strip lights buzzed overhead as the briefing continued. But nothing Brennan heard encouraged him to believe that they were making significant headway.

DI Bill Conroy was heading up the group tasked with sifting through all the footage from the traffic and security cameras. They'd so far come up with only the one short clip that showed the kidnapper walking along Penfold Street towards Streatham High Road carrying Molly, who looked as though she was crying. But the sequence lasted just seven seconds. The kidnapper kept his head down and his face couldn't be seen. But it was obvious to them all that they were looking at a man and not a woman. He was wearing a dark hoody and jeans and what looked like a pair of black trainers.

It seemed that Molly and the man hadn't been picked up on any other cameras so it wasn't known if they'd got into a vehicle or entered a house or flat.

'We're still trawling through the footage,' DI Conroy said. 'But it was a busy time of day. Plus, a couple of cameras in the area aren't working. However, the clip tells us that the bloke didn't have a car or van parked behind the house. Instead he chose to walk away from there carrying the baby. We know from the tape that he walked at least a few hundred yards along Oakdale Lane and Hopton Close. But beyond that he could have gone off in any number of directions.'

Another detective reported on the door-to-door inquiries.

'Unfortunately most of the properties in the area were empty when officers called,' he said. 'We're assuming the owners and tenants were at work, and most still are, so there's a good chance they wouldn't have seen anything. As yet, we have only one confirmed sighting of a man with a child. A woman named Tina Redgrave was returning from the school run when she spotted them in Penfold Street. But it was as she was pulling onto her driveway, so she didn't see the guy's face.'

Brennan wasn't surprised. Londoners rarely noticed things that weren't relevant to their own busy lives. This was especially true of people hurrying to and from work. They were usually listening to music, playing with their smartphones or fretting over what the day ahead held in store for them.

The team were then told that the techies hadn't managed to trace the origin of the messages. The perp was probably switching between unregistered phones or using an anonymous text app.

'So what do we know about the perps who DI Mason mentioned as having made threats against her?' Brennan said.

DC Amanda Foster was across this one and Brennan noticed

she was standing at the back of the room with her mobile phone to her ear. As he caught her eye she raised a hand in acknowledgement and quickly hung up.

'Sorry, guv,' she said, flicking a tendril of dark hair away from her face. 'I was just getting updated.'

'So what have you got for us?' he asked.

She read from her notes as she spoke. 'DI Mason gave you two names,' she said. 'One was the drug trafficker Frank Neilson who told her he would make her pay if he was convicted and sent down. I'm glad to say he's still behind bars.

'The other man was Edwin Sharp who she collared for rape five years ago. He hit DI Mason with a hammer and threatened to see to her when he got out. Well, I've just this second learned that he was released from jail a month ago. We have an address in Lewisham, but officers who called round there say the flat is empty. Neighbours say he only stayed there a week before moving out. We're now trying to find out where he's gone.'

Brennan felt his stomach tense and his spirits lift slightly.

'That sounds promising,' he said. 'I think it's fair to say we have our first suspect.'

12

Sarah

I was in a dreadful state by the time we got to the station. It had only just turned five p.m. and already it was the longest day of my life.

The latest text from the kidnapper had hit me hard. I'd bellowed like a wounded animal and Adam had had to put an arm around me to calm me down. I dreaded to think how much more strung out I'd be if not for the sedative that was sloshing around inside me.

The fear was like razor wire inside my mind. I'd finally stopped sobbing, but now I had trouble thinking, trouble seeing.

Adam said he thought it might be best if Sergeant Palmer took me back home, but I insisted on going up with him. I needed to find out what was happening and if my colleagues were in a position to offer us any hope. If not then I was sure that the fear and uncertainty would soon engulf me.

It felt weird to be entering the building for the second time that day. This morning I'd been a very different person – upbeat and energised after a long, lazy weekend. Now I was little more than a zombie, struggling to hold on to reality as my world tilted on its axis.

Several of my colleagues approached me as we made our way up the stairs and they told me they were confident that Molly would soon be found safe and well. Others just gave me sympathetic looks, while some pointedly avoided making eye contact, presumably because they didn't know how to react.

Brennan was waiting for us just inside the incident room. Beyond him I took in the familiar scene, detectives talking into phones and staring into computer screens. I also noticed the whiteboard with photos of Molly pinned to it. It turned my stomach to see my little girl's face there. I'd seen scores of children's faces over the years while working on cases they'd been involved in. Each one had been someone's son or daughter. But it was only now that I truly realised how desperate and helpless those parents would have felt.

'Let's go straight to my office,' Brennan said and steered us in that direction.

His office was small and cluttered and through the window rain clouds were now bruising the sky above South London.

Adam waited until we were all seated before he let rip. 'How in Christ's name did it happen?' he yelled. 'The kidnapper gave a clear warning. You were supposed to stop that photo being released.'

Brennan held up both hands, palms out, fingers splayed. 'I know and I feel as gutted as you do,' he said. 'But it was due to a breakdown in communication. It wasn't deliberate.'

He told us how a member of the media liaison team had released the picture of Molly and Adam responded by shaking his head and swearing.

'Well someone's head should bloody roll,' he seethed. 'God only knows what's going to happen to our daughter because of the force's rank incompetence. I don't fucking believe—'

I reached across and grabbed his arm, causing him to snap his head towards me.

'Stop it, Adam,' I said. 'Going on about it won't solve anything. I for one came here to find out how close they are to finding Molly. I feel as angry as you do, but there's no point ranting and raving over something that can't be changed.'

He seemed so angry that I thought he'd ignore me. Instead he closed his eyes briefly and took a deep breath. Then he opened them again and gave a slow nod.

'Very well,' he said. 'You're right. I'm sorry.'

'There's no need to be,' Brennan said. 'I completely understand why you're pissed off. I would be, in your position.'

Having calmed down, Adam sat back and listened to what Brennan had to say. We both did. But what he said did nothing to raise our hopes or allay our fears.

So far only the one woman had come forward to say she had seen a man with a child near my mother's home. The phone from which the messages had been sent had not been traced. And there was just one short clip of video footage from a street camera.

We viewed it on Brennan's computer and the sight of my baby in the kidnapper's arms sent my heart into freefall. The footage was in colour and slightly blurred, but I could tell straight away that it was Molly. She was looking back over the man's shoulder towards the camera, wide awake and clearly upset. One arm was wrapped around the kidnapper's neck and her head was raised and moving from side to side.

When Brennan paused and enhanced the image, I could see that her little face was scrunched up and her mouth was open.

I felt a cry in my throat but I refused to let it out. Instead

I just gazed at the screen as the muscles around my eyes tightened.

'Unfortunately we only have the rear view of the kidnapper,' Brennan said. 'As you can see he appears to be of average build and height, just as Molly's grandmother described him. He could be aged anywhere between twenty and forty.'

It was hard to tell because he was wearing a dark hoody and jeans and there were no distinctive markings visible on his clothes.

We watched the video through twice and after the second time I sat back in the chair and had to will the tears not to come.

Brennan asked if I was OK to carry on and I just nodded and wiped my eyes with a tissue.

'I'm still hopeful that by the end of this evening we'll have more to go on,' he said. 'We're still going door-to-door and people in the area are gradually returning home from work. It's possible a neighbour we haven't yet spoken to saw something. There's also the outside chance that someone has seen the photograph on the telly and recognises the room that Molly's in, which is obviously why the kidnapper didn't want it released.'

'I very much doubt that,' Adam said. 'There must be hundreds of thousands of white sofas in homes across London alone.'

Brennan then asked me a series of questions. Did I have any idea how the kidnapper got my number? *No.* Had I spotted anyone watching me or the flat in recent days or weeks? *No.* Did Molly have any medical conditions that required ongoing treatment? *No.*

He then asked Adam a bunch of similar questions. Did he know who the kidnapper might be? *No.* Did he know of anyone who had a grudge against Sarah? *No.* Did he himself have any enemies? *Yes, lots.*

Adam was in such a state that he was struggling to respond. I could tell that his mind was leaping in all directions and he was finding it hard to make sense of anything.

Finally, and almost reluctantly, Brennan told us about the two perps whose names I'd given him, the pair who had threatened retribution. He said Frank Neilson was still banged up, but the rapist Edwin Sharp had been released from prison a month ago and they were trying to trace him.

'I didn't mention him to begin with because I don't want to overstate the significance,' he said. 'Just because he's out, it doesn't mean he's been up to no good. It's more than likely he doesn't even remember making threats against you, Sarah.'

I thought about this for a moment and said, 'On the other hand it might be all he's been thinking about for the past five years.'

It didn't seem like five years ago to me. The Edwin Sharp case was one of those that had stayed with me, and I could remember every detail. In fact, I still had some of the newspaper cuttings in a file at home. That was because it was one of my most high-profile cases and even earned me a commendation.

Sharp was an arrogant cocaine-obsessed stockbroker who raped a 23-year-old woman after a drug-fuelled office party. It happened shortly after I joined Lewisham CID and just before they teamed me up with Adam.

I arrived at Sharp's terraced house with a WPC named Felicity Trant. When he answered the front door, it was clear he was high on drink and drugs. He was wearing a dressing gown with nothing underneath and his eyes were wide and glassy.

He became aggressive and abusive when I explained why we were there and he called us bitches and whores.

When I said I was going to arrest him and take him to the

station, he lost it completely. He leapt to his feet and punched WPC Trant in the face, sending her flying across the room. Then he dashed into the kitchen before I could stop him.

I was only a couple of seconds behind him, but by the time I reached him he'd armed himself with a hammer from a drawer and lashed out at me with it.

I suffered a painful blow to the shoulder before I managed to force him to the floor and put cuffs on his wrists.

And that was when his dressing gown fell open to reveal a small flaccid penis, which made him blush and bare his teeth.

'You fucking cunt,' he screamed. 'I won't forget this.'

The next day, during the formal interview, Sharp gave me a look that could melt wax and said, 'If I go down for this I'll make sure I'll see to you when I get out, Detective Mason.'

Sharp pleaded not guilty in court to rape and claimed the sex with the woman had been consensual. But the jury rejected his story and it took them just three hours to find him guilty of rape and assaulting police officers.

The judge condemned him for not showing any remorse during the trial, and as he was led out of the dock he looked across the courtroom at me and stuck up two fingers.

'I'm confident it won't take long to track Sharp down,' Brennan said, wrenching me back from the past. 'We're trying to reach his probation officer and the landlord of the flat he stayed in for just a week. We're also contacting his family and friends.'

'Sharp is a nasty piece of work,' I said. 'I wouldn't put it past him to try to finish what he started with the hammer. But it's hard to imagine that he would have it in him to kidnap my daughter.'

Brennan shrugged. 'Our prisons are filled with people who hold grudges, Sarah. For some of them the thought of eventually getting sweet revenge is what keeps them going. And it's often the case that the sweeter and more elaborate the revenge the better.'

13

Sarah

So was the man on the street camera footage Edwin Sharp? Was he the bastard who had abducted Molly after attacking my mother?

It was impossible to tell, of course, because his features weren't visible on the tape. But Brennan went on to point out that the very latest description of Sharp had him at five feet nine tall, with a slim build and dark hair cropped close to his head. He was aged thirty-six, and when he walked out of Wandsworth prison four weeks ago he was apparently in good health.

Brennan brought a photo of him up on his computer and I took a quick intake of breath.

'This was taken just before his release,' Brennan said. 'The prison sent it over a few minutes ago.'

It was amazing how little the man had changed. It seemed he had hardly aged. There were the strong cheekbones and dimpled chin, the mouth that was flat and narrow, the jaw that was dark with stubble. He still had the kind of face that gave him an air of unbridled arrogance.

'According to the prison he served the full sentence imposed because he didn't know how to behave himself,' Brennan said. 'He got into a few scuffles and was once caught in possession of drugs.'

'I don't understand how he can just disappear,' Adam said. 'Surely under the terms of his release he would have had to remain on the radar.'

Brennan agreed. 'Rest assured that's one of the questions I'll be asking.'

The DCI then looked at his watch and said he needed to get back into the incident room.

'I give you my word that I'll call you straight away if there are any developments,' he said. 'There's really nothing more I can tell you at this stage. But I do want you to know that more than fifty detectives are now working directly on this case. All leave has been cancelled and I've been given the go-ahead to bust the overtime budget.'

I exchanged an anxious glance with Adam. He shook his head and expelled a puff of air.

'I suppose we have to resign ourselves to a long night then,' he said, his voice cracking with emotion.

'The team will be working flat out until we get a result,' Brennan said. 'If we're not able to return Molly to you by tomorrow morning I intend to arrange a press conference and I'd like one or both of you to attend.'

I sat there, nerves jangling, as the dread pooled in my stomach and my eyes started tearing up.

Brennan got to his feet and came around his desk. He stood next to me and put a hand on my shoulder.

'I have no idea what your religious beliefs are, Sarah,' he said. 'But if you do believe in God then it might help to pray like you've never prayed before.'

*   *   *

Like a lot of police officers who are frequently exposed to the ugly realities of life, I'd always had a hard time believing in God. But that had never stopped me asking for his help.

I'd been mouthing silent prayers ever since I'd discovered that Molly had been abducted. Such was my desperation that I refused to accept the possibility that it was a waste of time.

'Please bring my baby back to me,' I whispered to myself as we left the station. 'And I beg you not to let that man hurt her.'

Sergeant Palmer was waiting outside for us next to her own car and she'd be driving us home.

Once we were settled in the back seat and she was behind the wheel, she said, 'The DCI wants me to stay with you at the flat tonight. Would that be all right? I have an overnight bag and I'll make myself comfortable in the living room.'

'It's not a problem,' I said.

'Thank you. What about you, Mr Boyd? Are you returning to the flat?'

'Of course,' he replied. 'I don't intend to go home just yet.'

I felt a surge of relief and reached out to touch his arm.

'You don't have to stay with me,' I said.

'I know, but I want to.'

There was a sudden clap of thunder and I realised that dark clouds were now clustered overhead. Within seconds big drops of rain were pounding the windscreen.

'I'd like to go and see my parents before I go home,' I said. 'They're staying with my aunt in Balham. I need to tell them about the latest message and I don't want to do it over the phone.'

On the short journey to Balham my phone rang four times and each time my heart leapt into my throat. But the callers were just friends and former colleagues who had heard the news about

Molly. I told them I couldn't speak to them, and it got to the point where I wished I could switch my phone off. But of course I couldn't because I had no idea if and when the kidnapper would make contact again.

My aunt Tessa lived with her husband Jeff in a terraced house off Balham High Road. She was four years older than my mother and had a son who lived in Australia.

It was a solemn-faced Jeff who answered the door. He was a thin, fragile man with hollow cheeks and wispy grey hair. He immediately pulled me into an embrace.

'Oh you poor darling,' he said. 'This is so terrible.'

'How's Mum?' I asked him.

'Come in and see. Are you by yourself?'

'I'm with Adam and a police officer. They're going to wait outside in the car.'

It was Adam's idea not to come in because he reckoned he would be a distraction. My parents hadn't seen him since before the divorce and there was no telling how they'd react. My father William was a curmudgeonly 64-year-old and had vowed never to speak to Adam again.

In the event, I didn't think it would have been a problem. My mum and dad were far too distressed to be concerned about anyone other than their granddaughter.

Naturally they were eager to know if there had been any news.

'That's why I came right over,' I said. 'The bastard has sent another message.'

I told them what was in it and they took it badly. My mother collapsed in tears and my father kept shaking his head and telling us that he feared we would never see Molly again. It was all very upsetting and I was actually glad to leave the house. It was just after eight p.m. by then and the evening was drawing in. The rain had eased off but the air was heavy and moist.

When we got to my flats we had to run the gauntlet of reporters and photographers again. Now there were even more of them outside the flats.

Upstairs, Sergeant Palmer offered to make us both something to eat, but neither Adam nor I had an appetite.

'I'll have a drink, though,' I said. 'Something stronger than tea.'

I told Palmer to help herself to whatever was in the fridge and went into the living room.

'You sit down and I'll pour you something,' Adam said. 'Is the booze still in the same place?'

I nodded and he went to the cupboard next to the dining table.

'You've got a bottle of whisky and half a bottle of gin,' he said.

'I'll have whisky and make it a double.'

I sat on the sofa feeling weak and empty. My mouth was dry and my chest was thudding. I had no intention of going to bed. What was the point when I knew I'd never be able to sleep? I had no option but to sit back and wait for news while destructive thoughts ran riot inside my head.

As Adam handed me a glass half-filled with whisky, I asked him how long he planned to stay.

'All night if that's OK with you,' he said.

I just nodded.

I fired down some whisky and felt it bite into the back of my throat. Adam poured himself a glass before switching on the TV.

A moment later we were looking at another photo of Molly, this time one that Adam had taken a few weeks ago on his phone. It showed her in the park throwing bread to the ducks.

'It's one of those I sent to Brennan,' he said.

There was no telling how the kidnapper would react to seeing it and this worried me, despite what Brennan had said.

There was nothing new to report and it was clear the media were still in the dark about the kidnapper's motive. But for how long? I wondered. Someone on the inside was bound to leak it sooner or later, perhaps even intentionally. It wasn't unknown for officers I'd worked with to take back-handers.

Adam flipped between the news channels while I finished off my whisky. It warmed me up inside and made me feel a bit light-headed.

'Why don't you go up and have a bath or shower,' he said. 'It'll help you relax. I'll have another drink ready for you when you come down.'

I decided it was preferable to listening to news readers telling me what I already knew.

I went upstairs, but instead of going to the en suite shower I was drawn into Molly's bedroom.

The emotional impact was immediate. My vision blurred and I had to blink away the tears. I stood in the middle of the room taking everything in: the cot with the SpongeBob duvet, the pink patterned wallpaper, the giant panda in the corner, the pile of her clothes on the chair that were waiting to be put away.

I pictured her standing up in the cot with her arms in the air, beseeching me to lift her out. It was always such a wonderful moment as I pulled her close to my chest and she'd put her arms around my neck. The feel of her warm body and her soft cheek against mine never failed to cheer me up.

Suddenly I felt completely overwhelmed, and I realised I was gulping at the air, forcing myself not to break down.

I turned and hurried across the hallway into my bedroom. I collapsed on the bed, my crying muffled by the pillow.

And there I lay, crushed by despair, until I heard Adam's voice after a few minutes.

I lifted my head and saw him standing next to the bed looking down at me, his breathing loud and laboured. He was holding my mobile phone in his outstretched hand.

'You just received another text message from the kidnapper,' he said.

I shot up, so fast it made my head spin.

'Have you opened it? What does it say?'

'That you should check your emails because he's sent you a video clip.'

14

DCI Brennan

Brennan could feel the pressure building as he cast his gaze around the incident room. His temples were pulsating and beads of sweat had popped up on his forehead.

He had a bad feeling about this case, and he could not ignore the chilling prospect that it might drag on for weeks or even months. If so, then it could well prove to be his last case before his retirement in September; his swansong in other words, the case that some would see as the defining aspect of his legacy.

If he couldn't solve it, if he couldn't return Molly Mason to Sarah, then he would have to live with the dark shadow of failure for years to come. And it wouldn't be just a professional failure. It'd be personal too given that Sarah was one of his closest colleagues. It wasn't something he wanted to contemplate, given that his future was already blighted by his wife's condition.

He was giving up work sooner than he needed to so that he could spend as much quality time as possible with Grace before the dementia took her from him. He wanted to give her his full attention, devote himself entirely to the woman he had loved for over thirty years. He didn't want to spend precious time consumed by thoughts of little Molly Mason and fretting over how he had let Sarah down.

The statistics he'd just been studying had only fuelled the pessimism. Child abductions were on the increase across the UK. According to one report, between 2013 and 2014 abductions and kidnappings of minors and teenagers under eighteen soared by 20 per cent. Another study showed that during 2014 alone around 900 child abductions were reported and almost half were taken by persons other than the child's parents. Fortunately most of the victims were recovered safely, but with long-lasting physical and mental scars.

Brennan was aware that under Common Law there was a distinction between kidnapping and abduction. Kidnapping was defined as taking away a person by force, threat or deceit, with intent to cause him or her harm, and it usually involved a monetary or political objective. Abduction, on the other hand, was generally regarded as taking someone against their will without making known the intent.

In cases of child abduction, the terms were usually interchangeable, which was why the man who had taken Molly was being referred to as a kidnapper. At this stage they couldn't be sure that his sole motivation was to 'punish' her mother. It was still conceivable, perhaps even likely, that he would eventually demand a ransom.

Brennan derived a small amount of comfort from knowing that during his career he had been involved in two major cases where children were abducted by strangers. And both had been resolved successfully.

In the first an eight-month-old baby girl was snatched from her bedroom by a woman who entered the house through an open back door while the mother was in the front garden. It turned out that the woman's own baby boy had died of meningitis a year earlier and she couldn't have any more children. So she had decided to steal one. They arrested her as she'd been stalking the mother for some days and was caught on CCTV.

The other case was even more disturbing – a 5-year-old boy lured into a car outside his home by a man who offered him sweets. Luckily the area was well served by number plate recognition cameras and the criminal's car was quickly spotted. He was a known paedophile and thankfully they managed to get to him before he laid a hand on his helpless victim.

But it was already obvious to Brennan and everyone else on the team that Molly's case was not going to be so easy to solve – not unless Edwin Sharp was indeed their man.

But Brennan didn't want to build up his hopes only to have them dashed if the guy had a cast-iron alibi for this morning. After all, the link to him was pretty tenuous since his threat against Sarah Mason had been made over five years ago, and even then it might well have been a throwaway remark spat out in the heat of the moment. After all, threats were made against the police all the time. Brennan himself had been threatened more times than he could remember by people he'd arrested.

He sucked in a breath and released it in a sigh. Then he started walking slowly around the incident room to check on what progress was being made.

It immediately became apparent that it was still slow-going. Frantic calls were being made and Sarah's case history was being delved into via computers. CCTV footage was still being trawled through and all known sex offenders tracked down.

There was still no word on Sharp, though. An officer had spoken to his former landlord who claimed he kicked Sharp out after a week because the ex-con tried it on with his 15-year-old daughter. The landlord didn't know where he'd gone and he didn't care.

They were still waiting to hear back from Sharp's probation officer who'd been on an away-day with his colleagues.

Brennan felt his spirits sag as he headed back to his office where he was due to take part in a conference call with his superiors, including the Commissioner. He wasn't looking forward to updating them with the news that they were no closer to finding Molly Mason.

His phone rang just as he was stepping through the door. He whipped it out of his pocket and saw that Sergeant Palmer was calling, presumably from Sarah's flat in Dulwich.

'What's up, Sergeant?' he asked. 'Is there a problem?'

'I think so, guv,' she said. 'DI Mason just received another text from the kidnapper.'

Brennan felt his veins flood with ice.

'What's it say?' he asked.

'Well it's just a one-sentence message telling her that he's sent an email to her personal account. She and Mr Boyd are about to check it.'

Brennan's heart slammed against his chest and his skin prickled. A video clip for pity's sake. He didn't want to imagine what might be on it.

When he next spoke the words felt like they were sticking to his mouth.

'Send it over as soon as it's been opened,' he said. 'And brace yourself, because I have an awful feeling that you're going to be dealing with two severely traumatised parents.'

15

Sarah

I had two email accounts – one for work and one for personal use. The kidnapper had sent the video to my personal Hotmail account and that in itself was worrying because very few people knew the address.

It was at the top of the inbox, and when I opened it up there was a brief message which read:

**THIS WAS YOUR FAULT, SARAH MASON. IF YOU
RELEASE ANY MORE OF THE IMAGES I SEND
YOU THEN IT'S MOLLY WHO WILL SUFFER.**

The sender's address was canttraceme@flash.com.

I felt my stomach clench as I clicked on the video attachment, but for some reason I couldn't open it up on my phone. It was a problem I'd experienced before and I was in too much of a hurry to seek a solution.

'It'll work on my laptop,' I said to Adam. 'It's on the dining table.'

My laptop was off so I had to fire it up, and while I waited I could feel the dread working its way through me, consuming every fibre of my being.

Adam stood behind me with a hand on my shoulder and Sergeant Palmer stood to my left, leaning forward, her breath smelling of mint.

None of us spoke and the only sound was the hum of the computer as it woke up from its slumber.

I stared intently at the screen as the acid churned in my stomach. A part of me wanted to turn away and leave Adam to see what the video clip contained. But I couldn't bring myself to do it. However distressing it was going to be, I had to see for myself what had happened to my baby.

Familiar images appeared on the screen as the laptop came to life and the adrenaline spike snatched my breath away.

Adam gently squeezed my shoulder. Palmer leaned in even closer. And the fear pressed down on me like a lead weight.

Finally the laptop was up and running and I went straight to my Hotmail account.

The message was there, along with the attached video, which I immediately dumped into the download file. I then went to the file but hesitated before opening up the clip.

'Would you like me to take a look first?' Palmer asked.

I shook my head and clicked on the mouse. The audio track engaged first and a child's ear-splitting scream tore into my soul a millisecond before Molly appeared. I had to fight back a violent urge to be sick again when I saw what the heartless bastard was doing to her.

16

DCI Brennan

Brennan called all his detectives together and told them that the kidnapper had made contact again.

'This time it's by email as well as text,' he said. 'Sergeant Palmer will send the email to us in the next few minutes. I want you to get straight to work trying to trace it back to the sender.'

He explained that the email had a video attachment that Sarah was about to view.

'I'm assuming it's in response to the fuck-up over the photo,' he said. 'If it is, then it could mean he's done something nasty to the child. Let's hope not, but we need to be prepared.'

He could see the concern etched on the faces of his detectives. Every man and woman on the team knew Sarah and most of them had worked with her. A good few had also met Molly and had made a fuss over her when Sarah had brought her into the office to show her off.

Brennan retreated to his office and got on the phone to tell his superiors he was pushing back the conference call so that he could provide them with the very latest information. Then he sat behind his desk to wait for Sergeant Palmer to call. But when his phone rang after about a minute it wasn't her on the line.

'It's me, guv.' Brennan recognised the distinctive Scottish voice of DC Phil Stewart who had been out of the office all afternoon, trying to track down Edwin Sharp.

'What have you got for me, Phil?' Brennan said.

'I just spoke to Edwin Sharp's probation officer, guv. She's confirmed that she did know that Sharp was evicted from the flat at the end of his first week out of prison. He made a point of telling her.'

'Does she know where he is now?'

'She's given me an address in Tooting. It's a flat that belongs to one of his old mates from his time in the city.'

'Terrific. Text it to me and we'll pay him a visit.'

Brennan hung up and then made a call to arrange for a tactical team to be put on standby and be ready to descend on Sharp's place in Tooting.

If Sharp had Molly, then they needed to move as quickly as possible. If he didn't, then at least they could eliminate him from their inquiries and focus on other suspects.

Brennan checked his watch. Several minutes had passed since Sergeant Palmer had called him. So why hadn't she phoned back?

17

Sarah

Watching the video clip was like having my heart cut out with a knife. It was painful beyond words.

I wanted to turn away but I couldn't. I felt compelled to bear witness to the cruelty that was being inflicted on my poor, defenceless daughter.

Molly was being held upside down by her right ankle and dangled naked in front of the camera.

The kidnapper stood to the left just out of shot. Only his hands were visible – one holding her up while he viciously smacked her bare bottom with the other.

She was crying like I'd never seen her cry before. Her eyes were squeezed shut but the tears were spilling from them.

The sound of his hand striking her flesh every two or three seconds hit me like a bolt of electricity. Molly's pale little body stiffened with every blow and phlegm sprayed out of her mouth and nose.

'Oh God, I can't believe this is happening,' Sergeant Palmer wailed suddenly.

And yet it was happening, and before our very eyes. My baby was being brutally abused, for no other reason than to teach me, her mother, a lesson. I could feel her pain, see the terror and confusion on her screwed-up face.

I instinctively reached out a hand towards the screen, towards Molly, thinking in a moment of madness that I could pull her away from her tormentor. But just as I did so the video came to an abrupt end.

However the images continued to play on a loop inside my mind, like a ghastly horror movie that I couldn't switch off.

I battled the impulse to scream, but I couldn't stop the tears from flowing, or the rush of nausea from sweeping through my body.

Adam dropped onto the chair next to me and when our eyes met his face crumbled. I'd never seen him cry in all the years we'd known each other, but it didn't surprise me. His love for Molly was as strong as mine and he was just as devastated by what we had just seen.

'We need to forward the video to the DCI,' Sergeant Palmer said, her composure regained. 'Would you like me to do it?'

'Let me look at it again,' I said. 'I want to see if there are any clues.'

I said it without thinking but realised that it was a subconscious reaction, a way for me to deal with the horror that was consuming me. Acting like a cop might stop me from falling to pieces and would help me to feel less useless.

'You should leave that to us,' Sergeant Palmer said. 'There's no point torturing yourself.'

'She's right,' Adam said, before I could argue the point. 'I doubt there'll be any clues. The clip only lasts twelve seconds. There was just a bare wall in the background and all we saw of the guy were his arms and hands. There were no tattoos or rings on his fingers and he didn't speak. We learned only that he's pretty strong and fucking cruel.'

His voice came out shaking and I could tell that he was fighting to calm it. Tears were spilling from his eyes and sweat sparkled like fine dew on his forehead.

I wanted to respond but I was too choked up to speak. All I had seen on the video was my daughter hanging upside down and screaming. I hadn't registered any other details.

Adam dipped his gaze, breaking eye contact, and I watched as he clenched and unclenched his fists.

'The man who has Molly is no fool, Sarah,' he said, his voice a hollow rasp. 'We have to accept that he's not likely to make any silly mistakes with the photos and video clips he sends to you.'

I was still trying to process this, and to accept the truth of his words, when Sergeant Palmer spoke up.

'That might not actually be the case,' she said, and we both looked at her as though she had suddenly entered the room.

'What are you on about?' I said.

She flicked her head towards the laptop.

'It's the way the video was shot,' she said. 'When it started I assumed the camera was in a static position, like it was on a shelf or something. But halfway through, it moved – only slightly, but enough to make me think that someone else was holding it.'

18

DCI Brennan

Brennan felt his eyes bulge as he viewed the video clip. He had seen some terrible things during his years on the job, but this was something to add to the list of dreadful sights that had affected him.

As he watched Molly Mason being held upside down and smacked, he couldn't help thinking about his own grandson, Michael. The boy wasn't much older than Molly and Brennan loved him with all his heart. He could imagine how he would feel if it was Michael who was being beaten like that.

His own reaction to the video was all the more intense because he felt partly responsible. If the photo of Molly on the sofa hadn't been released to the media by mistake then perhaps the kidnapper wouldn't have felt it necessary to hurt her.

He played the clip for the fourth time, hunched over his desk like a question mark. It certainly looked as though Sergeant Palmer was right. The camera did move slightly about halfway through. That could have been because the surface it was resting on – a tripod maybe – had shifted fractionally for any number of reasons.

Or it could mean that it was being held by another person – an accomplice. If so, then it was hugely significant, if not entirely unexpected.

Brennan sucked his lips in thought, his anxiety as taut as a membrane. The idea that the kidnapper might not be working alone gave rise to many more questions.

Was it some other lunatic who felt he had a score to settle with Sarah Mason?

Was it a friend or relative of the kidnapper who had been drawn into it willingly or against their will? A girlfriend even? It happened.

Or was this a gang-related abduction that involved a whole bunch of reprobates?

It was yet another aspect of the case that they would need to factor into the media strategy. Deciding how much to make public was a real dilemma, though, especially after the cock-up with the photograph. It was essential to control the release of information and yet at the same time keep the press onside in order to get as much help from them as possible.

The papers were already working up a head of steam because they sensed that this was not a straightforward child abduction. And after the Yard insisted that the photo of Molly be pulled, they'd become even more suspicious. Reporters had been hounding the press office for several hours and a number of detectives had been receiving calls from their contacts in the media. The story was getting bigger by the minute, but then, given the various elements, that was bound to be the case.

A fifteen-month-old child snatched from her grandparents' home in broad daylight by a man wearing a balaclava. And not just any child – Molly Mason was the daughter of two senior detectives in the Met. There was enough there already to make it big news across the country.

But once the hacks found out about the apparent motive behind the abduction, and about the photos and video clip, the story would become a worldwide blockbuster.

For that reason, Brennan wasn't looking forward to tomorrow's press conference. They'd be put on the spot for sure and it was going to be hard to justify holding stuff back – even though there was no telling how the kidnapper – or kidnappers – would react.

Brennan spent twenty minutes on the conference call updating his superiors. When he returned to the incident room, the operation was in overdrive, even though it was almost 11 p.m.

The team had seen the video clip of Molly being smacked and the impact on them had been profound. Two of the detectives – a man and a woman – had actually been moved to tears. Even Brennan found it difficult to control his emotions as he addressed them.

'If we didn't know before that the man who has abducted Molly Mason is a vicious psychopath then we do now,' he told them. 'And we also know that there is a strong possibility that he has at least one accomplice, and it could be a man or a woman.'

Brennan then announced that he was about to head up a raid on Edwin Sharp's new flat in Tooting. He nominated three officers to go with him and told the rest to chase down every conceivable angle.

'Prioritise all persons of interest,' he said. 'That includes everyone with an MO that fits the bill. And put pressure on the computer wizards. I want to know who sent that bloody email to Sarah.'

Brennan made one quick call before leaving the station. He wanted to say goodnight to his wife before she went to bed. Grace was a night owl who loved to sit up late watching box sets and movies. It was a simple pleasure that might soon be denied her.

According to her prognosis she had about a year before the dementia started to seriously impact on her life. No one could be sure to what degree it would impair her judgement and ravage her memory. But it was certainly going to change her from the fun-loving, intelligent woman that he'd married.

'I have to go out,' he told her. 'And I know for sure now that I won't be coming home tonight.'

'Is the little girl still missing?' she asked him.

'I'm afraid so.'

'Then I'll say a prayer for her and her mother.'

'You do that, sweetheart. And don't forget to take your pills.'

'And don't *you* forget to stay safe and not to take any risks.'

She said it whenever he phoned her from work and every time he left home in the morning. It was one of the many little things he loved about her. And it scared him to think that at some point in the not too distant future she would probably stop saying it.

19

Sarah

'Molly has never been smacked. She's only ever known people to be kind to her.'

I was rambling on as the haunted space in my heart grew with every single beat. I had never felt so scared, so helpless. My chest was tight and burning and my head was filled with my daughter's screams.

We were back in the living room and Sergeant Palmer had made me a cup of tea which sat untouched on the coffee table in front of me.

I was still grappling with what she'd said about the movement of the camera. Did it mean that the man had at least one accomplice? And if so, was that person just as vicious and heartless?

'It's making me sick imagining what he – or they – could be doing to her,' I sobbed. 'She's just a baby. She'll be thinking that I've deserted her.'

I choked on my own tears and started coughing. Adam lowered himself onto the sofa next to me and I felt his hand on my shoulder. When I stopped coughing he said something, but the noise in my head prevented me from hearing what it was. I didn't care because no words were going to erase the pain I was experiencing. I felt as if I had been torn inside out while a cold fist was squeezing my heart.

I saw then that lines of strain had appeared around Adam's mouth and his eyes were dull with shock. Sandpaper stubble coated his chin and the veins were bulging out of his neck.

The situation was taking its toll on both of us, physically and mentally. I felt sure that if I looked in a mirror I wouldn't recognise myself.

Molly's screams continued to echo in my head and when I closed my eyes I saw her face, the features distorted with distress.

I went to the drinks cabinet and poured another whisky. I downed it in one go and it made me shiver and gag. I then walked over to the window and pulled back the curtains.

'I closed them because of all the press outside,' Sergeant Palmer said behind me.

I could see a crowd of men and woman down below. They'd been pushed back by a couple of uniformed police officers into the parking area where they would no doubt spend the night.

I was spotted within seconds and there was a flurry of activity. Cameras flashed and I heard several people shout my name.

It suddenly occurred to me that there was no good reason not to talk to the media, given that Brennan was planning a press conference anyway in the morning if Molly hadn't been found.

So I asked myself why I shouldn't confront them now and make a direct appeal to the kidnapper. He was bound to be watching the news and it was just possible that what I had to say might weaken his resolve.

I thought about it for a few seconds and then found myself rushing towards the front door, intent on exiting the flat before

Adam and Sergeant Palmer realised what I was going to do and tried to talk me out of it.

Sergeant Palmer called out to me, but by then I was hurtling down the stairs, while desperately trying to assemble my thoughts.

I knew I looked a mess, but I was hoping that would work to my advantage. I wanted the kidnapper to see that he had already succeeded in punishing me. Perhaps then he would show some compassion and let Molly go.

As I walked outside, my gait was unsteady and the breath thundered in my ears. I told myself that I had to stay calm and put my message across as strongly and as clearly as possible. And when the questions came I would answer them truthfully and without hesitation.

I had grown used to confronting the media in my capacity as a detective. But this was different and it was not going to be so easy because now I was the distraught mother of a stolen baby and not an experienced copper doing her job.

My appearance outside sparked an immediate reaction and the crowd of reporters and photographers surged forward, leaving the two police officers on duty powerless to stop them.

Lenses were trained on me, questions were fired, and flashbulbs popped.

I stopped on the edge of the parking area and blinked against the harsh beam of light from a TV camera.

'Have you come to make a statement, Sarah?' one reporter shouted.

'Do you know why your daughter was taken?' yelled another.

I folded my arms tightly across my chest and felt a ball in my throat. I told myself to stay calm, that I couldn't allow myself to fall apart.

The man who has Molly needs to hear what you have to say. You have to try to convince him to end his brutal and sadistic mission.

My lips felt dry so I ran my tongue along them, then inhaled several times to help compose myself. The whisky still coated the inside of my mouth and I hoped that nobody would smell it on my breath.

I started to speak just as Adam and Sergeant Palmer appeared either side of me. Adam gripped my elbow and said, 'You shouldn't be doing this, Sarah. You're in no fit state.'

I pulled my arm free. 'I have to,' I replied through pinched lips. 'I can't just sit around doing nothing.'

He said something I didn't catch and stepped back, probably because he knew there was no point arguing with me.

I then raised a hand to stop the questions which were now coming thick and fast.

'I want to make an appeal,' I said, my voice thick and scratchy. 'I want to appeal to the man who has taken my daughter to please let her go. She's just a baby and I miss her so much.'

I paused, swallowed, let my arms drop to my sides.

'You claim that I've wronged you in some way and that this is how you intend to punish me,' I continued, speaking directly to the kidnapper. 'But surely you must know that making my daughter suffer is cruel beyond words. Please, please find it in your heart to return her to me. She doesn't . . .'

An image of Molly being smacked resurfaced in my mind suddenly and it made me catch my breath. I felt the heat in my eyes and I struggled to hold back the tears.

'Are you saying that the man who abducted your daughter has been in touch?' a reporter at the back of the crowd called out.

I nodded. 'He's sent text messages to me along with photos and a video.'

I realised I was giving away more than I'd intended, but now I wanted to let it all out, get it off my chest. I wanted people to know what was happening so that they could look out for Molly and call the police if they suspected someone they knew of being the kidnapper.

Sergeant Palmer stepped in front of me and tried to steer me back into the block, but I pushed her away.

'I want the man who took Molly to know I genuinely have no idea what I'm supposed to have done to him,' I said. 'I've racked my brain, but I just don't understand why this is happening. I am not a bad person and I wouldn't knowingly hurt anyone.'

I turned slightly to the right and stared into the lens of a TV camera.

'Whoever you are, I beg you not to hurt my Molly again. You say your aim is to make me suffer. Well you've done that by sending me the video. I can't describe the effect it's had on Molly's father and me. We're both crushed. So please, please let us have our little girl back.'

I didn't know what else to say so I just stood there, my ears buzzing from the adrenaline rush.

There were several seconds during which no one spoke and the only sound was the distant rumble of thunder. All eyes were on me and I could tell from the expressions on the faces of some of the reporters that what I had said had come as a shock to them. This convinced me that I'd been right to speak out now and not wait until the formal press conference tomorrow. Surely it would have a much greater impact.

'Can you tell us exactly what the kidnapper wrote in the text messages?' someone asked.

Before I could respond, other questions were lobbed at me and it quickly descended into a raucous free-for-all.

'Tell us about the video, Sarah. What's on it?'

'Why did the police get us to pull the photo of your daughter on the sofa?'

'Do you think this has something to do with your job as a detective?'

'Is it true that the man who snatched Molly might not be working alone?'

Sergeant Palmer seized control of the situation then and it was a relief because the noise and the pressure was suddenly making me dizzy and disoriented. She grabbed my arm and pulled me back, then nudged me towards where Adam stood.

'That's all for now,' she shouted. 'As you can see, Miss Mason is distressed and she needs to return to her flat.'

But as Adam led me back towards the entrance to my block, one female reporter raised her voice above all the others and asked a question that shut everyone else up and halted me in my tracks.

'Are you aware, Miss Mason, that in the last few minutes your colleagues have made an arrest in connection with Molly's abduction?'

I spun round and sought her out in the crowd. She was standing at the front, not ten yards away, a woman somewhere in her thirties with long brown hair and thick-framed glasses.

'Is that true?' I burst out.

She nodded. 'I just received a call from my news editor. A man has been detained after officers raided a house here in London. According to our contact, he's apparently someone who is known to you.'

20

DCI Brennan

The raid on Edwin Sharp's poky ground-floor flat in Tooting had gone without a hitch. The tactical team hadn't even had to batter down the front door because Sharp just happened to arrive home only seconds before they swooped.

That was an hour ago and the flat was still filled with bodies in padded vests and uniforms.

But there was no sign of Molly Mason, which had come as a huge disappointment. Sharp was insisting that he had no idea where she was. So far they hadn't come across any evidence to prove he was lying.

The sofa in the living room was brown, not white, and there was no cot in any of the bedrooms. Plus, they hadn't found a balaclava or a hoody like the one worn by the man in the street camera footage.

However, Brennan was convinced that Sharp was hiding something, which was why he hadn't whisked him straight off to the nick. Officers were in the other room checking his phone and laptop and Brennan wanted to question him in situ rather than waste valuable time going through the formal process.

He'd made it clear to Sharp that he was their prime suspect but had so far ignored his pleas to speak to a solicitor.

'Five years ago you told Detective Mason that you would see to her when you got out of prison,' Brennan said to him. 'And it seems like too much of a coincidence that only weeks after you're released her daughter is abducted.'

Sharp was sitting across from Brennan at the table in the small, cluttered kitchen. He was wearing a tight, black T-shirt and baggy jeans. His skin was pale, eyes sunken, and he looked slightly undernourished. He was smoking a rolled-up cigarette and before responding to Brennan he sucked on it so hard it made his cheeks bulge.

'I've told you it's got nothing to do with me,' he said, his tone desperate. 'I can't even remember making any threats against that copper. And even if I did, she shouldn't have taken it seriously.'

'I don't believe you,' Brennan said. 'I'm willing to bet that you've stewed on it for five years and snatching Detective Mason's daughter is your way of punishing her for bringing you down.'

Sharp's face tightened. He exhaled a ribbon of smoke and said, 'That's not true.'

Brennan's mouth twisted into a cynical smile. 'Oh come off it. You're a fucking rapist. You like having power over women, and the fact that it was a woman who collared you must have been a hard thing to swallow.'

Sharp took another drag on his cigarette, then twisted it out in an ashtray on the table. Grey smoke spiralled towards the ceiling.

Brennan stared at him, examining every feature of his face, which was a mixture of fear and fury. He had smoker's lines around his mouth and tiny spidery veins in his cheeks.

He might have been good-looking once, but now he was gaunt and pasty, as though something vital had been sucked out of him.

'Look, you've got the wrong man,' Sharp said after a long pause. 'I've seen the news so I know all about what's happened. But it's got nothing to do with me and I'm not even that interested in it. As I've already told you, I wasn't anywhere near Streatham this morning when the kid was taken.'

Brennan nodded. 'But you can't prove that can you, Mr Sharp? You say you were in bed, but no one can corroborate that so it's hardly a cast-iron alibi.'

'But it's the truth. I didn't get up until eleven. I haven't got a job yet so there's no need to.'

Brennan clicked his tongue against the roof of his mouth and sighed.

'The problem is that you don't sound very convincing, Mr Sharp. You're coming across like someone who's been caught out because you didn't expect us to make the connection between you and Detective Mason.'

Sharp's eyes peeled wide. 'This is bollocks and you know it. You've seen for yourself that there's no kid here. And you haven't found a shred of evidence that links me to her or her mother.'

'Except that it was Detective Mason who was responsible for getting you banged up in spite of the fact that you claimed you were innocent.'

'I was innocent, but that doesn't mean I set out to get my own back on her. And even if that had been my intention, I wouldn't have snatched her baby. That's fucking sick.'

103

'So is rape, Mr Sharp. And yet you were convicted of that.'

Sharp jerked back in his chair, as though recoiling from a punch.

'If you're going to arrest me then do it,' he said. 'Otherwise go away and leave me in peace.'

'I have no intention of leaving here until you tell me what you've done with that little girl,' Brennan said. 'I'm assuming you've just come from wherever it is you're holding her. Maybe it's the home of an accomplice.'

Sharp shook his head. 'You're not listening to what I've been telling you. I am not a child snatcher. I went out for a walk earlier this evening and then before coming home I visited the all-night supermarket in the High Street. I've shown you the receipt to prove it.'

Brennan plucked a sealed plastic evidence bag from his inside pocket and held it up. It contained a wrinkled supermarket receipt.

'So you bought three things,' he said. 'A pint of milk, a book of stamps and an envelope.'

'That's right.'

'And you say that you used the envelope and a stamp for a letter which you posted while there.'

'Correct.'

'So how long were you out before you arrived at the supermarket?'

He shrugged. 'I'm not sure. Three, four hours maybe.'

'That sounds more like a hike than a leisurely walk.'

'It's my way of beating the boredom. Sitting in all day does my head in.'

'Then I'll ask you again. Where did you actually go on this marathon walk?'

'I can't remember exactly. The High Street, the heath. I dropped in at the Rose and Crown on Brompton Road about eight. But the rest of the time I just wandered aimlessly like I always do.'

'We'll be checking CCTV,' Brennan said.

'Good. It'll show that I'm not lying.'

Brennan began to experience the first inkling of doubt. Could it be that he was reading this wrong? Was he clutching at straws because he so wanted Sharp to be the kidnapper, despite the lack of evidence?

'Have you got a minute, guv?'

Brennan turned to see DS Fleming standing in the doorway, an anxious look on his face.

'What is it?' he asked.

Fleming lifted his brow. 'There's something you need to see.'

Brennan told Sharp to stay put, got up and followed Fleming along the hall and into the living room where two other officers were leaning over Sharp's laptop which was resting on the coffee table.

'We've found some interesting stuff,' Fleming said. 'Seems Mr Sharp has spent a good deal of time trawling the news sites for stories about the abduction. It started soon after the story broke. For some reason, he also printed off the photo of Molly on the sofa, although it doesn't appear to be here in the flat.'

Brennan stared down at the computer screen as one of the officers clicked through the sites that Sharp had been visiting.

'I agree it's interesting,' he said. 'But it still doesn't prove that he's the one who grabbed her. Only that he's been following the story.'

'But it's not all we've found,' Fleming said. 'The idiot hasn't bothered to delete the contents of his history file since he started using this laptop a few days after he got out. It's full of some rather incriminating stuff, much of which he's downloaded onto a file that he's neglected to conceal.'

Brennan was shown the various websites that Sharp had been visiting and also the contents of a file labelled: Private.

What he saw caused his breath to lurch in his chest and the blood to boil in his veins.

Back in the kitchen, Brennan had to fight to control the anger that was balled inside him like a fist.

'So it turns out you've told us at least one big fat lie, Mr Sharp,' he said.

Sharp's eyes flashed like shards of glass caught in the sunlight. He started to speak but Brennan talked over him.

'You told us you weren't interested in the abduction story and yet you've been following it religiously online. You even printed off that photo of Molly Mason and I'd love to know why.'

A sudden panic flamed on Sharp's face and his teeth played nervously against his bottom lip.

'I don't see what difference it makes,' he said, with false bravado. 'I was just a bit curious, like most people probably are. It's not as if I've committed a crime.'

'Oh, but you have,' Brennan said. 'You've been downloading child porn and that's a serious offence. It's going to put you right back behind bars where you belong.'

Sharp was speechless. He cast a desperate look at the other people in the room and then dropped his head into his hands.

'You're under arrest,' Brennan said. 'And we now have even more reason to believe that you are involved in the abduction of Molly Mason.'

Brennan read him his rights and got one of the uniformed officers to cuff him.

To the others in the room, he said, 'I want a forensic team to tear this flat apart. And gather as much CCTV footage as you can. We need to know exactly where this pervert has been today, and God willing, the trail will lead us to Detective Mason's daughter.'

21

Adam

Brennan finally returned Adam's call just after midnight. He confirmed what the reporter had said outside, that a man had been arrested during a raid on a house in Tooting.

'It's Edwin Sharp,' the DCI said, before going on to crash Adam's hopes by revealing that Molly hadn't been with him. 'He's denying any involvement in the abduction, but we have reason to believe that he could be lying. We're about to question him formally and at the same time we're checking on his movements today.'

'Has he got an alibi?' Adam asked.

'Not as such. He claims he was at home in bed when Molly was kidnapped. But there's no one to back it up.'

'So what makes you think he might have something to do with it? And please don't keep us in the dark. That will only make us more anxious.'

Brennan hesitated a moment, then said, 'Look, you need to keep this to yourselves, OK?'

'Of course,' he said and felt his heart miss a beat.

'Well we found some child porn on his laptop, and he can't really account for his whereabouts this afternoon and this evening. He claims he's been walking around town, so we're having to check CCTV cameras.'

Adam's jaw clenched involuntarily at the mention of child pornography and he had to force himself to remain calm.

'Have you had a look at his phone?' he asked.

'We have, and it wasn't the one used to send the text messages and email to Sarah. Or to take the photos and video of Molly.'

A beat of silence passed, then Adam said, 'So there's every chance that he's telling the truth?'

'It's possible,' Brennan conceded. 'But it's early days. We can't—'

Adam abruptly severed the connection. He'd heard enough. A crushing disappointment flooded through his system and the breath rushed out of him.

For a short time they had been given a frisson of hope, but now it was gone and he was drowning again in a cauldron of despair.

He should have known it was too good to be true. Edwin Sharp had been put in the frame only because Sarah remembered something he'd said to her over five years ago; and because they were scratching around for potential suspects. No way was he a solid, credible lead, even though he was into child porn.

Adam padded into the living room to give Sarah the bad news. She was sitting next to Sergeant Palmer on the sofa. She looked exhausted, drained of energy and emotion. Her haunted eyes were blackened with mascara and her hair was limp and greasy.

Adam's heart was up in his throat as he told her what Brennan had said.

'If Sharp does know where Molly is then you can be sure that Brennan will get it out of him,' Adam said, forcing calm into his voice.

Disbelief crossed her face like a shadow and she got to her feet.

'I'm going upstairs,' she said through the tears. 'I need to be alone for a while.'

She hurried out of the room and Adam resisted the urge to go after her. Instead he stood there, fisting his hands as the sudden, heavy silence pressed against his eardrums.

'Perhaps she needs to be prescribed something stronger by the doctor,' Sergeant Palmer said.

Adam nodded. 'You're probably right. I dread to think what it will do to her if Molly isn't found soon.'

'You look in a bad way yourself, sir,' Palmer said. 'Are you planning to stay here for the rest of the night?'

'I am. I'll crash in the spare room. I don't think I should leave her. I can go home and freshen up in the morning before the press conference.'

'Well I'll be here if either of you need me.'

'I appreciate it.'

Just then he felt his phone vibrate in his pocket with an incoming text message. He took it out and felt a stab of guilt when he saw who had sent it.

'I have to make a call,' he said to Sergeant Palmer. 'I'll go outside on the landing . Feel free to stretch out on the sofa. I won't disturb you unless I have to.'

'Thank you, sir,' she said. 'But I don't suppose any of us will get to sleep tonight.'

Adam stepped out onto the internal landing and walked to the far end, past two other flats, to a window that was slightly ajar and overlooked the parking area below. He stood close to it and hauled in a deep slice of evening air before opening the text message to read it again.

Hope you're bearing up. Call me again if you can. Please. H xx

Her name was Helen Casey and he'd been dating her for six weeks. She was a financial adviser who he'd met through an online dating agency. He enjoyed her company and even more so the sex. On Saturday they had spent the night at the hotel in Windsor before she flew off on a business trip to the States on Sunday. And that was when she'd revealed that she had fallen for him big time and wanted a full-on, monogamous relationship.

His cowardly response had been to tell her that he was smitten with her too. In truth, though, he wasn't yet ready to commit and was reluctant to get too involved too quickly.

He had spoken to Helen earlier on the phone while Sarah was with her parents, and he'd told her then what had happened. She'd been shocked and sympathetic and had offered to fly home so she could be with him. But he'd told her not to because he was confident that Molly would soon be found, which of course was a lie.

He decided now that it wouldn't be prudent to have another conversation with her tonight. At best it would exacerbate the guilty feelings that were stirring inside him. At worst it might cause him to lose his temper, because right at this moment he regarded her as an unnecessary distraction.

So he replied to the text, saying:

Sorry can't speak. With the police. Will call you tomorrow. A x

Adam sagged against the wall, feeling sick. Through the slightly open window he could hear the voices of the reporters and photographers downstairs in the parking area and it ignited a hot rage inside him.

He'd always had a low regard for the British press. Through experience, he'd come to view them as insensitive vultures who didn't give a shit for the people they wrote about.

He'd had more than a few run-ins with tabloid tossers over the years and had once punched a *Sun* newspaper crime reporter in the face.

To them this story was like manna from heaven. He'd seen the excitement on their faces as Sarah poured her heart out to them earlier. They hadn't been thinking about how much she was suffering, only about how they would write up what was turning into the juiciest human interest tale of the year.

He still couldn't quite get his mind around the fact that this story was all about his own daughter. His baby. The little girl who gave meaning to his life.

In trying to stay strong for Sarah, he had so far succeeded in delaying the full shocking impact of what was happening. But it was there all the same, bubbling below the surface like a raging volcano.

After composing himself he went back inside to find Sarah. He thought she'd be lying on her bed, but instead she'd retreated to Molly's room where she was sat on the floor with her back against the wall and her legs stretched out.

Just being in the room sparked a series of images in Adam's head: his daughter crawling across the floor, the way she giggled as he tickled her ribs, then sobbing because he was leaving her to return to his flat in Mitcham.

He squeezed his eyes shut, trapping the tears, and when he opened them Sarah was looking up at him, her face illuminated by the flickering night light on top of the chest of drawers.

'I'm trying to imagine that Molly is sleeping in her cot,' she said, her voice weak and strained. 'And that the last fifteen hours didn't happen.'

'Do you want me to sit with you?' he asked.

'I'd rather be by myself if that's OK.'

He was a little hurt but he hid it by flashing a faint smile.

'Of course it is. I quite understand.'

She turned to face the cot again and he wondered if she was able to sense their daughter's presence. He couldn't himself, but if Sarah could then he hoped that it was in some small way comforting for her.

Stepping out of the room, he gently closed the door behind him. Then he went to the bathroom, emptied his bladder and washed his face. He found an unused toothbrush in the cupboard above the sink and used it to clean his teeth. To say that it felt strange going through the motions again in the flat that used to be his home would have been a gross understatement. It felt positively weird, but he was sure that being back in his own flat right now wouldn't have felt right either.

The spare room was sparse but comfortable, with a double bed and a stand-alone wardrobe. The walls had been given a fresh coat of magnolia paint since he'd moved out and there was a new patterned rug on the floor.

He closed the curtains and switched off the light. Then he took off his shoes and stretched out on top of the duvet without taking his clothes off. He didn't for a single second believe that he would be able to sleep, so he wouldn't even bother to try. He just stared up at the shifting patterns on the ceiling and wondered where his daughter was and what she was doing. He prayed that she was asleep and recovering from the beating she had taken. He tried not to dwell on other nightmarish scenarios, including the possibility that she was being sexually abused. The thought of it made his chest hurt and his eyes water.

He had to force his mind to move in another direction and found himself reviewing the events of this terrible day, starting with the shock on Sarah's face when he first saw her in the

113

neighbour's kitchen. Then the text messages from the kidnapper, that ghastly video and finally talking to Brennan about who might be behind it.

It didn't seem possible that so much had happened in such a short time. Was it really only fifteen hours?

When his daughter was snatched, he was at the Old Bailey waiting for the jury to return a verdict on Victor Rosetti. And Brennan broke the news to him over the phone just after Rosetti was whisked away in his Mercedes having been found not guilty of drug trafficking.

Adam hadn't thought about the Romanian gangster since that moment. But now, suddenly, he was reminded of the brief conversation he'd had with him through the Mercedes window.

'*We may have lost the battle, scumbag,*' he'd said to the man. '*But not the war. It won't be long before I collar you for something you won't be able to wriggle out of.*'

'*Don't waste taxpayers' money,*' Rosetti had said. '*It will never happen. Besides, I should be the least of your worries.*'

'*What's that supposed to mean?*'

'*You'll find out soon enough – word is, you're in for a nasty surprise.*'

Adam let out an involuntary gasp and sat bolt upright on the bed. Rosetti's words rang in his ears and sent blood pulsing through his veins. He hadn't thought about that conversation before now because he'd been trying to concentrate his mind on who might have a grudge against his ex-wife – not on who would want to punish him. But what Rosetti had said suddenly seemed hugely significant.

'*. . . word is, you're in for a nasty surprise.*'

What had the bastard meant by that? Had it simply been an idle threat? Or had he known that something bad was going to happen?

114

The air seemed to disappear from the room suddenly, as a series of alarming questions pummelled his brain.

Was it conceivable that Rosetti had instigated the abduction? Was it him or one of his heavies who had smacked Molly on the video? And was he just pretending that it was an act of revenge against Sarah so that the police wouldn't make the connection?

The mere thought of it caused Adam's heart to flip over and, as he leapt off the bed, he realised that he was struggling to breathe.

22

Sarah

I was in the middle of yet another prayer when Adam burst back into the room. He was in a state of high agitation and could barely get his words out.

He gave me a hurried account of his brief encounter with Victor Rosetti outside the Old Bailey and what the Romanian had told him. I experienced a flash of anger and frustration, but it was quickly replaced by a ray of hope that this might turn out to be a genuine lead.

'Why didn't you mention this to Brennan?' I said.

'Because I pushed from my mind everything that happened before I heard that Molly had been snatched,' he said. 'I just failed to make the connection until just now.'

'Then you need to tell Brennan.'

'I will and he'll have to take it seriously. Rosetti is an evil bastard and he has it in for me. I wouldn't put it past him to do something like this.'

He tried ringing Brennan straight away but got no answer on his mobile phone.

'Shit.'

He rushed down the stairs and I followed him into the living room, my breath coming in loud, shallow puffs.

Sergeant Palmer was still awake, sitting on the sofa watching one of the news channels.

'I've just remembered something that happened this morning,' Adam told her. 'It could be relevant and you need to check it out.'

She muted the TV and listened to what he had to say. Then she urged him to calm down and called the incident room.

A minute later she was through to Brennan and the DCI asked to speak directly to Adam.

'Shall I make you something to drink?' Palmer asked me after she had handed over her phone. 'Tea or coffee perhaps?'

But I shook my head, too hyped up to provide a coherent response.

I paced the room instead, my heart a heavy weight in my chest.

When Adam hung up he told us that Brennan was going to move swiftly and organise a raid on Victor Rosetti's home in Fulham, West London.

'He's taking Rosetti's remark seriously,' he said. 'And he's liaising with my lot at the NCA. We have a file on all the Romanian's criminal associates.'

I could tell that Adam was frustrated and he instinctively wanted to go looking for Rosetti himself. But Palmer persuaded him to sit down and insisted on making him a cup of tea.

He complied, albeit reluctantly, and then at her request he wrote down exactly what Rosetti had said to him.

I didn't know what to make of it myself. It was easy to believe that Victor Rosetti was capable of getting one of his gang members to abduct Molly, but harder for me to accept that he would take the risk, especially as he was acquitted by the jury.

When I put this to Adam, he said, 'When Molly was taken,

Rosetti was still waiting for a verdict. He might have decided that the outcome was irrelevant and that he was going to punish me whatever the result. So he could well have got his people to act around the time the jury were due to deliver.'

It struck me as an improbable scenario, but as a detective I'd learned long ago never to rule anything out, especially when the motive is revenge.

However, despite Adam's reasoning, I didn't share his fervour for Rosetti being the new prime suspect. I was convinced from what the kidnapper had written in the text messages and email that it was me he wanted to punish, not Adam.

I was about to ask Sergeant Palmer what she thought when I caught sight of myself on the TV. I grabbed the remote control from the coffee table where she'd placed it and turned the volume back on.

'I want to appeal to the man who has taken my daughter to please let her go. She's just a baby and I miss her so much.'

I almost didn't recognise myself and it sounded to me like someone else's voice.

The coverage of my impromptu appeal was being screened unedited and as I watched it I couldn't help wondering what the kidnapper would think and if he'd be encouraged to respond.

The sequence ended with a close-up of my face after the reporter revealed that a man had been detained.

I looked like someone who'd had the blood drained from her body. My skin was pale and stretched and there were new, deep lines across my forehead.

I was reminded for a moment of all the other distressed mothers who had appeared on TV over the years to beg for the safe return of their children.

And I wondered just how many times their emotional appeals had actually brought about a happy ending.

My mother called within minutes of my appearance on TV, despite it being nearly two in the morning. She was distraught and demanded to know why I hadn't told her about the video. She broke down on the phone and my father came on and I had to go through it all again for him.

Afterwards, I left Adam and Sergeant Palmer downstairs and went upstairs to lie on my bed. But I came nowhere near to falling asleep. I was coiled like a tight spring, hounded by the unendurable terror that someone was harming my baby.

Adam came in several times to inform me that there had been no further developments and that my phone – which he was holding onto – had received several text messages but only from friends and well-wishers.

By the time daylight filtered into the room I'd shed so many tears that my pillow was soaking wet.

I went over to the window and peered through the curtains. The sky was a fragile blue, and in the parking area the reporters and paparazzi were still gathered.

I hauled myself into the en suite and my stomach twisted at the sight of myself in the mirror. My eyes were rimmed with purple shadows and my hair looked as though it had been flattened with a heavy coat of wallpaper adhesive.

I spent a long time in the shower, hoping the hot jets of water would make me feel more able to cope with the day ahead. But I felt just as lifeless after I got out and towelled myself dry.

I applied a minimal amount of make-up to cover the blotches and shadows and then put on a pair of jeans and a light brown crew-neck sweater. Finally I scraped my hair back in a tight bun and went downstairs.

Adam and Sergeant Palmer were waiting for me and I discovered that they had both been up all night watching the rolling news channels. Neither of them had showered and Adam told me he would soon shoot home to shave and get changed.

I was handed a mug of steaming coffee and some toast. The coffee I was desperate for, but I forced down the toast because I knew I had to eat something or risk collapsing.

It was a strange feeling being in the flat with Adam and a police officer I didn't really know. I was so used to it being just Molly and me. The mornings were always such a rush as I prepared for work and got Molly ready to go to her grandparents' house.

The fact that she wasn't here hit me hard suddenly. I felt the sting of tears in my eyes as I pictured her sitting in the high chair and making a mess of herself as she dug into her cereal.

But I managed somehow not to break down and took a couple of deep breaths to regain my equilibrium.

Then Sergeant Palmer updated me as I drank the coffee. Brennan and his team had been at it all night and two hours ago Victor Rosetti had been taken in for questioning.

'But I regret to say that there was no sign of Molly at his house in Fulham,' she said. 'They're now searching the place and checking out any other properties he's connected with.'

'It doesn't mean it wasn't him,' Adam said. 'Why else would he say that he'd heard I was in for a nasty surprise?'

My mind conjured up an image of Victor Rosetti, one of the most notorious of the Eastern European gangsters who had muscled in on the drugs and prostitution rackets in London in recent years. I had never met the man, but I knew all about him and his fearsome reputation. Like most detectives within the Met,

I'd followed his trial with interest and found it astonishing that the jury had seen fit to clear him.

Palmer was now telling us that preparations were under way for a press conference to take place at noon at the Yard, and Brennan wanted us both to attend.

'There have been scores of calls overnight in response to your appeal,' she said to me. 'Most are from people claiming they think they've spotted Molly, but as you yourself know, a fair number will be cranks and time-wasters. However, every call will be followed up.'

It was what made this case different to most. Adam and I both knew what to expect and just how difficult it was for the investigating officers.

A huge amount of information would be flooding into the incident room. Dealing with all the interviews, the computer searches, the CCTV footage and the door-to-door inquiries would be enormously time-consuming. Making progress would be slow-going unless they got a lucky break. And that was what everyone would be hoping for.

I drank a second cup of coffee with my first smoke of the day. I hoped it would help me to relax, but it didn't.

Time moved on as though in slow motion and it wasn't until just after ten that there came another chilling development.

A fourth text message from the kidnapper arrived on my phone. I experienced an almost paralysing panic as I opened it up and read it.

Morning Sarah. Molly had me up at the crack of dawn. She was upset when she realised that her mummy wasn't here. But she'll get used to that in time. I'll be sending you another video clip later so be prepared. And btw I enjoyed your little performance in front of the cameras. Very touching. It even made Molly smile.

23

DCI Brennan

'I have done some very bad things during my forty-three years on this planet, but stealing a child is not one of them.'

Victor Rosetti spoke with a deep, heavy accent, his voice gravelly from too many cigarettes.

He had a round face, low brow, fleshy lips. He was wearing an open-neck shirt, the sleeves rolled up to reveal a spider's web tattoo on his right arm just below the elbow.

Brennan gave him an assessing look across the table in Interview Room One. The Romanian was sitting next to his solicitor, a cocky individual in his thirties named Mark Finn, who sported a smart grey tapered suit and oversized glasses. The fourth person in the room was DC Foster.

Rosetti had refused to answer any questions until Finn arrived ten minutes ago. Now he was claiming to have no knowledge of Molly Mason's whereabouts, which was not unexpected.

'So what were you referring to when you told Detective Boyd that you'd heard he was in for a nasty surprise?' Brennan said.

Rosetti sucked a breath through his teeth and shook his head.

'Boyd is lying. I didn't say that to him.'

'So are you denying that after you left the court building you crossed over the road and spoke to Detective Boyd through your car window?'

'Not at all. We pulled over and I told him to cheer up, that he had to accept that you win some and you lose some. I can remember the exchange word for word. He wasn't happy and so we drove off because I could see he was about to lose his temper. I've given you the names of my two friends who were in the car with me. They heard what was said.'

Brennan did not believe a word of it. This was his first encounter with Rosetti, but he knew him to be a slippery customer from reputation, and the fact that he had just managed to avoid a long and well due prison sentence was proof of that.

'So why would Detective Boyd make it up?' Brennan asked him.

Rosetti shrugged. 'That's a good question. I can only assume it was to give you people another excuse to raid my home.'

'That makes no sense,' Brennan said.

'Really? The NCA are furious because I was cleared by the jury. They'll do everything possible to make life difficult for me from now on.'

'That's nonsense.'

'Not from where I'm sitting. I've been out for less than twenty-four hours and I'm already back in a police station being grilled about something I didn't do.'

'I insist you release my client right away,' the lawyer said as he leaned forward across the table. 'You have no grounds to hold him since it's clear that Detective Boyd has misled you.'

Brennan curled his lips. 'That's highly unlikely, Mr Finn. The man's daughter is missing and sending his colleagues on a wild-goose chase wouldn't help us find her.'

'Then perhaps his distress is causing him to act irrationally,' Finn said. 'He wants to blame someone and has decided to target my client.'

Brennan moved his neck from side to side to loosen it. He was exhausted, and his eyes were heavy and gritty. Having missed out on a night's sleep he was feeling knackered.

He had earlier spent over an hour questioning their other suspect, Edwin Sharp, and that session had been just as frustrating and unproductive.

Now both men were flatly denying any involvement in the kidnapping and there was so far not a scrap of evidence to prove they were lying.

Yet Brennan's gut told him that neither man could be trusted. Sharp was a convicted rapist after all and Rosetti a notorious drugs baron. And it could reasonably be argued that they each had a motive for wanting to abduct little Molly Mason.

'I intend to lodge a complaint over the way that you and your officers have conducted themselves,' Finn said. 'You forcibly entered my client's home without a warrant and caused unnecessary alarm among his guests. As you know, one of them suffered a physical injury in the process.'

'Are you talking about the woman who fell and broke her nose?'

'That's right. It happened as she was trying to defend herself.'

'Defend herself, my arse. She was off her head on drugs and booze and she tried to punch one of my officers.'

She was also one of several prostitutes who'd been paid to attend Rosetti's coming out party, which had been in full swing when the tactical team turned up.

Brennan looked at his watch and decided it was time for a break. He wanted to find out if the search of Rosetti's house had turned anything up. He also wanted to review the statements of

Rosetti's two minders who had apparently heard the conversation he'd had with Boyd.

But the decision to suspend the interview for half an hour prompted the Romanian to thump the table with the flat of his hand.

'This is harassment on the part of the police,' he barked, and his pupils became wildly dilated. 'I have rights that are being violated and I don't—'

Brennan cut him off as the anger rose in his blood. 'Do you really think I give a shit about your rights when a small child has been abducted and we strongly suspect you of arranging it?'

The detective didn't wait for Rosetti and his brief to respond. Instead he got to his feet abruptly and stormed out of the room, leaving DC Foster to turn off the recorder.

Brennan went straight to the incident room and convened a meeting to find out the latest state of play.

The first thing he learned was that Sarah had received another message from the kidnapper, who had informed her that he would soon be sending her a second video.

This time the tech team were monitoring her mobile phone, so they would see it at the same time she did.

It was a shock to Brennan because the message was unlikely to have come from either Sharp or Rosetti, who had both been in custody at the time. Sure, it was possible the text had been on a time delay but he couldn't see why either man would have gone to the trouble since they wouldn't have known that they'd be in no position to send it. So either it was sent by an accomplice or they genuinely hadn't been involved.

Brennan then listened to the various reports with a growing sense that they were getting nowhere fast. There was discouraging news from the search teams who had found no evidence that Molly Mason had ever been inside Sharp's flat or Rosetti's house.

Examination of the suspects' phones and computers had also drawn a blank, apart from the child porn on Sharp's laptop. And they still hadn't managed to trace the source of the text messages and email.

What's more, the CCTV footage so far collected from around Sharp's home in Lewisham did indeed show him wandering the streets during the late afternoon and evening. In one clip he was seen buying stamps and an envelope in a Tesco store and then sitting on a bench to write something on a sheet of paper that he produced from his pocket. He then posted the letter in a box outside the entrance.

Brennan wanted to know what Sharp had written on the paper. In fact he was so curious that he told two detectives to haul him back to the interview room from his holding cell so that they could ask him.

'You'd better alert the duty solicitor,' he told them. 'He's probably in the canteen.'

Brennan was then briefed about the response to Sarah Mason's appeal and the CCTV clip of the man in the hood carrying Molly away from her grandparents' home.

'At the last count we'd received a hundred calls,' he was told. 'Most from people who say they think they've seen Molly. Some are even claiming they know where she is. Needless to say it's taking time responding to each and every one.'

Brennan then called Sergeant Palmer and asked how Sarah and Adam were coping.

'They're still struggling,' she said. 'The latest text message has made things worse. Miss Mason is very upset.'

Brennan asked to speak to Sarah but it was her ex-husband

who came on the line demanding to know what was happening with Victor Rosetti.

'He's claiming that he didn't say that you were in for a nasty surprise,' Brennan said. 'And he's denying all knowledge of Molly's abduction.'

'The bastard's lying,' Adam said, his voice tight with adrenaline. 'I know what I bloody well heard. I'm only sorry I didn't recall it sooner.'

'Well proving it is not going to be easy.'

'Then let me bloody well talk to him. I'll get—'

'You know that won't be possible,' Brennan cut in. 'You can't get involved. You have to trust me and the rest of the team to do our jobs.'

'Then get him to tell you what he's done with our daughter. He knows where she is. I'm sure of it.'

Adam was becoming hysterical so Sergeant Palmer took her phone off him.

'The poor man's very distraught,' she said to Brennan. 'He's convinced himself that Victor Rosetti took Molly in order to punish him.'

'Well that may well be the case,' Brennan said. 'But you need to calm him down before the press conference. I don't want him to lose it in front of the cameras.'

Brennan then had a quick word with Sarah, assuring her that the team were still working as hard as they could to find Molly. He gave her a brief update on both suspects and said he would see her in a little while at New Scotland Yard.

'I wish I could give you more positive news,' he added. 'But we are where we are. If there are any developments between now and the press conference I'll get straight back to you.'

Brennan pocketed his phone and headed for the vending

machine to help himself to a coffee. But before he got there he was approached by Jade Law, one of the admin staff. She gave him an urgent message from the detectives who were interviewing Sharp.

'They want you to go to Interview Room Two right away, sir,' she said.

'Do you know why?'

'Well apparently Edwin Sharp is insisting on talking to you. He's saying he's ready to come clean about what he's been up to.'

24

Sarah

It took Adam a while to calm down after he spoke to Brennan about Victor Rosetti. He stomped around the living room cursing, his face puce with rage.

I was reminded of when we were together and he would fly off on one when he didn't get his own way. But this time I felt that his anger was fully justified.

He firmly believed that the Romanian gangster was somehow involved in Molly's abduction.

'Why else would he have insinuated after his acquittal that something bad was going to happen to me?' he kept saying.

While he talked it over with Palmer, my thoughts returned to the latest text message which had made my blood run cold.

In a weird conversational tone the kidnapper had said that Molly had woken up at the crack of dawn and was upset because her mother wasn't there for her.

But she'll get used to that in time, he'd written.

And of course he was right. My daughter was at an age when memories don't last, when children live in the present and instantly forget things. So how long, I wondered, before she forgot me, her mother? Would it be a matter of months or just weeks?

I suspected that the answer would be out there on the internet, posted by a bevy of child psychologists, behavioural therapists and people who'd been separated from their parents at an early age. But I resisted the temptation to do a Google search because I knew it would only add to the weight of my despair.

I was about to spark up a cigarette to ease the tension inside me when my attention was drawn to the TV screen.

Sky News were showing the front pages of the morning newspapers and they were dominated by our story. The headlines were big and bold and beneath them were photographs of Molly.

'*Daughter of London cops abducted,*' Sun.

'*Mum of kidnapped toddler makes dramatic appeal,*' Mail.

'*Kidnapper taunts mother of stolen child,*' Express.

'*Two men held over child abduction,*' Guardian.

'*Massive hunt for kidnapped baby,*' Metro.

The photos that had been published were those that Adam had provided and thankfully no publication carried the one the kidnapper had sent to me showing Molly on his sofa.

Sky News then ran their latest report on the story. It included shots of my parents' house, the CCTV footage showing the kidnapper taking Molly, my appeal for him to hand her back, and a short clip of Brennan confirming that two men were being interviewed under caution. But their names were being withheld, although the reporter ended his piece-to-camera by saying, 'We understand that the two suspects are known to Detective Mason and her ex-husband. Both are believed to have a criminal background.'

A breathless cry came from my mouth and I felt a weight crashing through my chest. I dropped onto the armchair and my eyes filmed over with tears.

'What if the kidnapper gets upset because the CCTV footage of him with Molly is shown?' I said.

Adam didn't know what to say. He stood in front of me, ramrod stiff, his face a confusion of emotions.

Neither of us moved for perhaps a full minute. Then Adam announced that there was no time for him to go back to his flat to change and freshen up. I told him to go and shower upstairs.

When he'd left the room, Sergeant Palmer told me that she would be going home as soon as we were on our way to the Yard.

'I'll be back later,' she said. 'Meanwhile don't hesitate to call me if you have a problem or just need to talk to someone. You have my mobile number.'

I was glad I didn't have to face the prospect of being cooped up in the flat all day, wondering what the next video from the kidnapper would contain. Just thinking about it gave me palpitations. Would it show him beating Molly again or would I have to watch my baby enduring something far worse?

I needed to be involved in the effort to find her. If I couldn't be a part of the investigation then I'd make another appeal to the kidnapper, even though the thought of it made me nervous. At least then I'd be doing something constructive instead of floundering hopelessly in my own personal hell.

There was another media scrum when the time came to leave. Television crews and photographers jostled each other for the best position, and we were showered with questions. But this time I kept my head down and refused to respond.

There were more uniforms on hand to control the pack and help us through to Adam's car, a shiny black Audi. He was insisting on driving himself to the Yard, so I sat in the passenger seat and we set off with a police escort.

The sky had turned a harsh grey, the sun having fallen victim to a layer of thick clouds.

Every sinew in my body began to tighten as we drove. I wasn't looking forward to what lay ahead. Police press conferences were invariably tense and unpredictable, and I had always felt sorry for the distraught relatives of victims when they were thrust into the harsh glare of publicity. I could never have imagined that one day I'd find myself in that same position, pleading for help from the British public. Everything that was happening still seemed so unreal and my head was filled with a thousand thoughts.

'Have you got your phone?' Adam said suddenly.

'It's in my bag.'

'Are you sure you'll be able to hear it if a text comes through?'

He had a point. It was noisy in the car, what with the sound of the engine and the hum of the traffic from outside.

I reached down into the footwell and delved into the shoulder bag which rested between my legs. I pulled out the phone and checked to make sure that I hadn't missed any calls or messages. I hadn't.

'Let's just suppose that Molly wasn't taken by either Sharp or Rosetti,' Adam said. 'Have you given any more thought to who else it might be?'

'Of course I bloody well have,' I snapped.

'OK, don't bite my head off. I just thought I'd ask.'

'Well it was a stupid question. In between crying all I've done is search my memory for an answer to what's happening. But it's not there, or if it is I'm not seeing it.'

'Then you need to think harder, Sarah. Surely if you've given someone a reason to have such a massive grudge against you then you wouldn't forget it.'

'We've already been over this with Brennan and Sergeant

132

Palmer,' I said. 'I really have no idea why anyone would feel the need to punish me like this. I honestly don't, Adam. If I did I'd tell you.'

He opened his mouth to say something else but thought better of it and turned his attention back to the road. I watched him for a moment, noting that a vein in the side of his neck was pulsating. It always did that when he was stressed, and I remembered that when our marriage started to fall apart it never seemed to stop.

I turned away from him and looked out of the side window. I found myself wishing that things had worked out differently, that Adam and I had stayed happily married and that he hadn't cheated on me. Perhaps then both our lives would have been less difficult and more fulfilling. And our only daughter would not have been taken from us.

The distant past loomed up out of nowhere and I recalled when Adam and I first met. The memory made my breath catch in the back of my throat.

He was the first detective to speak to me when I joined Lewisham CID, and I was immediately drawn to his warm smile and come-to-bed eyes.

There was something about him that set him apart from the others and drew me in almost from day one.

Before long we were seeing each other in secret and we were both delighted when the powers-that-be decided we'd make a good team.

For nine months we worked together and it proved to be a successful partnership. We made some high-profile collars and what I found so touching was that, wherever possible, he sought to give me the credit. It was his way of helping me to win the respect of a male-dominated team that was rife with prejudice and sexism.

One particular case had always stuck in my mind. The perp was Bobby Knight, a leading figure in a South London gang involved in everything from drugs to people trafficking. He was engaged to the gang boss's daughter and therefore thought he was untouchable.

But then one day my most reliable snout told me that Knight had a large stash of heroin in the house waiting to be shipped out across the country. I told Adam and he advised me to treat the intelligence with caution because he doubted that it was credible. He reckoned that Knight was too smart to keep anything incriminating in his own house. But I told him that I trusted my source and wanted to go for it. So he backed me when I took it upstairs and got them to approve a dawn raid on the property.

Luckily for me the information proved reliable. We found two small bags containing Class-A drugs including heroin, cocaine and methadone. The size of the haul was disappointing – it had a street value of only about £5,000 – but fortunately that wasn't all we found. In one of his bedroom drawers I myself happened to find an automatic revolver.

It gave me great satisfaction to be the one to arrest Knight and put the cuffs on him. It was a tremendous result, and Adam made sure that everyone knew it was down to me.

Knight was convicted and jailed for eight years for illegal possession of drugs and a gun, though, throughout, maintained he was innocent and accused us of stitching him up. And it led to my promotion from detective constable to detective sergeant.

Shortly after that the professional partnership between Adam and me ended when he transferred to the National Crime Agency.

But that made it easier for us to be open about our relationship and within months we were married.

Back then it was all so wonderful, and I felt like I'd been blessed. I had a great job and a terrific husband. I was looking forward to starting a family and to growing old with the man I loved.

But that wasn't how it panned out because Adam decided that for him it wasn't enough.

25

Sarah

By the time we got to New Scotland Yard I had a dull headache and my mouth felt uncomfortably dry.

It said something about the importance of the case that the press conference was being held there and not in Wandsworth. I soon discovered that it was partly due to the fact that the Commissioner himself was keen to be on hand to give interviews. According to Brennan, he wanted it to be known that the case was a top priority – not just because it involved a child, but also because the parents were two serving police officers in the Met. I'd never met the man but it sounded like he was genuinely concerned and I appreciated his input.

As soon as we arrived, Brennan ushered us into an office he'd been allocated. I could tell that like the rest of us he hadn't had any sleep. His face was lined with emotion and fatigue, and there were bags under his eyes.

'The press conference begins in fifteen minutes,' he said. 'In a moment I'll go through how we intend to approach it. But first I need to give you an update.'

He started with Victor Rosetti. The Romanian was still in custody and still insisting that he didn't tell Adam that he was in for a nasty surprise.

Adam started to speak but Brennan raised a hand to stop him.

'Right now it's just your word against his, I'm afraid. And his two minders are backing him up. Plus, the search of his house hasn't turned up anything at all to link him to your daughter.'

Adam's face contorted in anger. 'So that's it? You're just going to let him go?'

'We'll hold him as long as we can while we make further inquiries. We're talking to his associates to find out who does and doesn't have an alibi for yesterday morning when Molly was taken.'

Adam shook his head and blew out his cheeks. He was poised to pursue the subject but Brennan didn't give him the chance.

'We've made more progress with Edwin Sharp, though,' he said. 'A short time ago Sharp finally decided to tell us what he's been up to. However, from what he said and what we know I'm 99 per cent sure he didn't snatch your daughter.'

'Why have you come to that conclusion?' I said. 'Given that the man's a paedophile and he threatened to see to me when he got out of prison.'

Brennan covered his mouth with his fist as he cleared his throat. 'There are CCTV cameras at either end of the street where he lives in Tooting,' he said. 'An hour ago we were able to view the footage from yesterday and he doesn't appear until midday, which tallies with what he told us about staying in bed until eleven.'

'But you said he'd been monitoring the story and had even printed the picture of Molly,' I pointed out.

'That's right. He says he was keen to know what was happening because he was pleased that it was happening to you. He admits he still harbours a grudge against you but never had any intention of doing anything about it upon his release. He printed the picture so that he could upset you more by defacing it with crude drawings of penises and smiley faces. He also wrote on it that he hoped Molly would be raped and murdered and that it was her mother's fault for leaving her.'

I gasped and my skin suddenly felt hot and prickly.

'He put the picture in an envelope last evening and posted it to you from outside his local superstore,' Brennan said. 'It would have arrived at the station later today or tomorrow. He says he saw a way to get back at you and seized the opportunity. In other words, he decided to ride on the kidnapper's back and add to your agony by sending the picture.'

'The sick bastard,' Adam said.

Brennan nodded. 'Needless to say you won't have to see what he did. The post was picked up this morning from the postbox in question, but I've got an officer down at the sorting office to intercept it.'

I scrunched up my eyes, trying to focus on what he was saying, but the image in my head of Molly's photo being defaced in that way was a powerful distraction.

'We'll continue to question the scumbag,' Brennan said. 'I've already charged him with downloading child porn from the internet, but I'm inclined to believe him when he says he's not involved in Molly's abduction. He was in custody when you received the latest text. I know it's theoretically possible that he triggered it on a time delay, but I don't think he did. And we haven't uncovered any evidence to suggest he has an accomplice.'

None of this was what I wanted to hear. It seemed our hopes had been raised for no good reason. As a police officer, I'd grown used to such disappointments during an investigation. But as the mother of a stolen child they were like daggers being plunged into my heart.

Brennan looked at his watch. 'It's almost time, so let me thank you for agreeing to do this press conference. I appreciate that it's not going to be easy, especially now that the media know much more about what's going on. They'll have questions about the text messages and about the video. But I'll provide most of the answers during the introduction. It'll then be up to you, as Molly's parents, to appeal for information and for your daughter's safe return. Explain what Molly means to you and ask the public to be vigilant. What you said outside your flat last night had a significant impact, Sarah. This press conference will enable us to keep up the momentum and reach an even wider audience.'

Brennan looked from me to Adam and then stood up, buttoning his jacket as he did so.

'So are you ready, guys?' he said.

I took a moment to swallow down the growing lump in my throat, then gave a slow nod.

A moment later my stomach was cramping with nerves as I followed my boss and my ex-husband out of the office.

As we walked into the room, we faced a blizzard of flashing lights. There must have been fifty reporters and photographers and at least two TV camera crews.

I felt my knees wobble as we took our seats behind a table covered with microphones.

Adam and I sat side by side and Brennan sat on my left. A man I recognised as the head of media relations filled the chair next to Adam. He was the one who got the ball rolling by introducing the DCI.

Brennan remained seated as he thanked everyone for coming

and then said, 'Molly Mason's parents are here so that they can appeal for help in finding their daughter. They're desperately worried about Molly who was abducted yesterday from her grandparents' house in Streatham. In a moment I will invite them to speak, but can I ask that any questions be directed at me as the senior investigating officer on this case?'

Brennan then gave a pretty detailed account of everything that had happened. He told them about the text messages and the reason the kidnapper had given for taking Molly. He also mentioned the photographs and video and explained why the images were not to be made public.

'The texts and emails were sent anonymously,' he said. 'But experts within our High Tech Crime Unit are trying to identify the sender. If they're successful, then it could help us to establish Molly's whereabouts.'

There followed a raucous Q and A session in which Brennan was asked about the two suspects who were being held. He was forced to admit that one of them would probably be released shortly while the other faced a charge in connection with an unrelated crime.

'So does it mean that Molly's kidnapper is still out there?' a reporter asked.

'I'm afraid it does,' Brennan said. 'That's why we urgently need help from the public on this case, which is one of the most bizarre the Met has ever had to deal with.'

The time came for us to say a few words and Adam followed up on his offer to go first.

'Sarah and I were divorced some time ago, but we've remained close because of our daughter Molly,' he said. 'She means the world to us. She's a beautiful, sweet little girl and we can't bear to think that bad things are happening to her. If the man who took her is watching, then I'm begging him to return her to us. Please. He's breaking our hearts.'

He stopped there and pressed his fingers into his eyes, but not before a couple of tears sluiced down his cheeks.

The hairs on my neck bristled when I realised that all eyes in the room were then on me. For a split second I didn't think I had it in me to speak. But after I exhaled a long, shaky breath the words tumbled out.

'I miss my baby so much,' I said. 'Every second she's not with me is sheer agony. I don't know why this is happening. The man who took her claims he did it in order to punish me. But he won't tell me what I'm supposed to have done. I can't help thinking he's made a mistake, that it's someone else and not me he wants to hurt.'

That was as far as I got before an emotional wave slammed into me. I didn't cry or break down. Instead I shuddered violently and lost my train of thought. My head dropped and I stared down at the table as around me the noise level rose dramatically.

I felt myself being pulled up. My chair scraped across the floor. Someone called out my name. Then I became aware that Adam was pushing me towards the door and Brennan was telling everyone that the press conference was over.

Adam put his arm around me and led me out of the room. A woman in a dark trouser suit was waiting for us in the corridor. She quickly introduced herself as Frances from the press office and said, 'Are you all right, Miss Mason?'

I nodded, unable to speak.

'Just take a breath then,' she said. 'We've set aside a room so that you can relax and have another chat with DCI Brennan before you go. There's tea, coffee and soft drinks.'

The room was small but contained two leather sofas and a coffee table. The drinks were on a hospitality trolley.

Frances invited us to sit down and asked us what we wanted. We both opted for tea.

'My brain just seized up in there,' I said to Adam. 'There was so much more I wanted to say. But I froze.'

'Me too. But at least we got our message across.'

Just then Brennan walked in and asked if we were all right and we both nodded.

'Well, calls are already coming in apparently and we've got dozens of officers on standby to answer them,' he said.

I started to ask a question, but at that moment I heard the familiar and now dreaded sound of my phone pinging with another incoming text message. I had already taken it from my bag and it was gripped in my right hand.

'It could be anyone,' Adam said.

But I had a feeling it was the kidnapper, and I was right. There was a message with an MP4 video attachment.

I pressed my thumb against the attachment before reading the message, so anxious was I to see what was on it. I half expected it not to work like before but this time it did play and my heart jumped when I saw Molly sitting in a bath surrounded by thick white foam.

But there was something different about her, and when I realised what it was I let out a strangled cry.

26

DCI Brennan

Sarah's reaction to the video made everyone jump. She turned her stricken gaze on Brennan and held up her phone for him to take.

He grabbed it from her as Adam rushed across the room and the two of them viewed it together.

The relief the detective felt was electrifying. This time the kidnapper wasn't smacking Molly. Instead she was splashing around in a bath while clutching a small rubber duck. And she appeared to be content rather than distressed. But he knew what had sparked Sarah's reaction and Adam confirmed it.

'My God, look what he's done to her hair,' Adam shrieked. 'He's cut it short and dyed it brown.'

Brennan then read aloud the text message that accompanied the video.

Hi Sarah – Seems my little darling has already forgotten what happened to her yesterday. I'm sure it won't be long before she forgets you as well! Hope you like her new look – I much prefer it. But don't forget if any part of this video is made public Molly will suffer. Next time I might be tempted to take her virginity.

Adam reacted angrily by kicking out, his shoe striking the drinks trolley, sending two glasses and a plate of biscuits flying across the room.

Brennan placed a hand on Adam's shoulder and his fellow detective turned to look at him, his eyes brimming with tears, his nostrils flared like a bull's.

'I swear I'm going to find that cunt and kill him,' he snarled. 'I'll make him wish he'd never been born.'

Brennan shared this sentiment and at that moment he would have gladly throttled the kidnapper with his bare hands regardless of the consequences.

'He's messed with her hair so that it'll be more difficult for people to recognise her,' Sarah said, her voice a hoarse whisper. 'I bet it's another reason he doesn't want the photos and clips to be made public. The man's sick and evil.'

Brennan was already thinking ahead and wondering whether they should doctor one of the photos they had of Molly so they could show the public what she looked like now. Or would that antagonise the kidnapper and give him another excuse to hurt her?

His threat to rape the child was a chilling reminder that they were being forced to play by his rules. Trouble was, he hadn't spelled out exactly what those rules were.

'I need to get out of here,' Sarah said as she rose suddenly to her feet.

Adam offered to take her home but she shook her head.

'I don't want to go home. I want to go and see my mum.'

'Then I'll take you,' Adam said.

27

Sarah

Adam dropped me off at my aunt's house and said he would call me later. When I walked inside, any semblance of control broke down. I cried into my mother's shoulder until there were no more tears left to shed. My mother cried with me and my father stood to one side as though in a state of shock. They both looked utterly exhausted, and it was clear that they were finding it just as hard to cope as I was.

There was no way I could have gone back to the flat. The latest instalment from the kidnapper had left me badly shaken. I kept going over in my head what he'd written and the words drilled into my blood.

Next time I might be tempted to take her virginity.

How could he even contemplate such a vile act on a fifteen-month-old child? It was sick and loathsome and it terrified me.

But there were other parts of the text message that also made my flesh crawl.

There was his reference to Molly as *my little darling,* followed by, *it won't be long before she forgets you as well!*

At least in the video she wasn't being smacked. But the clip was shocking just the same. Her beautiful hair, for heaven's sake. What a horrible mess he had made of it. That in itself was a form of physical abuse. And try as I might I couldn't imagine Molly just sitting there quietly while he did such a thing to her. She was one of those children who hated her hair being brushed or put into bunches. Sometimes it even led to a full-blown tantrum.

My parents and aunt insisted on seeing the video of Molly in the bath, but I made a point of not telling them what was in the text message. Their reaction was predictable; relief on seeing that Molly was still alive and seemingly unharmed. But shock and outrage that the bastard had made such a crude attempt to change her appearance.

Throughout the afternoon I tried not to dwell on what it would be like if I continued to receive photos and video clips showing her growing up without me. How would I feel seeing her laughing, being potty-trained, putting proper sentences together, spending her birthdays in someone else's house?

A part of me couldn't imagine that it would be worth carrying on. But there was also a voice telling me that that would be like abandoning my daughter, because as long as she was alive there would always be hope.

That very point was touched on in at least one of the many TV reports we watched on the news channels. The reporter rounded off his commentary by saying, 'For Molly's mother, viewing these videos and photographs will be sheer torture. But it's impossible to believe that she won't feel compelled to endure it no matter how long it goes on.'

My brain did not allow a moment of respite from the panic

and fear that gripped me. But as the evening approached, exhaustion finally overcame me and I wasn't able to resist it any longer. I fell asleep lying on the sofa, my head resting on my father's lap.

28

Adam

Sleep eluded Adam. His brain had slowed down and his body felt as though it had been on a long-haul flight. But he couldn't relax enough to drop off.

Since leaving Sarah with her parents he had wandered from room to room in his flat, willing the phone to ring and praying it would be DCI Brennan on the other end of the line with some good news about Molly. But as the evening wore on, the more despondent he became. He felt more alone than at any time in his life.

He spoke briefly to Helen and she told him that she was going to return to the UK at the earliest opportunity. It should have cheered him up, but it didn't, and to him that was further evidence that their relationship was either moving too fast or going nowhere. In fact, he came close to telling her that he wanted to end it, that he now realised he still had feelings for his ex-wife. After all, it was the truth, and surely it was only fair that Helen was made aware of it. But instead of biting the bullet he told her he had to go but would stay in touch.

He'd spent the last half an hour scrolling through pictures and video clips of Molly that were stored on his phone. The images of his little girl made him smile through the pain. She was such a funny little thing and how he wished he had spent more time with her. His heart was filled with shame and regret, and a loud, persistent voice in his head kept repeating the words, *if only, if only, if only.*

If only he had taken his marriage vows more seriously. *If only* he had been satisfied with what he'd had instead of looking for something more exciting. *If only* he hadn't been drawn into an affair with a younger woman who gave his pathetic ego a boost.

He had made too many mistakes, and that was partly why it had come to this. If he hadn't fucked up his marriage it wouldn't have happened. Sarah wouldn't have felt the need to work and Molly wouldn't have had to spend so much time with her grandparents.

The television had been on the whole time and he'd been switching between news channels. Molly's abduction was the main story on all of them, including CNN and Fox. There was footage of the press conference, interviews with Sarah's neighbours in Dulwich who said what a delightful child Molly was. One described Sarah as a caring mother who doted on her daughter.

The BBC was running a new angle about a Find-Molly Facebook page that had been set up and had already attracted 90,000 likes and 8,000 comments. Most of the comments were from people saying they were praying for Molly's safe return. But some trolls had been critical of Sarah for going to work instead of staying at home to look after her child.

The anger smouldered in Adam like hot coals. He had avoided drinking because he'd been fearful of getting drunk. But now he realised it might be the only way to get through the night without trashing the TV in a fit of pique.

He got up and poured himself a large brandy. But just as he put the glass to his lips the Beeb announcer said there had been a development in the Molly Mason abduction story.

Adam's heart stopped beating and for a split second he feared the worst.

But dread turned to anger when the announcer said, 'The police have just confirmed that one of the men being questioned about the abduction has been released. Victor Rosetti, the Romanian national who was cleared by a jury yesterday of drug offences, had been in custody for almost twenty-four hours.'

Adam reacted by throwing the glass across the room. It smashed against a wall, splattering brandy everywhere.

'This should not be happening,' he screamed at the television. 'The bastard knows something.'

Adam collapsed back on the sofa as he fought to bring his breathing under control. His thoughts spun in all directions, and after several minutes he decided that if Brennan and his team couldn't get Rosetti to tell the truth then he would have to do it himself.

Adam knew that he was taking a huge risk, but he felt he'd been given little choice.

Word is, you're in for a nasty surprise.

Rosetti had said that and now he was denying it, which meant that Brennan's hands were tied. There was only so far he could take it unless he had evidence linking Rosetti with Molly. Without it they'd have struggled to keep him locked up.

But Adam wasn't going to allow himself to be constrained by

rules and regulations. He wouldn't rest until he knew why Rosetti had made the comment. There had to be a reason.

Rosetti lived alone in a rented three-bed detached house in an affluent part of Fulham. The money used to pay for it was funnelled through two legitimate businesses – a West End nightclub and a minicab firm in South London. Both were fronts for his far more lucrative drug distribution racket.

Adam had visited the house a few times during the NCA's ill-fated investigation, so he knew where to go.

It was just gone 11.30 p.m. when he arrived and parked across the street. There were no lights on in the house and no cars on the short driveway. But it didn't mean that Rosetti wasn't at home.

Adam realised that there was no easy way to go about this. He had no idea what to expect and how Rosetti would react to him suddenly turning up on his doorstep. Or how he himself would react if Rosetti had company. But he wasn't going to let that deter him from confronting the bastard. There was no time to waste and too much at stake to worry about getting into trouble. Molly was his main concern now, and he was prepared to cross any line in order to get her back.

So before allowing any doubts to settle in his mind, he got out of the car and walked across the road towards the house.

There was no gate, and as he stepped onto the driveway, he patted the side pocket of his leather jacket. The bulky hardness of the gun he was carrying sent a bolt of adrenaline tearing through his body.

As Adam approached Rosetti's front door, a sensor light came on, catching him by surprise. He snapped his head round but saw no one watching him.

High hedges either side blocked the view of the neighbouring properties, but he did spot a security camera above one of the ground-floor windows. There was no light showing so he couldn't be sure if it was switched on.

His pulse accelerated as he rang the doorbell and he kept telling himself that he had to do whatever it took to find out what Rosetti knew.

Blood hummed in his ears as he waited for the door to open. He could only hope that Rosetti wouldn't see him through a window and be panicked into calling the three nines. If so, then it would only be a matter of minutes before a patrol car turned up and he was escorted from the premises, or cautioned even.

Undeterred by that possibility, Adam rang the bell again. When there was no response, he felt sure that the house must be empty. He briefly toyed with the idea of trying to break in, but decided against it because the last thing he wanted to do was set off a burglar alarm.

He checked his watch. It was fifteen minutes to midnight. So he decided to wait in the car in the hope that Rosetti would arrive home soon and wasn't spending the night elsewhere following his release from custody.

He repositioned the Audi so that the moon's glow did not hit the windscreen and make him more visible. Then he settled back in the driver's seat and prepared himself for a long wait.

But he got lucky. After only thirty-five minutes a pair of head-lights approached along the quiet road, prompting him to duck down out of sight until the car passed by.

He then watched in the rear-view mirror as it stopped in front of Rosetti's driveway.

The car was a black Mercedes, and Adam would have put money

on it being the same one that had picked Rosetti up from outside the Old Bailey.

A rear door was opened and a man stepped out onto the pavement. The door was then slammed shut, and as the car drove off, the man turned to walk up the driveway.

That was when Adam saw that it was Victor Rosetti. There was just enough light to make out the short, stumpy frame and shaved head. He was wearing a white open-neck shirt and jeans.

This is it, Adam told himself. *Just hold your nerve and do it for Molly.*

He exited the car as quietly as possible and eased the door shut behind him. A quick look to make sure that nobody else was around, then he moved swiftly across the road to the driveway, arriving just as Rosetti was inserting a key into his front door.

Adam broke into a run and managed to cover the distance between them before Rosetti heard him and turned round, whiplash fast.

Rosetti had no time to react before Adam rammed into him with all the force of an express train.

They both went crashing through the open front door into the house.

Rosetti stumbled backwards and lost his balance, falling to the floor just inside the hall.

But Adam managed to stay on his feet and immediately unleashed a power kick that connected with the back of Rosetti's head. The Romanian cried out and rolled up against the wall. It gave Adam the precious seconds he needed to get his bearings in the gloom, switch on the hall light, and close the front door behind him. He then whipped the revolver from his pocket before Rosetti even realised what was happening.

When Rosetti saw the gun being pointed at him, his eyes widened alarmingly and a muscle tightened in his jaw.

'Are you fucking crazy?' he screamed.

A tight smile twisted on Adam's lips. 'Absolutely. Which is why I've come here to kill you.'

Rosetti struggled to a sitting position, his back against the wall, his breath coming hard and fast.

'Th-this is a joke, right?' he managed. 'You're a copper, for Christ's sake.'

Adam aimed the gun at Rosetti's chest, a look of feral rage on his face. 'I'm also the father of the child you've abducted,' he said. 'And since you won't say what you've done with her I'm not prepared to let you live.'

Rosetti started shaking his head. 'But I've got nothing to do with what has happened to your kid. I've told your lot already. They know I'm telling the truth which is why they let me go.'

'But you lied to them. You claimed that you didn't tell me I was in for a nasty surprise.'

Rosetti stared at the gun, his mind ticking over, and Adam felt a wave of fury rattle through him.

'The only way to save yourself is to cough up,' he said. 'If you didn't do it but you know who did then you should tell me to save yourself.'

Rosetti swallowed hard. 'But you wouldn't dare. You'd be done for, finished.'

'That's where you're wrong. I've got a friend outside in the car waiting to drive me away from here and he's also ready to give me an alibi for tonight. You've got lots of enemies, so there's no way that I'll be among the suspects.'

'But this is fucking crazy. You need to calm down. Please. I'm not your man. I really don't know anything.'

154

'Then why did you say that outside the court?'

'I was winding you up. That was all there was to it. Honest to God. And I'm not just saying that because you've got a pistol pointed at me.'

Adam narrowed his eyes. 'I don't believe you. It was too much of a coincidence that my daughter was kidnapped that very morning.'

'But that's all it was. A coincidence.'

Adam bent over and pressed the muzzle of the revolver into the flesh beneath Rosetti's chin. 'I'm going to count to ten. If you don't come clean, I'll blow your fucking head off.'

In desperation, Rosetti made a grab for the gun and Adam was too slow to react. He lost his grip and the gun fell into Rosetti's lap.

A violent struggle ensued as both men rolled around the narrow hallway, punching, kicking and scrambling for the weapon.

Rosetti was clearly the stronger of the two, but Adam's strength came from a fierce rage that had spiralled out of control. He was like a man possessed, and it made him oblivious to the blows that struck his head, stomach and chest.

But Rosetti made the first serious mistake by dropping his guard in order to reach for the gun after it slipped onto the floor.

Adam seized the opportunity by cracking his fist into Rosetti's temple, causing his head to slam against the wall with a heavy thud. He followed through with a savage punch to the Romanian's throat that snatched his breath away and made his body go limp.

Adam quickly retrieved the gun and hauled himself to his feet, while Rosetti was too dazed to stop him.

Adam then stepped back and bared his teeth.

'You're a no-good scumbag,' he yelled. 'And you deserve everything that's about to happen to you.'

Rosetti's eyes were still trying to focus as Adam aimed a brutal kick at his face. The heel of his shoe struck Rosetti on the mouth, pushing a couple of teeth through his bottom lip. Blood sprayed the front of his shirt.

Instinct screamed for Adam to carry on beating the man until he opened up about Molly. He was in such a demonic rage by now that he didn't give a shit about the consequences. Later he would reflect that Rosetti must have seen the madness in his eyes, which was why he elected to save himself before it was too late.

'OK, OK, enough!' the Romanian yelped, raising his arms defensively. 'Don't hit me again. Please. I'll tell you what you want to know.'

Adam froze and stared down at him, his heart pounding, legs shaking.

'Does that mean you did abduct my daughter, you evil shit?'

Rosetti swallowed as he wiped his bloody mouth with the back of his hand.

Then he took a long, slow breath and said, 'No it doesn't. I swear I didn't take her. But I think I know who did.'

29

Sarah

It was approaching midnight when I arrived back at my flat. My parents had tried to persuade me to stay at my aunt's, but I'd felt compelled to return home after sleeping for a couple of hours.

As the taxi dropped me off, a uniformed police officer appeared as if by magic. It didn't surprise me that he was still here because so was the media. Two photographers and a reporter rushed over as soon as they spotted me.

The officer put himself between me and them and said, 'We weren't sure if you'd be back tonight, ma'am. Would you like me to get the family liaison officer to come over?'

'No, I'll be fine,' I said. 'But thank you.'

'Well I have instructions to alert Sergeant Palmer if you turn up.'

'Then tell her I'll see her tomorrow.'

'Will do, ma'am. And rest assured I won't be letting those hacks bother you.'

As if to prove his point, he turned, held up his hands and told them to leave me alone. But that didn't stop the reporter from asking me where I'd been or the photographers from taking a bunch of pictures as I entered the building.

I wondered how long it would take for the story to burn itself out and their interest to wane. Would they be hassling me in six months if the situation hadn't changed?

This thought stayed with me as I closed the front door to my flat and turned on the lights. And it pulled me down even further into the depths of despair.

Could this nightmare really go on for that long, or perhaps even longer?

The only person who knew the answer was the man in the balaclava. The kidnapper. The psycho whose stated aim was to punish me.

I'd been intending to make myself a coffee, but I suddenly felt the need for something stronger to help numb the pain. So I went straight to the fridge, grabbed the half-full bottle of Chardonnay and poured myself a large glass.

I started drinking it while standing with my back against the sink. My thoughts returned to the man who had stolen my child, not because he wanted to love and nurture her, but because he wanted to use her as a weapon against me. I knew that in that scenario it was hardly likely he would treat her well. He'd be impatient with her and short-tempered. He'd neglect and abuse her until he finally got fed up with her or decided that he had punished me enough.

And what then? Would he let me have her back or would he . . .?

I didn't want to contemplate the awful possibilities, but that was going to be difficult, because as long as Molly was at his mercy I'd be cursed by the cruelty of my own imagination.

A shuddering sob erupted from me and with it came a sudden

urge to be sick again. I put the glass down on the worktop and rushed into the downstairs toilet.

I retched into the basin a few times but all that came up was acid and wine. I wiped my lips on toilet paper and rinsed my mouth with water before looking in the mirror.

My face was as pale as skimmed milk and the whites of my eyes were tinged red. I looked like a zombie from *The Walking Dead*.

I retrieved my wine from the kitchen and went and sat on the sofa in the living room.

The silence pressed heavily against me, while exhaustion gnawed at my bones.

I sat there for a while, deep in melancholy thought, my mind rolling back to the day before yesterday. I wanted to rewind time to the moment I walked into Molly's room to wake her up. If only I had decided to let her sleep on and to take the day off work. Then she wouldn't have been with my mother and the man wouldn't have been able to take her. But it was clear from his messages that he would have struck at another time anyway. After all, he had probably been watching and stalking for days or weeks so that he could acquaint himself with my routine.

I started to ransack my shaken memory, trying to remember if there was anything unusual that I should have picked up on, something that ought to have alerted me to the danger ahead.

But it was hopeless. Events before that fateful morning were too vague to make any sense of.

I downed some more wine and then stared across the room as I rolled the stem of the glass between my fingers.

My precious little girl stared back at me from a wall-mounted frame. It was a blown-up picture taken on her first birthday. She was pointing at the camera with one hand while holding Peppa Pig by the ear in the other.

My eyes filled with fresh tears and my insides balled into a tight knot. It seemed cruelly ironic suddenly that Adam and I were both police officers and yet we hadn't been able to protect our daughter.

But that didn't mean we couldn't use our experience and expertise to help find her. We just needed to work out the best way to go about it.

30

Adam

'So come on,' Adam urged. 'Who do you think has taken my daughter?'

Victor Rosetti tried to stand up but Adam shook his head.

'Stay where you are and start talking or so help me . . .'

Rosetti sat back down and his lips curled as though he'd tasted something sour.

'What I'm going to tell you is the frigging truth,' he said, his voice a hard-edged whisper. 'So for Christ's sake give me your word that you won't kill me.'

Adam nodded. 'You'll live, but only if I believe you. So you'll need to convince me that you're not feeding me a load of bullshit just to save your sorry arse.'

Rosetti lapsed into a nervous silence for a few moments, his jaw agape, a mist of sweat on his forehead.

Adam's breath thundered in his ears as he waited, his mouth full of saliva that he couldn't swallow.

Eventually Rosetti began.

'A few months ago I met a guy in prison. I was on remand and he was only weeks away from being released. We got talking about how we had both wound up inside, and it turned out we had something in common. And that something, or rather someone, was you, Detective.'

Adam felt his eyebrows knit together, and his head started reeling with questions. But he said nothing. Just waited for the Romanian to explain himself.

Rosetti wiped a dribble of blood from his chin before continuing.

'You were one of the arresting officers in both our cases, so we spent a lot of time slagging you off. But this guy was even more pissed off than me because he claimed he was fitted up and evidence was planted against him.

'He'd served four years of an eight-year stretch and they were letting him out. But he wasn't just blaming you. He reckoned you had a partner in crime. A fellow officer who was the one who charged him and then went on to lie in court about what he'd done. He said he'd been trying to think of ways he could punish her when he got out.'

'Her?'

Rosetti tilted his head to one side. 'That's right. The officer was Sarah Mason.'

Adam felt a darkness move inside him. He licked his lips and tried again to swallow, but couldn't.

'The guy didn't actually know that you two had got married and divorced while he was banged up,' Rosetti said. 'He was surprised when I told him. And he was even more surprised when I mentioned that you'd had a kid together.'

'Why did you tell him that?'

Rosetti shrugged. 'He was asking lots of questions and I had no reason not to answer them.'

'But how come you knew so much about me?'

'I'd made it my business to find out. You were the one leading the investigation aimed at putting me away. I was looking for some leverage to use against you.'

Adam took a moment to process what he'd heard. So far it sounded all too credible and that scared him. 'So what makes you believe he snatched my daughter?' he asked.

'During our last conversation he said he'd come up with a plan to get back at Detective Mason. He wouldn't elaborate and I didn't push it because I didn't really want to know. He said he was going to punish her, but that you'd both be in for a nasty surprise. They were his words, not mine.'

Adam stood there, shaking, as a chill spread through him.

'So now you need to give me this bloke's name,' he said. 'And if it's one I don't recognise I'll know you've been lying to me.'

Rosetti was quick to respond. 'His name's Bobby Knight, a villain who was part of Tony Kemp's gang south of the river. You got him for drugs and possessing a firearm.'

Any doubts Adam had about Rosetti's story were swept away by the mere mention of Knight.

Bobby Knight was indeed a name that Adam recognised. The day they raided the man's home and arrested him was scorched on his memory.

It was a collar that earned Sarah promotion and the respect of all her colleagues in Lewisham CID.

And now it seemed that what had happened on that day might have come back to haunt them both.

'So that's it,' Rosetti said. 'I've told you everything. Because of what Knight said I think it's a fair bet that he's the one who took your daughter. He was released a couple of months ago.'

'Have you heard from him since then?'

'No, and I didn't expect to. We weren't mates. We just got involved in some heavy conversations. It happens on the inside.'

Something stirred in Adam at that moment, something primal and dangerous.

'Why didn't you tell this to Brennan when he interviewed you?' he said.

'Because I didn't want it to come back on me.'

'So you were prepared to leave my daughter at the mercy of that psychopath just so you weren't implicated in any way.'

'It wasn't like that. And anyway I can't be certain that Knight has her. It's up to you to find out.'

'But you suspected that something was going to happen,' Adam said, his voice rising almost to screaming pitch. 'And when it did you kept your mouth shut.'

Rosetti was in full panic mode now. He started wheezing, as though the air was having trouble leaving his lungs. And his eyes were popping out on stalks.

'You really are the pits,' Adam said. 'And no way do you deserve to live.'

There had been times in the past when he'd harboured murderous thoughts, but they'd never been as strong as those that filled his head right now.

The scumbag had withheld information that might have led the police to Molly. He'd been prepared to let the whole ghastly situation play out for purely selfish reasons.

'Please don't do anything stupid,' Rosetti said. 'You know you'll regret it.'

'I don't think so,' Adam said. 'But I do know that if I don't find my little girl soon then I will regret not having killed you when I had the chance.'

Adam held the gun in both hands and aimed it at Rosetti's head. The Romanian started shaking violently, while pleading for his life.

Adam's response was to smile as he pulled the trigger.

31

DCI Brennan

Brennan came awake with a jolt, his heart pumping furiously. At first he didn't know where he was, but he was glad he'd left the dream behind, that damn recurring dream that made him feel empty and afraid. In it Grace no longer knows who he is and looks at him as though he's a complete stranger. When he tells her that he's her husband she gives him a cryptic smile and says, 'No you're not. I don't know who you are. Get away from me.'

As always when he surfaced from the dream his brain was slow to engage. So it was several seconds before he realised that his mobile phone was ringing, the screen a throbbing rectangle of light in the darkened room.

As he reached for it, he felt Grace stir beside him.

'Is that the alarm?' she croaked.

'It's my phone, sweetheart,' he said. 'I'm sorry. I'll take it in the other room.'

'Don't be daft. It might be important.'

It had better be, he thought, as he pressed the answer button and saw that it was only just after midnight.

'Brennan here,' he said and was taken aback by the sharp, urgent tone of the voice that responded.

'This is Adam Boyd. I've got a lead on Molly and you need to follow it up straight away.'

'I'm sorry, Adam. I didn't catch what you said. You woke me up and my brain's not yet in gear.'

'What? For fuck's sake don't tell me you're in bed. You're supposed to be looking for my daughter.'

'Calm down, Adam. I was dead on my feet and needed a few hours' sleep. But the team are working through the night.'

'And you should be with them, not taking time out for a nap.'

Brennan had to consciously resist the urge to sever the connection.

'Look, I know you're upset, Adam. And I realise that the pressure you're under is enormous. But yelling at me won't make you feel any better. So if you've got something urgent to tell me then please get on with it.'

Adam exhaled heavily into the phone. 'OK, sorry. But look, I've got a name for you. It's a bloke who Sarah and I arrested four years ago when we worked at Lewisham together. He recently got out of prison, but while inside he told Victor Rosetti that he was going to get his revenge on the both of us.'

Brennan was at once alert. 'Rosetti! Are you serious?'

'Yes. He lied about not knowing anything, just like I told you.'

'How do you know this? Have you been to see him?'

'Never mind that. You're wasting time. The guy he spoke to in prison is Bobby Knight. You need to find him. He's a crazy fuck and he used to be part of Tony Kemp's firm.'

Brennan knew of Bobby Knight, and he remembered his trial which took place before Sarah moved from Lewisham to work in

167

Wandsworth. But he was more familiar with Tony Kemp, one of the main villains operating in South London.

'I'll get right on it,' he said. 'But first I need to know that you haven't done something stupid, Adam – like approaching Victor Rosetti after we let him go.'

'So what if I did? At least I got him to fucking talk, which is more than you managed.'

'Oh, Christ, Adam. You're not supposed to be getting involved. You know that.'

'All I know is that some lunatic has my little girl and I'll do whatever I have to do to get her back.'

Brennan felt a stab of apprehension.

'So what exactly have you done?' he said.

'Nothing I'm ashamed of.'

Brennan shook his head. These cryptic responses were making him more anxious by the second.

'What does that mean, Adam?'

'It means I'm not prepared to say any more about it because it's not important. Finding Molly is. So please just do your job and go get Knight.'

Adam hung up then and Brennan let loose a string of expletives, which prompted his wife to lean across the bed and put a hand on his shoulder.

'What's wrong, my love?' she said, her voice quiet and tentative.

'It's nothing for you to worry about, but I have to go to work.'

'Then while you get dressed I'll make some tea.'

'You don't have to, Grace.'

'I know, but I want to.'

He touched her hand and smiled as she got up and slipped on her dressing gown. When she left the room he switched on the bedside lamp and called the incident room. DC Amanda Foster answered. He told her to track down Bobby Knight who he believed had just been released from prison.

'Pull out all the stops,' he said. 'This is a credible lead and there's a strong possibility that he's the guy who has Molly Mason.'

Before ending the call he gave Foster Adam Boyd's mobile number.

'At the same time I want an urgent trace on that phone. I need a location and I need it pronto. So ring me straight back.'

Brennan's eyes felt gritty and heavy even after he had showered. But at least he didn't feel so tired. Those three hours of sleep had been so desperately needed. Exhaustion had begun to blunt his senses and slow him down. Pressing on regardless had not been an option.

DC Foster called back while he was getting dressed.

'We've got a location on the phone, sir,' she said. 'The signal was triangulated to a property in Fulham.'

When she told him the address he recognised it immediately as belonging to Victor Rosetti.

'Send a patrol car to pick me up right away,' he said. 'I need to get to that address as soon as possible.'

It was only a couple of miles from his home in Battersea to Rosetti's place in Fulham. But given that he didn't know what he was going to find when he got there – or how long he'd have to stay – he thought it best to be chauffeured rather than have the hassle of taking his own car.

Grace was waiting for him in the kitchen and a lump rose in his throat because he was reminded of that awful dream in which the dementia had wiped all memories of him from her mind. But the lump became dislodged when she smiled as she handed him a mug of steaming tea.

'Get that down you before you go out,' she said.

He thanked her and watched as she sat down at the table and sipped her own tea. She was flushed and her eyes looked tired, her skin sallow. He wanted more than anything to take her back to bed and perhaps even make love to her for the first time in weeks. He could tell from the way she looked at him that she was thinking along the same lines. But they both knew it wasn't going to happen. As had been the case too often during their marriage, his job was going to have to come first. But that would change as soon as he retired and made it his business to spend every waking hour with her.

She asked him what had happened that sounded so serious. But as he started to speak the pulsating light of a police car splashed against the curtains.

'I'll tell you about it later,' he said. 'I have to go.'

She smiled again. 'Let me know when you'll be home and I'll make something to eat. Stay safe and don't take any risks.'

'I wouldn't dream of it,' he said.

32

DCI Brennan

As Brennan sat in the back of the patrol car his head was filled with a mix of hope and fear. He hoped to God that this was a genuine breakthrough in the case, and that they'd be a step nearer to finding Molly Mason. But he was also fearful that her father may well have stepped over the line by confronting Victor Rosetti in his own home.

It was easy to imagine Boyd beating a confession out of the Romanian. How else would he have got him to open up? But if that was what he'd done then he'd be in deep shit, despite the circumstances.

Brennan was halfway to Rosetti's house when he received another call from DC Foster. She wanted to let him know that the phone traced to the address in Fulham was now on the move.

Brennan felt a trickle of dread as he made the decision to carry on to the house.

It took them ten more minutes to get there and the first thing Brennan noticed were the lights on inside. It was one a.m. and the rest of the houses in the street were in darkness.

The patrol car pulled onto the empty driveway and Brennan jumped out along with the two uniforms. A sensor light came on as they approached the front door.

Brennan stuck his finger on the bell push and felt a shiver of unease when there was no answer after thirty seconds. But just as he was about to instruct one of the officers to check the rear of the house, the door was jerked open suddenly and they were greeted with: 'Why the fuck can't you leave me be?'

It was Rosetti and he was standing in the doorway with a swollen bottom lip and blood on his open white shirt.

'I think you know why we're here,' Brennan said, somewhat relieved to find that Rosetti wasn't more seriously hurt. 'We need to have a talk.' Brennan didn't wait for an invitation. He stepped over the threshold. 'Please lead the way to somewhere more comfortable, Mr Rosetti.'

The Romanian gave a resigned shrug, much to Brennan's surprise, and then stomped along the hallway into the living room. There, Brennan told him to sit on an armchair and asked him if he needed an ambulance.

Rosetti shook his head. 'All I need is to be left alone so that I can go to bed.'

Brennan narrowed his eyes and said, 'I received a call from Detective Boyd who I believe was here until a few minutes ago. Is that correct?'

'He was waiting for me when I got home.'

'And is he responsible for the injury to your mouth?'

'No he isn't.'

'Then how did you—'

'I drank too much vodka tonight and fell down the stairs.'

'Was that before or after Detective Boyd came here?'

'Before.'

172

Brennan didn't believe him. He leaned forward, elbows on knees.

'If you were assaulted by Detective Boyd then you should tell me,' he said.

Rosetti managed a weak smile. 'What I've told you is the truth. If you want me to make up a story that won't be a problem. I can say that he came here and threatened me with a gun that turned out to be a replica, and that he smacked me around a bit. But if I do that we'll all be dragged into a long drawn-out investigation and I'm sure that wouldn't please you and your superiors.'

Brennan smiled inwardly. He didn't condone what Molly's father had done, but he understood it. Rosetti had got what had been coming to him. That in itself was a result. And the fact that he did not want to press charges against Adam was doubly satisfying.

Brennan cleared his throat and took out his notebook. 'So let's get down to the serious business of what you told Detective Boyd,' he said. 'It's my understanding that you lied to us when you said you knew nothing about his daughter's abduction.'

'I didn't lie,' Rosetti said. 'I just didn't remember what Bobby Knight had told me until I got back here and Boyd started asking me questions.'

Brennan blew out a sigh. 'Well I suppose we should all be grateful that the memory surfaced eventually.'

'Yeah, I reckon we should.'

Brennan could have hauled him in for withholding information, but he knew it would be more trouble than it was worth. Instead he chose to go with the easy option. 'So now I want you to tell me exactly what you told Detective Boyd,' he said.

Twenty minutes later Brennan walked out of the house, having listened to Rosetti recalling his conversations with Bobby Knight.

He'd advised the Romanian that he would have to make a formal statement later in the day and then be expected to testify in court against Knight if it came to it.

Rosetti was subdued and compliant, and Brennan could only think that Adam had put the fear of God in him. He just hoped that Adam wouldn't go off on his own again because it might not work out so well for him the next time.

As Brennan was getting back into the patrol car his phone rang. He fumbled it from his pocket and saw that the caller was DC Foster.

'I'm about to head back to the station,' he said. 'Have you got anything on Knight?'

'Indeed we have, sir. He was released from prison two months ago and went to live with his mother in Peckham.'

'Have you got an address?'

'Yes, sir, but first there's more you need to know.'

'Oh?'

'Well Knight's mother actually reported him missing two weeks ago. What's more she told the officers who went to see her that she's convinced her son has been murdered.'

33

Sarah

It was almost two in the morning and I was still wide awake. For the past hour I'd been sitting on the floor next to Molly's cot, my brain grinding away at a multitude of memories.

A pale, vaporous moon lit the room, throwing all of Molly's things into sharp relief.

Forcing myself to think about the joyous moments I'd had with her was the only way I could stop myself asking the same questions over and over.

Was she awake? Was she crying? Was she thinking about me? Was she being abused?

Not knowing the answers was becoming increasingly unbearable. It was like having my brain squeezed in a vice. I just couldn't see myself holding it together for much longer. The mental anguish was crippling me.

I tried telling myself that other mothers whose children had gone missing or been abducted had managed to cope despite the pain. They'd dug deep within themselves to find the strength to carry on.

But they hadn't been forced to look at pictures and video clips of their children. So in that sense my situation was terrifyingly unique. I had seen what the kidnapper had done to Molly's hair. I'd seen him holding Molly upside down and smacking her. And I had no doubt in my mind that there was worse to come. Much worse.

My body started to tremble as more unanswerable questions invaded my thoughts.

Was her nappy being changed regularly? Was she being given enough to eat and drink? Was she being teased and tormented? Was she at the mercy of more than one evil predator?

The nausea was building up inside me again and I suddenly felt faint.

I got up and stumbled out of Molly's room, went downstairs to pour myself a glass of water. My body was cold and clammy and my stomach was making unpleasant noises. I probably needed to eat something but I knew I'd never be able to hold it down.

I opened the medicine drawer in the kitchen to see if there was anything I could take to still my nerves and settle my stomach. But as I rummaged among the out-of-date tablets and used tubes of ointment, the doorbell rang.

It was the last thing I expected, and it triggered a new rush of adrenaline through my veins.

A mounting sense of trepidation closed in on me as I hurried to the front door.

On the way, my right leg banged against the hall table, but the pain was swamped by the adrenaline.

When I opened the door I expected to see Brennan or Sergeant Palmer on the landing. But instead it was Adam who was standing there.

He was wearing a brown leather jacket and a shirt that was loose around the neck. And there was a strange look on his face that stole my breath away and made me stiffen.

'Oh God, Adam. Please don't tell me you're here because something bad has happened.'

He shook his head. 'No, no, no. Not bad. But it could be good. That's why I came straight over.'

'What is it?'

'Well let me in and I'll tell you.'

He went straight into the living room and poured himself a large glass of whisky without asking if I minded. It was then that I realised his face was covered in sweat and his hands were shaking.

He gulped down the whole glass of whisky and poured himself another. I just stood there watching him with bated breath, the blood thumping in my ears.

After he had downed the second glass, he grated his fingers through his hair and turned to me. His face seemed to sag with exhaustion, and the emotional strain he was under radiated out of his eyes.

'I went to see Victor Rosetti,' he said, his voice soaked with emotion. 'At first the bastard tried telling me what he told Brennan – that he hadn't known that something bad was going to happen to me. But I managed to force a confession out of him, along with the name of the man he thinks abducted Molly.'

My brain was slow to make sense of what he'd said, and his words hung in the air for a few moments like an echo.

'I've already spoken to Brennan,' he continued excitedly. 'He's getting straight onto it.'

My heart began to race and I had to take a breath before I could speak.

177

'Who is it?' I said, my voice shaking with desperation. 'Do I know him?'

'You do. Bobby Knight. D'you remember him?'

It came as a tremendous shock, in part because I'd thought about him only yesterday. But not in my wildest imagination would I have linked him to Molly's abduction. He was just another villain who claimed he was innocent despite the weight of evidence that proved he wasn't.

'He got out two months ago apparently, probably on licence after serving just over half his sentence,' Adam went on. 'But while he was inside he crossed paths with Victor Rosetti. They had a few conversations, during which he told Rosetti that he planned to seek revenge against you for getting him sent down.'

Adam went through what the Romanian had said to him and as I listened I poured myself a whisky and dropped onto the sofa.

The Knight case was in the distant past but I was still able to bring to mind most of the details. The raid on his home, the discovery of the gun and drugs, him insisting he was innocent and accusing us of planting the evidence. Then the subsequent trial, including my own testimony. I even remembered how his mother broke down in court when the jury returned a guilty verdict. And then later, when sentence was passed, his father stood up in the public gallery and shouted at the judge, claiming that his gangster son was the victim of a blatant miscarriage of justice.

'After the news broke that Molly had been abducted, Rosetti suspected that Knight was behind it,' Adam said. 'But he'd just been acquitted so he kept quiet because he was happy to see me suffer. His mistake was to approach me outside the Bailey and tell me that he'd heard I was in for a nasty surprise. If the smug cunt hadn't said that we'd be none the wiser.'

My thoughts spun wildly, but out of the chaos an image

emerged – Bobby Knight standing in the dock. He was twenty-eight back then – so thirty-two now – and he looked every inch the villain that he was. Slicked-back dark hair, broken nose, rubber lips, a scar on his left cheek from a knife attack in his youth. He was suited up for the big occasion, complete with smart tie and red poppy in his lapel. I remembered thinking at the time that he was the stereotypical gangster, in the mould of Ronnie and Reggie Kray, and just as ruthless as those two were.

He'd worked for the still-notorious gang boss Tony Kemp, whose daughter Lauren he was planning to marry. She turned up in court every day of the trial, a pretty young thing with red hair and a taste for expensive designer clothes. I wondered if she had waited for him to serve his sentence or had decided to cut him loose and get on with her life.

'Do you really think he could be the kidnapper?' I said to Adam.

Adam sat down beside me, a fresh glass of whisky in his hand.

'I'd stake my life on it,' he said. 'The guy was a right nutjob. That was why we were all so keen to put him away. We knew he'd been responsible for at least two gangland murders and God knows how many blags. But we could never pin anything on him until you got the tip about the drugs.'

'Which he claimed we planted, along with the gun.'

'Of course he did. They all do when we catch 'em bang to rights.'

I sipped at my whisky, savouring the gentle burning sensation in my gullet.

'But he never threatened me like Edwin Sharp and Frank Neilson did,' I said.

'That doesn't mean anything.'

'But the kidnapper has made it clear that it's me, not you, he wants to punish.'

'And from what Rosetti told me you were the one Knight

179

was planning to target before he learned that we were married and had a daughter together. It appears he then decided to hurt us both.'

The more I thought about it, the more credible it seemed. By now my heart was going like the clappers.

'Hopefully it won't take them long to find him,' Adam said. 'I'm assuming his family are still living here in South London and I expect he had a probation officer.'

I desperately wanted Adam to be right and it was impossible not to feel excited. I could tell from his expression that he was convinced that Knight was the kidnapper. But then he'd had longer to get his mind around it. He was the one who had confronted Rosetti, the one who'd got off his arse and done something, the one who'd deserve the credit if our nightmare was soon to be brought to an end.

This line of thought started alarm bells ringing in my head.

'Just a sec,' I said. 'You told me that you forced a confession out of Rosetti. What exactly did you do to him?'

Adam shrugged. 'If you must know, I kicked him in the mouth and threatened him with a fake gun. You should have seen his face, the fear in his eyes. It was priceless.'

I clapped my hand over my mouth and looked at him aghast.

'It's all right,' he said. 'He's not seriously hurt, and I warned him that if he puts in a complaint I'll make sure he regrets it.'

'But what if he does?'

Another shrug. 'I'll say the fucker attacked me when I went to see him. It'll be my word against his. Plus, I've dumped the gun and there were no witnesses to what happened.'

I didn't know what to say. On the one hand I feared that he might have torpedoed his career in the police, but on the other I was glad he'd done what he'd done, however reckless it was. He'd managed to elicit crucial information from a good-for-nothing drug trafficker that would, God willing, lead us directly to Molly.

I put a hand on his knee and said, 'Whatever happens, I want you to know that I'm proud of you, Adam. I've been telling myself that we should be doing something and that's exactly what you've gone and done.'

Adam stared back at me and I saw his eyes start to fill.

In that moment I didn't care that we were no longer married, or that he cheated on me. All that mattered was that he was Molly's father and he'd put his love for her before everything else, including his job.

So when he started to sob I reached over and pulled him against me. And as he cried into my shoulder I stroked the back of his head, and for a while it was as though the last few years had never happened.

34

DCI Brennan

Brennan and his uniformed companions headed back across the Thames into South London.

Peckham was part of his patch, an area that had always been a breeding ground for people like Bobby Knight. Even at this early hour, the city was teeming with life; shift workers going about their business, homeless people looking for somewhere warm and safe to bed down, revellers walking home after a night out. And on the roads the ceaseless hum of traffic, mostly red buses and black cabs.

Brennan watched it all through the window of the patrol car, but he took nothing in. He was too busy thinking about how events were unravelling following the unlawful actions of Molly Mason's desperate father.

DI Adam Boyd had put his job on the line by attacking Victor Rosetti in his own home. But, as a result, there was now a new suspect in the frame – except that Bobby Knight had apparently disappeared and his mother believed he'd been topped.

It was an extraordinary development and one that had Brennan wondering what the hell was going on.

According to DC Foster, a missing persons report was filed two weeks ago after Knight's mother, Emily, said she hadn't heard from her son for twenty-four hours. His probation officer confirmed that Knight had failed to turn up for meetings and had given no indication that he was going to drop out of sight.

Mrs Knight had also told officers that she was convinced her son had been murdered by his former boss, Tony Kemp. The reason she gave was that after his release Knight started stalking and making threats against Kemp's daughter, Lauren, whom he'd been engaged to. But she moved on while he was inside. The mother had absolutely no evidence to back up her claim. Nevertheless detectives from Peckham had interviewed Kemp who'd acknowledged that Knight had been pestering his daughter, but had emphatically denied doing anything about it, except to warn him off.

What Brennan had to do was find out, and quickly, whether all this was in any way connected with little Molly's abduction. If not, then there was every chance that he was about to waste more precious time.

But there were questions that needed to be answered.

Did Bobby Knight follow through on his threat to punish Sarah by snatching her child? And did he drop out of sight in order to do so? Or did something happen to him before he got the chance to abduct her? If so, then someone else must have been responsible.

Yet again Brennan reflected on how grotesque and bizarre this case was, and how it revealed the true depths of human depravity. Any man who could steal a child and then torment the mother with pictures and videos had to be the devil incarnate.

From what Brennan had learned about Bobby Knight the guy would probably fit the bill. He'd been a violent criminal before he was sent down and although he'd never been convicted of murder, it was strongly believed he'd committed several while working for Tony Kemp.

Brennan doubted that the guy had been rehabilitated during his spell in prison. And from the sound of it, he'd come out even more bitter and twisted than when he went in.

Estate agents like to tell prospective clients that Peckham is no longer one of London's most dangerous inner city areas. But Brennan knew that to be total bollocks.

Despite the gentrification and influx of white-collar workers, it was still a place where shootings and knife attacks were fairly common.

The latest near-fatal stabbing had taken place only three nights ago and he had actually asked Sarah to go and interview the victim in hospital. Of course that was before she received that first text from the kidnapper.

Peckham had for years been blighted by a brutal gang culture, and Brennan was reminded of it as they drove through the area's dark, dingy streets.

It was at the epicentre of Tony Kemp's criminal empire and where Bobby Knight and others like him had cut their teeth as wide boys and villains.

The Kemp firm was one of several operating across South London. It was second in size and reach only to the outfit run by Danny Shapiro, another top dog in the underworld. Brennan had met them both and they were very different characters.

Shapiro was in his thirties, good-looking and quite personable. He was once married to a television soap star. But Kemp was a rougher diamond. He was an ugly, fat thug of pensionable age who was renowned for his vicious temper.

Brennan had questioned Kemp a year ago in connection with a double murder. A Polish prostitute and her pimp were both shot in the head and their bodies dumped on a piece of waste ground in Clapham. The victims were linked to an Eastern European gang that had ignored warnings not to set up business on Kemp's manor. So the finger of suspicion naturally pointed right at him, but unsurprisingly he claimed he didn't kill them and didn't pay someone to do it for him. Brennan and his team weren't able to prove that he was lying, though he so obviously was.

During the interview, Kemp came across as a charmless oaf who got his rocks off by intimidating people. He swore a lot and made it blatantly clear that he had no respect for any form of authority. In fact, Brennan came away with the distinct impression that Kemp wouldn't baulk at targeting anyone who upset him or he felt threatened by – and that included police officers of any rank.

It was why the detective wasn't looking forward to another unpleasant session with the man. But as things stood it would probably have to happen at some point if he followed through with this current line of inquiry.

Emily Knight actually lived in one of the better parts of Peckham. Her semi-detached house overlooked the common and was set back from the road behind a narrow grass verge.

Brennan had only been told that she was a widow aged sixty-six and retired.

He had no intention of going in heavy-handed. The house was in darkness, and if she was at home they were about to wake her, which was bound to come as enough of a shock.

He was hoping she'd cooperate after he told her why they were there. This wasn't about her son's links to organised crime

185

or his failure to meet probation commitments by disappearing. This was about finding a fifteen-month-old child who'd been abducted. That was the overwhelming imperative for Brennan and his team. And he hoped that as a mother Emily Knight would understand that.

An upstairs light came on seconds after he rang the bell. Brennan looked up to see someone pull back the curtain and peer out. Shortly after, more lights were switched on and the front door was opened by a grey-haired woman wearing a dark blue towelling robe, belted at the waist.

'Emily Knight?' Brennan enquired.

'Yes,' she said, and her startled eyes flicked beyond him to the two uniformed officers.

Brennan held up his warrant card. 'Detective Chief Inspector Brennan. I'm really sorry to be bothering you . . .'

'Is this about my son?' she interrupted. 'Has he been found? Is that it?'

'No he hasn't, Mrs Knight. But we do need to talk to you about him. It's very important, which is why we've had to disturb you in the middle of the night. So may we come in?'

She looked confused and then suspicious. But curiosity prompted her to wave them in.

They followed her into a brightly lit kitchen where she went straight to the sink to fill the kettle.

The two officers stood just inside the door while Brennan sat at the table. He looked around and decided that there was something oppressive about the house. The kitchen walls were a bilious shade of green and everything looked a little dated.

When the kettle was boiled, Mrs Knight turned to face them. But before she spoke she pulled a pack of Marlboro Lights and a lighter from her dressing gown pocket.

Brennan studied her as she lit up. He'd seen photos of her son and he could see him in her face, especially the full lips and sharp features. She was heavy-bodied and fleshy, with eyes that were rheumy and unfocused. Below them pads of flesh stood out and broken capillaries mapped her cheeks. It occurred to Brennan that here was a woman who'd had a tough life.

'So why are you here?' she said, fixing him with a steady gaze.

'Firstly can I ask if anyone else lives here with you, apart from your son Bobby, of course?'

She shook her head, and her cheeks hollowed as she drew on her cigarette.

'Before Bobby moved back in I'd lived here by myself since my husband's death three years ago. My other son, Noah, has a flat in Norwood.'

'I see. And can I just confirm that you reported Bobby missing two weeks ago?'

'That's right. He left here the day before to go to the job centre. He said he'd be back later. But he didn't come home and I've not heard from him since. That's why I know that something bad has happened to him. Bobby always stayed in touch and if he'd planned to go away he would have told me.'

'So why did you tell the officers who were looking into his disappearance that you believed he'd been murdered?'

'Because it's bloody obvious. That arsehole Tony Kemp had already threatened him twice. He said if Bobby didn't stay away from his daughter Lauren then he'd make him regret it.'

'So did you actually witness these threats?'

'Well no, but Bobby told me and I believed him.'

She puffed vigorously on the cigarette, the smell of tobacco permeating the room.

'The problem was he couldn't get over the fact that the bitch had moved on while he was in prison,' she said. 'He was still obsessed with her, besotted. He refused to accept that she didn't love him anymore and he thought he could get her back even though she's now engaged to someone else.'

'So what did he do?'

She shrugged. 'He kept phoning her and going over to her house in Greenwich. He even followed her a couple of times. I told him that he should stop and was wasting his time. But he didn't want to listen.'

This was all very interesting, Brennan thought, but he wasn't sure how relevant it was to Molly Mason's abduction.

'Look I don't understand why I'm having to tell you all this again,' she said. 'Your colleagues already know it. Don't you lot talk to each other?'

'Well I've not been part of that investigation, Mrs Knight,' he said. 'You see, I'm investigating the abduction of a child named Molly Mason. You've probably heard about it.'

'Bobby has got nothing to do with that,' she responded sharply. 'He would never take a baby from her mother.'

'You don't seem surprised that his name has come up in connection with the case,' Brennan said.

She swallowed hard and then switched her gaze to the glowing tip of her cigarette.

'That's because as soon as I saw it on the news I realised who the mother was,' she said. 'She was the one who planted the evidence that got my son convicted.'

Brennan thought about picking her up on that remark, but instead he bit his tongue and said, 'And did you know that while he was in prison he plotted revenge against her?'

Her eyes moved back to Brennan and she flung up a dismissive hand.

'He was angry with her and he had every right to be. Going to prison didn't just cost him his freedom. He lost the woman he was going to marry and he lost his dad as well.'

'His dad? I don't understand.'

'My husband had suffered depression for a couple of years,' she said, her voice beginning to crack with emotion. 'Bobby being stitched up like that pushed him over the edge. He slit his wrists in the bath upstairs a year after Bobby went to prison.'

'I didn't know that,' Brennan said. 'And I'm truly sorry for your loss.' He left it a beat before carrying on. 'But what I need to know, Mrs Knight, is if your son was planning to make Sarah Mason suffer as a way of getting his own back.'

Tears began to glisten in her eyes as she spoke. 'When he first went inside he made all kinds of idle threats. But that's all they were. He was never going to do anything when he was released.'

'So are you saying that he didn't mention Sarah Mason when he got out?'

'No he didn't. After four years locked up he'd come to his senses. And anyway, he couldn't have taken that girl because he must have been dead by then. Tony bloody Kemp killed him. I know it.'

Now she started to cry, and Brennan got up to guide her to a chair while one of the officers offered to make her a cup of tea.

The cigarette was still trapped between her fingers and she didn't seem to know what to do with it. So Brennan took it from her and dumped it in an ashtray on the table.

'I want to call Noah,' she said. 'I need him to come over. This is all too much.'

'We'll call him for you,' Brennan said. 'Meanwhile, I wonder if we could have permission to look in your son's room.'

She wiped her eyes on her sleeve. 'Is that necessary? Your

people searched it after he disappeared. They said they were looking for clues.'

Brennan sat down, pulled out his handkerchief and gave it to her. She took it and put it against her mouth.

'Look here, Mrs Knight. A little girl has been kidnapped and we're trying to find out where she is and who has her. Like it or not, your son's name has come up in connection with it. So we have no choice but to investigate. I understand that you believe your son is no longer alive, but you know yourself that you can't be sure. And neither can you be sure that he didn't snatch Molly Mason to punish her mother. So your cooperation would really be appreciated.'

He sat back while she tried to compose herself. She was asked by the officer making the tea if she wanted sugar and she nodded.

'It won't take me long to have a quick look round,' Brennan said. 'While I'm doing that one of these gents will ring your other son for you.'

She lifted her head and stared at him.

'It's the door on the right at the top of the stairs,' she said. 'I haven't changed anything since he was last in there.'

Before going upstairs, Brennan had a quick look in the living room. It was smaller than he had expected and rather cluttered.

The first thing he noticed was the colour of the sofa. It was brown, not white, and therefore not the one that Molly was sitting on in the first photo that was sent to Sarah's phone. But he knew, of course, that it didn't rule Knight out.

Upstairs, he checked the bathroom first and saw for himself that it wasn't the one that Molly had been photographed in. This one was pale blue and in the photo the bath was white.

Bobby's room overlooked the back garden. There was nothing

unusual about it. Double bed, fitted wardrobes, dressing table, wall-mounted television. Shirts and trousers were hanging up in the wardrobes and the rest of his clothes, most of which looked new, were folded in the drawers. There was little in the way of other personal belongings. It appeared as though he hadn't accumulated much since his release.

Brennan wondered if the officers called in to investigate his disappearance had bothered to carry out a thorough search of the room. He doubted it, but would need to find out. He'd also have to ask them if they'd taken stuff away, such as a laptop or tablet, because there was no sign of any.

It seemed unlikely that if Knight was still alive, and had indeed abducted Molly, that he would have brought her here to his mother's house. There certainly appeared to be no evidence to suggest that he had. But Brennan did not want to leave until he'd had a good look around. So he took a pair of latex gloves from his pocket and got to work.

He searched the pockets of Bobby's trousers and jackets. He went through the drawers, checked under the bed, rifled through a documents file containing information pertaining to his release from prison.

He was about to accept that he was wasting his time when he realised that he hadn't looked under the mattress. And that, as he'd discovered over the years, was where many people concealed things.

He didn't actually expect to find anything, so when his fingers brushed against something hard and cold he felt his heart stutter.

It was a Samsung smartphone and it came to life when he switched it on.

Goosebumps broke out along his limbs as he began to click on the various apps. There weren't many, and it quickly became evident that the phone had never been used to make calls or send messages. But it had been used it to take photographs. And when Brennan saw what was in the picture gallery he felt a cold blast of terror sweep through his body.

35

Sarah

For Adam and me it was as though time had slowed down. It felt like the night would never end.

We were desperate to know what was happening but there was no point bombarding Brennan with calls. I assured Adam that my boss would let us know as soon as there was a development.

Being together was making the waiting more bearable for both of us. The issues that had driven us apart were pushed aside so that we could concentrate our minds on the only thing that mattered – our daughter.

We sat in the living room and talked about her. Adam asked me to dig out the CD with her photos, so I did and we watched the slideshow on the TV, which soon brought tears to our eyes.

There were pictures taken in the hospital on the day she was born, red-faced and tiny, swaddled in the pink blanket that was still upstairs in her room.

Adam appeared in a couple of those early photos and the pride in his expression back then was there for everyone to see. But in his eyes there was also a hint of regret because he knew that he was destined only to be a part-time father because of what he'd done.

My favourite pictures were those that showed Molly turning from a baby into a little girl. The pretty dresses, the unruly hair, the mischief in her eyes, the way she smiled on cue for the camera.

There were video clips amongst the photos too and these really hit the spot, causing a rush of heat to burn in my chest.

One was filmed on her first Christmas when she was ten and a half months old. In it she was surrounded by all her presents and didn't know what she was supposed to do with them. The look on her face was a joy to behold.

Another, shot on Christmas night, showed Adam throwing her in the air and onto the sofa. She giggled and screamed and then cried when he told her that he couldn't keep doing it because he had to go.

Molly had grown used to having a part-time dad now. She always looked forward to seeing him, but she seemed happy enough when he wasn't there. The arrangement seemed to work for everyone, which in the circumstances had to be a good thing.

I found myself thinking that when – not if – Molly came back to us, it would be impossible to achieve any degree of normality in our lives. I couldn't possibly go back to work again. I'd almost certainly been transformed into an overprotective mother, the type who never wants to let their children out of their sight. But I wouldn't care, not if it meant that Molly would be safe and that nobody could ever take her from me again.

'Another drink?'

Adam was reaching for my empty glass as he spoke. I'd been so lost in thought that I hadn't realised the slideshow had come to an end. I rubbed my eyes and felt their wetness.

'I'm not sure I should,' I said.

The two glasses of wine and a whisky I had already consumed were buzzing through my body. But I had to admit that it felt good.

'Just one more,' Adam said. 'You're a long way from being drunk, but at least it's helping us both get through the night.'

I let him take my glass and watched him cross the room to the drinks cabinet.

'Are you sure you don't have to go home?' I said.

He nodded. 'Positive. And in case you're wondering, I still live by myself so there's nobody waiting there for me.'

'So you're not seeing anyone then?'

He left it a beat and I wondered if he was deciding whether or not to tell me.

Then he said, 'There is someone on the scene. Her name's Helen and we've been dating for about six weeks. She's in Chicago right now on business.'

'Is it serious?' I said, and it came as quite a shock when I experienced a tiny flutter of jealousy.

He shrugged. 'She seems to think it is, but I'm not so sure.'

He poured us each a drink and then came and sat back down. I didn't want a prolonged conversation about Adam's love life so I raised the subject of Victor Rosetti again and what he'd said about Bobby Knight.

Neither of us had known that Knight had been released from prison early on licence. But even if we had it wouldn't have worried us because we wouldn't have expected him to still be holding a grudge.

'What I never understood back then was why he was so adamant that we'd fitted him up,' I said. 'I mean, the gun was in his bedside drawer and although his prints weren't on it there were traces of his DNA.'

195

'I told you,' Adam said. 'It was his only defence. He wanted to make the jury believe that one of us had planted it.'

'But there was something about the way he insisted that he knew nothing about the gun or the drugs,' I said, recalling how he responded to the allegations both during questioning and in court. 'In fact, there was a point when he almost had me convinced.'

'He's a career criminal, Sarah. Lying comes naturally to him.'

I shook my head. 'I'm not so sure now. I couldn't help wondering if one of the officers who took part in the raid wanted to make sure it wasn't going to be a waste of time. I remember how you yourself told me that you didn't think Knight was stupid enough to have drugs in his home.'

'But I was proved wrong,' Adam said. 'And don't forget that you were the one who actually found the revolver when you searched his bedroom.'

Suddenly my mind took me back to that house four years ago. Parts of what happened had blurred over time, but other parts were as clear as day.

I remembered how we'd barged in mob-handed. Knight had been in the living room watching television. Armed officers moved quickly through the house to make sure there was no one else there.

And I remembered waving the search warrant in Knight's face and telling the team to get cracking.

I made it clear in my report that I was the officer who searched his bedroom. And that was why, throughout the process that followed, he kept accusing me of planting the gun.

'*You were the first copper to go in the bedroom,*' he said. '*You must have put the fucking gun there. It doesn't belong to me. I've never seen it before.*'

But there was one detail I didn't put in my report because it didn't seem relevant. But now I was reminded of it and suddenly it did seem relevant. I felt it prick my conscience and force the breath from my lungs.

Turning to Adam, I said, 'You went into Knight's bedroom before I did. So I wasn't the first. You were coming out of the room when I reached the top of the stairs.'

He frowned. 'So what?'

'Well, you told me to search his room because you said you were going to check the other rooms.'

'Did I?'

'Yes you did. I didn't think anything of it then, but looking back it should have made me suspicious. You'd gone into that room first and yet you hadn't searched it. I should have asked why.'

He suddenly looked very uncomfortable.

'It was you, wasn't it?' I said, with a calmness I didn't feel inside. 'Did you plant the gun for me to find?'

If he'd been quick to deny it I probably would have believed him, but he hesitated and his face paled.

'It's true, isn't it?' I said.

His eyes held mine for a brief second, and then looked away as if in shame.

I knew then that the weight of his guilt had suddenly become a burden that was too heavy to bear.

36

DCI Brennan

After walking out of Bobby Knight's bedroom, Brennan checked all the other rooms in the house as well as the small back garden. He saw nothing to suggest Molly had been there, but the pictures on the phone found under the mattress convinced him that Knight had kidnapped her.

He then called DC Foster in the incident room and asked her to contact the detectives who looked into Bobby Knight's disappearance.

'I need to talk to them,' he said. 'And I also need to have a word with Tony Kemp. So find out where he is and let me have an address. And tell the rest of the team that I strongly believe Bobby Knight abducted Molly Mason.'

Emily Knight was still sitting on the same chair when he walked back into the kitchen. She had a cup of tea in one hand and a freshly lit cigarette in the other.

He took the seat next to her and held up the evidence bag containing the phone he'd found.

'Have you seen this before?' he asked her. 'It was in your son's bedroom.'

She put the cup down and squinted at the bag.

'That phone is black,' she said. 'Bobby's phone is white. I know that for sure because I went with him to get it.'

'This was under his mattress,' Brennan said. 'He must have hidden it there.'

'I don't understand. The police who came here before said they didn't find anything in his room.'

'Well I doubt they carried out a thorough search.'

'But why is this such a big deal? Who cares if my son had more than one phone?'

Brennan, still wearing the latex gloves, gently removed the phone from the bag. He went straight to the picture gallery and touched a finger against the tab to open it up.

'Your son was using this phone as a camera,' he said. 'And the photographs he took provide proof that he was planning to abduct Molly Mason.'

Brennan showed her the first photo and a frown tightened her forehead as she stared at it.

'This is the first of several photos showing the block of flats where Miss Mason and her daughter live in Dulwich,' he said. 'The date indicates it was taken five weeks ago.'

He flicked onto the next photo.

'This is Molly Mason's grandmother's house. It's where she was when she was abducted. The photo was taken four and a half weeks ago.'

The next photo showed Sarah Mason outside her mother's house with her daughter in her arms.

'I'm guessing your son either followed Miss Mason or else he was waiting for her to turn up,' Brennan said. 'It was taken a month ago when Miss Mason dropped Molly off as she usually does before going to work.'

He paused there to let her take it in and he could tell from her face that she was struggling to do so.

'The seventh and last photo taken on the camera is this one, and as you can see, it was snapped in a park,' Brennan said. 'The woman pushing Molly on the swing is her grandmother. That photo is dated three and a half weeks ago and there are none after that.'

It was a significant point, Brennan knew, because it meant that the photos and video clips that were sent to Sarah had not come from this phone.

'This can't be right,' Mrs Knight said, shaking her head sharply. 'I don't believe it. My Bobby would never have done this. It's not possible.'

'You have to believe it,' Brennan said. 'These photos prove that your son was stalking Sarah Mason after he got out of prison. It can only be because he was developing a plan to snatch her daughter.'

'But even if that were true he didn't go through with it. He couldn't have. He went missing two weeks before that baby did.'

'That's correct, Mrs Knight. Your son went missing. But that doesn't mean he was murdered.'

She shook her head. 'And it doesn't mean he took that child either.'

Brennan wasn't sure how much of what Emily Knight was saying he believed. She was clearly distressed and confused, but there was a degree of calmness in her demeanour that seemed misplaced. Perhaps, he thought, it was because lying and covering up for her son came naturally to her. After all, he'd been a villain for most of his adult life.

Brennan explained to her that there were more questions he needed to ask and that he wouldn't be leaving anytime soon.

He also told her that he was going to obtain a warrant so that the house could be searched more thoroughly.

'I hope you can appreciate why we have to move quickly on this,' he said.

He took from his pocket a colour photograph he'd had printed of Molly sitting on the white sofa. He placed it on the table in front of her.

'This little girl was abducted by a man wearing a mask. You'll know from the news that he's already subjected her to physical abuse. He actually sent a video clip to her mother showing him smacking the child. In his latest message he even threatened to rape her.'

The muscles in her jaw flexed as she stared down at the photo.

'My Bobby wouldn't do that,' she said. 'Not to a baby.'

Brennan tapped the photo. 'Do you recognise that sofa and the room she's in?'

She drew heavily on her cigarette before leaning forward to have a closer look.

'No I don't recognise it,' she said. 'It's not somewhere I've been.'

Brennan left the photo on the table and took out his notebook and pen.

'You said your son had another phone. Do you know where it is?'

'He had it with him when he went out that day.'

'Do you know the number?'

'It's in the address book in the living room. I gave it to the coppers who came here before. I've been ringing it since the day he left but it's not switched on.'

'Does he have a laptop or a tablet of some kind?'

She shook her head. 'He said he didn't need one. His phone was enough.'

'What about a car? Does he have one?'

'He's been using mine. It's parked out on the road. On the day he vanished he said he didn't need to take it.'

Brennan made a note and said, 'Now let's assume for a moment that Bobby has not been murdered. That he's alive but doesn't want you or us to know about it. Where might he have spent the past two weeks?'

She stubbed out her cigarette in the ashtray and gulped down a mouthful of tea.

'I really don't have a clue,' she said. 'I don't know any of his friends.'

'So where did he live before he went to prison?'

'With Lauren. They rented a house in Eltham. A couple of months into his sentence she had all his belongings sent back here and moved to another place in Greenwich.'

'Am I right in assuming that Bobby doesn't have a job?'

'He's been looking around for one, but it's not easy for ex-cons.'

'So why didn't he just go back and work for Tony Kemp?'

Her eyes grew hard. 'While Bobby was in prison he wrote lots of letters to Lauren pleading with her to wait for him. Some of them weren't very nice after she told him their engagement was off and their relationship over. It pissed Kemp off and he got a couple of other inmates to rough Bobby up. They passed on the message that Kemp wanted nothing more to do with him.'

'But that didn't stop Bobby going after Lauren.'

'Like I said before he was besotted with her still. He went to Lauren's place within days of getting out and demanded to talk to her. He even followed her to and from her boyfriend's house. She threatened to call the police and I feared he'd be arrested and sent back to jail. But instead Kemp came here one night and said he wanted a word with Bobby. I was told to go upstairs and I heard them shouting. Afterwards Bobby told me that Kemp had threatened to hurt him if he didn't back off.'

'When did this happen?'

'Three weeks before he disappeared. After that he didn't go to the house anymore, or so he told me. But I'm not sure if he stopped following her.'

It sounded to Brennan as though Bobby Knight was obsessed with two women – Lauren Kemp and Sarah Mason. One he loved and the other he hated. And he seemed intent on putting them both through hell.

'You mentioned your other son, Noah,' Brennan said. 'Are him and Bobby close? Would Bobby have confided in him?'

'Noah's the youngest and yes, they are close. Noah has always idolised his big brother. They tell each other most things.'

As if on cue the doorbell rang and Mrs Knight said, 'That'll be Noah now. When I called him he said he'd come right over.'

The man who walked into the kitchen introduced himself to Brennan as Noah Carter. In response to Brennan's puzzlement he explained that he began using his mother's maiden name some years ago because of his brother's notoriety.

'It was Bobby who persuaded me to change it by deed poll,' he said, after hugging his mum. 'He didn't want me to suffer because he was such a high-profile face in the underworld.'

Carter bore no resemblance to his gangster brother. He had soft features, a small mouth and ears that stuck out like jug handles. He looked fit and muscular in stone-washed jeans and a short-sleeved shirt that gaped at the neck. His hair was cut close to his scalp and when he spoke he had a slight lisp.

He stood next to his mum with one hand on her shoulder as Brennan explained why he was there.

Brennan expected him to react angrily to the fact that they had woken his mother up in the middle of the night. But instead Carter listened without interrupting until Brennan mentioned the phone he had found under his brother's mattress.

'It's news to me that he had another phone,' he said. 'I only ever saw him with an iPhone.'

'And how often did you see him before he went missing?'

'At least twice a week. Either I came here or he came to my flat. We also went out to the pub a few times.'

'Do you know what he got up to when he wasn't with you?'

'He went out looking for work and probably visited his old haunts, but don't ask me where because I don't know.'

'Your mother doesn't believe he's disappeared of his own accord,' Brennan said. 'She seems to think that his former boss, Tony Kemp, killed him. Is that what you think?'

'Of course. There's no question in my mind and that's what I told your colleagues when they came to see me. But they said that without a body and any evidence to prove that Kemp did it there's nothing they can do.'

'So how well do you know Kemp?'

'I don't know him. I've never met the guy. I'm a business consultant, Inspector, not a criminal. I love my brother and he's always meant the world to me. But I've followed a different path in life and I've always steered clear of the people he mixes with.'

'But you have met Kemp's daughter, Lauren. Your brother was engaged to her.'

'I only ever met her a few times when he brought her here. She's a spoilt brat, but Bobby is – or was – madly in love with her. It broke his heart when she dumped him and he just couldn't believe that she meant it. It became an obsession.'

'Your mother told me all about that,' Brennan said. 'But I'm more interested in your brother's obsession with Sarah Mason, the woman who arrested him.'

He told Carter about what Victor Rosetti had said and about the photographs on the phone.

Carter shook his head and when he spoke his voice was full of bile. 'My brother told me that Detective Mason must have planted the evidence that got him convicted,' he said. 'I know he stewed on it while in prison and he felt she destroyed his life. It's no wonder he hates her.'

'So do you accept that if he is alive he might well have taken her daughter as punishment?'

He looked down at his mother before answering.

'I suppose that in view of these photographs you've found it has to be possible,' he said. 'But I can tell you that Sarah Mason hasn't been occupying his thoughts as much as Lauren Kemp has.'

Mrs Knight had become even more distressed while listening to her son. Her sobs were now loud and pitiful.

'My officers are going to be here for a while,' Brennan said. 'I'm obtaining a warrant for a proper search and a forensic team will be coming here. So it might be sensible if your mother went somewhere else until we're finished.'

Carter nodded. 'I'll take her upstairs and she can get dressed. Then we'll go to my flat.'

'That's good. I'd like some officers to accompany you, though, and I trust you won't mind if they take a look around inside.'

Carter raised his brow. 'Is that because you want to see if my brother is there?'

Brennan nodded. 'It's necessary, I'm afraid, and it'll be best for all concerned if we don't have to obtain a warrant.'

Carter forced a smile. 'It's no problem. I understand. I've got nothing to hide.'

Brennan jotted down the address of the flat on his pad and watched Carter lead his weeping mother out of the kitchen and up the stairs. Then he took a moment to think through what he'd learned.

The most significant discovery was that Bobby Knight had most definitely put in motion a plan to abduct Molly Mason. Why else would he have spent time taking photographs of Sarah's flats and her mother's house?

But did he actually get to finish what he'd started? That was the million-dollar question and it served to complicate things still further.

Brennan was highly sceptical of the idea that Knight had been murdered. But he knew the theory couldn't just be ignored. It would now have to form part of the investigation and he'd have to take it seriously. But at the same time he would have to make sure that it did not distract the team from their main objective which was to find Molly Mason and bring her safely back to her mother.

37

Adam

'So this is all your fault, Adam. Our daughter has been abducted because four years ago you did something that was stupid, reckless and downright criminal.'

Sarah's face was dark as thunder as she screamed at him. Tears burned in her eyes and her body shook with anger.

Adam just stood there, rigid with shock, his chest so tight he could hardly breathe.

He hadn't intended to confess to planting the gun and drugs in order to ensure they got a conviction against Bobby Knight. But when she'd confronted him with the question, he'd suddenly discovered that his conscience wouldn't let him lie.

Sarah had a right to know that she was being punished for something she hadn't done. It was entirely his fault. Not hers. He was the one who had fucked up. Four years ago he could never have imagined the appalling consequences of his actions.

'I will never forgive you, Adam,' she said, her voice dropping from hysterical to low and threatening. 'I might never get my baby back because of you.'

'I'm so, so sorry, Sarah,' he said. 'At the time I thought I was doing a good thing.'

'Really? How in the name of God did you work that one out?'

He swallowed a huge lump. 'Knight needed to be brought down and I saw an opportunity to do it. He'd got away with murder for too long and the force had got nowhere playing it by the book.'

'But that was my collar. I was the one who got the tip about the drugs and persuaded the powers-that-be to authorise the raid on his house.'

He nodded. 'And that was another reason I decided to plant the evidence. I knew it was unlikely he'd have drugs in his own home and I didn't want you to look stupid. That was why I got you to search his bedroom. I wanted you to take credit for finding the gun.'

Sarah narrowed her eyes. 'But the gun had his DNA on it.'

'I was the first up the stairs,' he said. 'I went into the en suite and found his toothbrush. I used it to contaminate the gun with his DNA.'

She pointed a finger, said, 'You had no bloody right to do that. And you can't excuse what you did by saying he had it coming. You should be ashamed of yourself.'

'Oh come on, Sarah. It's not as if it doesn't happen all the time in the Met. I did it once; others make a habit of it.'

'That's no fucking excuse either, and it still makes you a bent copper. And if I had known it back then I would not have married you.'

Her words were tremulous, angry, vengeful and they hurt like hell.

'You can't make me feel any guiltier than I do already,' he said. 'I couldn't possibly have known that the bastard would react like this when he got out.'

'So what *did* you think, Adam? That he would thank you for stitching him up? Or after brooding on it for four years he'd forgive you? Or rather me, because I'm the one he blames. Which is why he's made it his mission to punish me.'

Sarah had been pacing the room. Now she dropped onto the armchair and gave him a look that made his stomach curl in on itself.

'Look, I'll let it be known that it was me,' he said.

'And what good would that do? You're Molly's father. So Knight is hardly likely to hand her back because the truth is out. He still went to prison as a consequence of what you did.'

Adam felt the life drain out of him. He wasn't thinking straight. It was as though the guilt and the shame had knocked all the sense out of him.

He snapped his gaze away from Sarah and went over to the drinks cabinet to pour himself another whisky.

'I would rather you didn't,' Sarah said.

He turned back to her.

'What?'

'I'd like you to go. Right now. I really don't want to have to talk about this any more tonight and if you stay we will.'

'But what I've told you doesn't change the fact that we need to help each other through this,' he said. 'Now is not the time for either of us to be alone. If we're going to help find Molly then we should work together.'

'I don't think you understand how upset I am, Adam. It's taking every ounce of my willpower not to come over there and smash my fist into your . . .'

She trailed off mid-sentence because her mobile phone message alert sounded. The phone was resting on the coffee table and they both heard it.

The atmosphere in the room changed in a heartbeat from anger to fear.

They both stared at the phone and then at each other. Adam was the first to speak.

'It's not necessarily him,' he said.

She shook her head. 'My gut tells me it is.'

She reached for the phone, and Adam dashed across the room to stand behind her. What had been happening between them a moment ago was instantly forgotten as she opened up the message.

'There's another attachment,' Sarah said, but she went to the text first and as soon as Adam started reading, his heart froze over.

Thought it was time I introduced myself. I'm Molly's new dad, here with my little angel. We're gonna have so much fun together. I hope it causes you unbearable pain, Sarah. It's no more than you deserve.

The attached photo then filled the screen. It was a grotesque selfie of someone wearing a black balaclava. It had three small slits for the eyes and mouth. The eyes were squeezed almost shut so you couldn't see their colour, and the mouth was stretched into a thin smile that showed just a hint of teeth. The camera was angled so that in the background you could see Molly lying fast asleep in a cot.

38

Sarah

I felt a sickening wave of despair rush through me. The evil bastard had done it again; he'd managed to raise the fear factor inside me to a whole new level.

I wanted to howl and scream, but I was too shocked to do either.

Adam took the phone from me and studied the photo as he walked over to the sofa. He sat down and I could see the pain in his eyes.

'If I ever get my hands on this evil fucker I'll kill him with a thousand cuts,' he exclaimed.

I was tempted to remind him that he was indirectly responsible for what was happening and there was a part of me that wanted to beat the shit out of him no matter how sorry he was. But anger was an emotion I couldn't afford to indulge right now. So instead I closed my eyes and tried to mentally erase the image of the man in the balaclava from my mind. But it wouldn't budge and I realised it never would for as long as I lived.

'I wonder when this picture was taken,' Adam said. 'Molly is spark out by the look of it so it could have been tonight.'

I tried to respond but the words wouldn't form, and I felt the hot sting of acid in the back of my throat.

'It terrifies me to think that he wears that hood when he's around her,' Adam said. 'Can you imagine how scared she must be and what it will do to her little mind?'

The thought of it caused my blood to surge. I pictured Bobby Knight's grinning face beneath the mask and remembered how he'd grinned when four years ago I'd produced the bagged semi-automatic pistol from behind my back and held it up in front of him. But his amused expression instantly turned to one of abject horror when I told him I'd found it in his bedroom.

I knew now that his reaction had been genuine and it was the first time he had seen it. So I could understand why he'd kept insisting he was innocent. And I could see how his rage must have festered and grown while he languished behind bars for all that time. But I couldn't accept that he was justified in pursuing such a brutal act of revenge that impacted on my child as well as on me. Adam was the one who planted the evidence against him, the one who had committed an act that to me was wrong and shameful.

Molly had played no part in what was done to him. She hadn't even been born, for Christ's sake. And yet she was paying the price, mentally and physically. What he was doing to her negated any sympathy I might have had for the man.

'We have to tell Brennan about this,' Adam said.

I sucked in a breath through my teeth. 'There's no need. You're forgetting that they're monitoring my calls and messages. They'll have received it at the same time I did.'

'I'm calling him anyway,' Adam said, and I watched him take out his phone and tap at the digits. 'He should have bloody well told us by now what's going on.'

He stood up and walked over to the window while waiting for his call to be answered. As he pulled back the curtain to look outside, I saw that it was still dark. But dawn could only be a few hours away and then we would have to endure another day of not knowing what to expect.

Would more photos and video clips be sent to me? And if so, would they show Molly sleeping, eating, bathing, or just looking confused? Or would they show her being subjected to unimaginable forms of abuse?

My bottom lip began to quiver and I felt a wave of heat roll up my back.

I stood up and shuffled into the kitchen to pour myself a glass of water. I swallowed a couple of paracetamols with it because I sensed a headache coming on. Or maybe it was a dreaded migraine.

I could hear Adam talking in the living room, but before going back in I had a few puffs on a cigarette.

I was still puffing away when Adam appeared at the door. The look on his face told me he did not have good news to impart.

'I spoke to Brennan,' he said. 'He's just seen the photo and read the text. He says he'll be over later.'

'Was that all he said?'

His eyes flared as he swept a hand back over his hair.

'He reckons Bobby Knight had definitely been plotting the abduction. It appears he was stalking you a few weeks back and he even took photographs of you with Molly. Brennan found them on a phone at his mum's house in Peckham.'

The breath rushed out of me. 'Do they know where he is?'

He shook his head. 'Knight's disappeared apparently. But that's not all. His family believe he may be dead.'

39

DCI Brennan

Brennan ended the conversation with Adam and rubbed his eyes, fatigue catching up with him.

They had talked briefly about the latest text message and about how the intelligence provided by Victor Rosetti had been spot on. But Brennan hadn't mentioned the means by which Adam had extracted it from the Romanian. He felt there was no need to since events had moved beyond that now.

Naturally Adam had been gutted to hear that Knight was missing and they still didn't know where Molly was. Brennan hoped he'd be able to give them some better news before the day was out.

He was briefing the two uniforms about what was going to happen next when Mrs Knight and her son came down the stairs. She was now wearing loose black trousers and a red cardigan buttoned up to the neck. Her grey hair was fastened tightly back, exposing a heavily wrinkled forehead.

'Thank you again for being so understanding,' Brennan said. 'I really do appreciate it.'

'Well make sure your people don't make a mess of the place. I don't want to have to clear up after you.'

'Don't you worry about that. You won't even know they've been here.'

'I hope you're right.'

'But before you go I need to ask you both again if you're absolutely sure that you have no idea where Bobby could be.'

'We've told you,' Carter said, his face full of emotion. 'He's dead, and his body is probably buried where it will never be found.'

'Well with respect, Mr Carter, we can't be sure of that. So until we have concrete evidence to the contrary we have to assume that your brother is alive and that he's holding Molly Mason in a house or flat somewhere.'

They both looked at him, their expressions blank, and he realised that they did not want to accept that Bobby was a child snatcher. It was easier – and less shaming – to believe that he'd been murdered for harassing his former boss's daughter.

Brennan decided to adopt a shock tactic in an attempt to open up their minds. He took out his phone and pulled up the photo that had just been forwarded to him.

'Molly's mother just received this from the kidnapper,' he said, holding it up so they could both see the photo. 'I accept that it's impossible to identify the man in the balaclava. But I believe that this is Bobby and that he's not dead. He just wants us all to think he is.'

The photo had the desired effect. Mrs Knight stifled a sob by putting her hand over her mouth. Carter instinctively wrapped an arm around her as he stared with undisguised revulsion at the photo.

'That's horrible,' he said. 'But let's be honest, Inspector. You can't even tell if it's a man or a woman.'

215

'I don't think there's any doubt that it's the man who abducted the child,' Brennan said. 'The same man who rendered her grand-mother unconscious with chloroform and tied her to a chair.'

Mrs Knight shook her head and struggled for words.

'I really don't know what to think anymore,' she said. 'I'm shocked and stunned by everything that's happened. But I really couldn't tell you where Bobby might be if he isn't dead. He's kept very much to himself since his release and I'm pretty sure he doesn't own another property that we're not aware of.'

'Has he been in touch with any of the people he was involved with while working with Tony Kemp?'

It was Carter who chose to answer this question, saying, 'My brother has always kept us away from that part of his life, Inspector. Most of what we knew about what he got up to we got from other people and from newspaper stories. It was how he wanted it.'

'OK, now what about the day he disappeared? Was he behaving differently in any way? Did he say anything to make you think something might be going on?'

'He seemed perfectly fine,' Mrs Knight said. 'He was in a good mood because he was going to splash out on some new clothes.'

'You said that he was going to the job centre.'

'That's what he told me,' she replied. 'And after that to the shops. But when the other detectives made inquiries at the job centre they found out that he didn't show up there.'

'Tony Kemp probably had him picked up while he was on his way,' Carter said. 'It was me who first suspected that something was wrong because we'd arranged to have a pub lunch together and he never showed. When he still hadn't been in contact the next day I told Mum to call the police.'

Brennan chewed on his tongue as he mulled this over. There were too many unanswered questions. Like why did Knight choose that day to disappear? Was his disappearance part of a carefully constructed plan? Did something happen that made it necessary for him to go off somewhere without telling his family? Could it be he dropped out of sight in order to avoid being seized by Tony Kemp's heavies?

For now Brennan had to accept that what Mrs Knight and her youngest son were telling him was the truth and they were not holding anything back. Nevertheless, he told the uniforms to go with them to Carter's flat to check it out.

He then called DC Foster to check if she'd found out who in Peckham CID had looked into the disappearance. He was given a name – DI Stanley Coulson – and told that the detective had been contacted and was waiting for Brennan to call him.

Coulson was happy to chat despite the hour. He'd been shocked to learn that Bobby Knight was now the prime suspect in Molly Mason's abduction. He confirmed that he and a couple of other officers had only carried out a brief search of the mother's house but was still surprised that they'd missed the phone beneath the mattress.

'I can only assume we failed to check under the mattress,' he said. 'But we weren't sure what we were looking for. In all honesty, we weren't even sure how seriously to take the disappearance. For all we knew he'd gone off on a holiday somewhere.'

He told Brennan they'd visited the job centre and checked the CCTV footage for that day, which confirmed that Knight never made an appearance.

'We tried calling his mobile but it was turned off and therefore not transmitting a signal,' he said. 'His phone records show that he never actually used it that day and in the previous weeks most of the calls were to his brother and Tony Kemp's daughter, Lauren. There were a few to some of his old cronies. We interviewed them

217

but they all claimed they didn't know where he was and what he was up to.'

'What about Kemp? I take it you talked to him.'

'Of course. But he had a solid alibi for the entire day and said he had nothing to do with Knight's disappearance. He did tell us the guy had been pestering his daughter and that he'd had to warn him off. But he laughed off claims from the mother and brother that he'd killed him. Without proof there was nothing more we could do.'

Brennan asked him to email the case file to the incident room in Wandsworth and then thanked him before hanging up.

By then it was three in the morning. He decided to have a quick look round the house before heading back to the station. But the chilling image of the man in the balaclava with the child in the background kept forcing itself into his mind, making it difficult for him to concentrate.

40

Sarah

We were trapped in an ever-worsening nightmare with no end in sight.

The news that Bobby Knight was apparently the man who had kidnapped our baby was of course encouraging. But the fact that he had vanished two weeks ago had come as yet another terrible blow. It heightened the pain inflicted by the latest message and photograph.

The horrific selfie he'd taken was stamped on my retinas and it appeared every time I closed my eyes.

Sergeant Parker, our FLO, had called to say she'd be over about eight. My mother had phoned to tell me they'd been given the go-ahead to return home since the scene of crime officers had finished the forensic work in the house.

It was almost dawn now and light was bleeding through the curtains. I'd managed to get a grip on my tears, but the cold terror was still growing inside me. All I wanted to do was curl up in a ball and not think about what was happening to Molly. That wasn't an option, though. There was simply no escape from the horror that had consumed us.

I made things worse for myself by watching the television news.

Molly was still the top story and the hysteria surrounding it continued unabated. They put up photographs of Molly, although, thankfully, not the ones from the kidnapper, they interviewed police officers, my neighbours, our friends, and a whole range of so-called experts.

A child psychologist spoke about how Molly's response to what was happening to her would depend on how she was treated.

'She would no doubt have been traumatised when he held her upside down and spanked her,' he said. 'But at that age children are able to forgive and forget relatively quickly if the person who hurts them then demonstrates extreme kindness. The inborn survival instinct teaches them to engage with and trust the person or persons they are wholly dependent upon. The psychological damage that's done usually emerges much later in life.'

As I listened to him speak I felt a scream twitching at the back of my throat because I could well believe what he was saying. As a police officer I'd come across children who had been severely abused, usually by their parents or other family members, and it had shocked me just how many of them had managed to carry on a seemingly happy relationship with their abusers.

The thought that Molly would inevitably become emotionally attached to the man who was being so cruel to her filled my heart with despair.

I was reminded of the kidnapper's message that accompanied the photo of Molly in the bath.

Seems my little darling has already forgotten what happened to her yesterday. I'm sure it won't be long before she forgets you as well!

After the child psychologist, there was an interview on Sky News with a woman whose thirteen-month-old daughter was abducted fifteen years ago. The girl was returned to her mother after police found her living with a family of travellers four years later.

'She didn't remember me or her father,' the mother said as she sniffed back tears. 'We were complete strangers to her. It broke our hearts.'

My own heart crashed to the floor then and I could feel my whole body beginning to quake.

Adam was suddenly at my side, touching my chin, lifting my eyes to his and telling me that we'd get through this and that I had to stay strong.

But his words brought me no comfort, and before I knew it the dam had burst again and I was crying uncontrollably.

I had always regarded myself as a person who could cope and show unlimited resolve in any situation. After all, I'd earned a reputation as a tough and resourceful copper. But this ordeal made me realise that I was far more fragile than I thought I was. I felt like I was being dismantled bit by bit, exposing a core that was soft and weak and vulnerable.

I wanted the tears to stop flowing and my heart to stop beating so ferociously, but I knew it wasn't going to happen. I'd lost control of my emotions and there was nothing I could do about it.

Adam made me a cup of tea and I was drinking it when Sergeant Palmer arrived. She was wearing a dark blue trouser suit today and her long hair was swept back in a severe ponytail. There were dark crescents under her eyes which made me think that she hadn't had much sleep.

She told us she was across everything that had happened and that DCI Brennan would shortly be addressing his team at the morning briefing.

'But he's already launched a nationwide appeal for information on Bobby Knight,' she said. 'The news channels will be running it any time now.'

A few minutes later Knight's photo appeared on Sky News and my stomach tensed when I saw it.

The reporter did not mince her words. She described Knight as a convicted drugs trafficker and South London gangster and said he was wanted in connection with Molly Mason's abduction.

'He was recently released from prison after serving four years of an eight-year sentence for possession of drugs and a firearm,' she said. 'Throughout his trial he maintained he was innocent and accused the police of planting evidence to get a conviction. The two arresting officers were detectives Sarah Mason and Adam Boyd, Molly's parents. Police believe he's kidnapped their daughter as an act of revenge.'

They then cut to Brennan making a statement outside Wandsworth police station.

'Bobby Knight dropped out of sight two weeks ago,' he said. 'We know for a fact that he'd been stalking Molly's mother. We believe that having abducted Molly he's now hiding out in a house or flat somewhere. I'm appealing for anyone who knows where he is or thinks they may have seen him to contact us without delay. It could be that he's moved into a property close to you. Or perhaps you've heard a child crying next door and you're suspicious because you didn't realise there were any children living there.'

It was a powerful appeal and I felt sure it would have a huge impact on the public.

After Brennan's little speech the report cut back to Knight's photo and there was more from the reporter, but she made no mention of the claim that Knight was dead, having been murdered by gang boss Tony Kemp. However, it did say he'd been part of a South London criminal empire allegedly run by Kemp.

I recalled how during the formal interview process I'd tried to get Knight to place on record the fact that he worked for Kemp. I even told him that if he dished the dirt we'd pitch for a lighter sentence. But he refused and at the time I didn't blame him because grassing on Kemp would have put his family in peril.

Adam was also glued to the television. He was standing close to me, shifting his weight from foot to foot, his face still and grim.

I guessed he was wrestling with his conscience, wondering whether to own up to what he'd done and if it would do any good if he did.

I was now firmly of the belief that if he confessed at this time to planting the evidence it wouldn't make any difference and might actually prove counter-productive.

'There's something I want you to know, Adam,' I said and my voice seemed to snap him out of a trance.

I got up, gripped his elbow and steered him over to the window so that Sergeant Palmer wouldn't be able to hear what I was going to say. The sky outside was filled with clouds and a light drizzle fell like muslin over the estate.

'At some point you are going to have to answer for what you did to Bobby Knight,' I said. 'But now is not the time. I won't tell anyone and I don't want you to either.'

It wasn't that I forgave him. I just didn't want to be burdened by the prospect that it would almost certainly shift sympathy and police resources away from us, which wouldn't help Molly.

Adam rolled out his bottom lip.

'Thank you,' he said. 'I know I don't deserve it and I promise I'll do everything I can to get our daughter back.'

Despite all the trouble he had caused I knew that he meant what he said and I found a small crumb of comfort in his words.

223

41

DCI Brennan

Brennan delayed the start of the morning briefing until ten to give him and his team time to carry out some checks and make a few inquiries.

More than forty officers and civilian staff were assembled in the incident room. Some of them had worked through the night, others had managed only a few hours' sleep. But the room was buzzing with a sense of optimism. They were confident the kidnapper had been identified. Bobby Knight was the prime suspect and that was real progress. They were hopeful that the resulting publicity – including the appeal that had already gone out – would trigger further developments.

Brennan started by walking them through the events that had unfolded during the night. He said that Detective Adam Boyd had taken it upon himself to go and see Victor Rosetti and had persuaded him to tell the truth. The Romanian had then pointed the finger at Bobby Knight. Brennan didn't mention Rosetti's bloodied mouth or the fake gun that Adam might or might not have used to threaten him with.

Then Brennan signalled to the officer operating the projector and Knight's picture appeared on the large screen to his left.

'This is the man we're looking for,' he said. 'The man who made it clear that he wanted to punish Detective Mason because she headed up the team that arrested him. He believed he was stitched up and that the evidence that convicted him was planted. But that was bullshit then and it's bullshit now. For one thing, his DNA was on the gun that they found in his bedroom. He's just a bloody sociopath with a grudge and we have to find him.'

Brennan relayed the salient points of the conversation he'd had with Knight's mother and brother.

'They're convinced that Tony Kemp had Bobby killed for harassing his daughter, Lauren. But there's no evidence to support the claim and Kemp denies any involvement. I'll be visiting him myself after this meeting so I'll see what he has to say.'

Brennan gave the thumbs up to the projector operator who replaced Knight's picture with the kidnapper's selfie.

'This was sent to Detective Mason's phone a couple of hours ago,' he said. 'The weirdo in the balaclava is either Knight or an accomplice, but there's no way we can be sure.'

He then read out the message that had come with it, but most of those in the room were already familiar with the words.

Next it was the turn of individual detectives to report back on the tasks they'd been assigned.

The first provided an update on the phone found under the mattress. Bobby Knight's prints were all over it apparently and there were no others.

DC Phil Doncaster had carried out brief background checks on Knight's mother and brother.

'I'll start with Emily Knight, guv,' he said. 'You gave me the

225

impression that she's a sweet little lady. Well that may be the case these days, but it seems that she wasn't always so.'

'How'd you mean?'

'She has form for one thing. In her twenties she was a brass and got done for soliciting fifteen times. Then she turned to shoplifting and was collared twice. Paid a fine and did community service. She stayed out of trouble after she got married and had the two boys. But her husband didn't. Albert Knight was a small-time villain. He did a three-year stretch for burglary and then received a suspended sentence for assault. He had a heart attack eight years ago and after that suffered severe depression, which ended with him committing suicide three years ago.'

'So it's plain to see why their eldest son turned to a life of crime,' Brennan said. 'He was following in mum and dad's footsteps.'

'It's a familiar story in that part of London, guv.'

'So what about the youngest son, Noah?'

'Well it seems like he's played it straight, unlike his brother,' Doncaster said. 'He doesn't have a criminal record and his name doesn't appear anywhere on the system. But I've managed to establish that he's divorced and lives by himself. He's a freelance business consultant specialising in setting up websites. The uniforms have checked his flat and there was no evidence to indicate that his brother was living there or had been in the recent past.'

'So for now we need to focus on finding Knight,' Brennan said. 'That means tracking down and speaking to all his known associates and visiting his old haunts. Surely someone must know where he's holed up.'

'But what if his mum's right and he's dead?' DC Foster said. 'I know it seems unlikely, but it's not impossible. Maybe Molly is in the hands of an accomplice.'

Brennan inclined his head. 'I agree it can't be ruled out. Knight may well be in a shallow grave somewhere courtesy of Tony Kemp. And that's why we need to talk to everyone he's been in contact with since he got out. I'm betting that if he did involve another person in his kidnap plan then it'll be someone he's worked with before. And someone who is just as sick in the head as he is.'

Brennan ended the session and checked his watch. Eleven a.m. DC Foster had set up a meeting with Tony Kemp for noon. It gave him time to ring Sarah. He felt it was only fair to keep her in the loop.

42

Sarah

I was grateful to Brennan for bringing me up to date with the investigation. But when I came off the phone I wanted to scream.

It wasn't so much what he'd said as the way he'd said it. His muted tone failed to inspire me with confidence.

'He's on his way to question Tony Kemp,' I said to Adam. 'But I don't get the impression he thinks he'll get much out of him.'

'I guarantee he won't,' Adam said. 'The guy has been running rings around all of us for years. The NCA has a file on him five feet thick. If he did arrange for Bobby Knight to be got rid of he'll have made damn sure he kept his distance from it.'

Neither of us wanted Knight to be dead. If he was then it meant that someone else had Molly, someone whose identity was a mystery to us, and we were no closer to finding her.

Brennan was convinced that Knight was alive, but he hadn't been able to convince me. My mind refused to let go of the worst-case scenarios.

'I need to do my bit,' Adam said suddenly, his eyes hard and determined. 'I can't just wait around for something to happen.'

He grabbed his leather jacket from the back of the chair and slipped it on.

'Where are you going?' I asked.

'To the office first,' he said. 'I'll dig out what we have on Knight and then go visit a couple of his old mates. Maybe I'll get something useful out of them.'

'But Brennan's got things in hand. The team are out there now talking to his known associates.'

'And they'll get the runaround, just like they did when they talked to Victor Rosetti. I'll be taking a different approach.'

He looked at me, his unshaven face taut with stress, and it worried me that he might take things too far and even obstruct the investigation.

'I'm not sure that's sensible, Adam,' I said. 'You'll get yourself into trouble.'

'I really don't care, Sarah. I caused all this so it doesn't matter what happens to me. It's what's happening to our daughter than I'm concerned about.'

Sergeant Palmer rushed into the living room at that point, having overheard the conversation. She started to speak, but Adam raised a hand to stop her.

'Whatever you're going to say don't bother,' he said. 'I'm getting involved in this no matter what.'

He then turned back to me, leaned close and whispered, 'The only way I can assuage the guilt I feel is to get out there, Sarah. I need to take my mind off what I did before it tears me apart.'

He then rushed out of the flat.

Sergeant Palmer immediately seized her phone and I assumed she was going to alert Brennan. But before she made the call she asked me if I was all right.

'I'm going upstairs to have a shower,' I said. It wasn't an answer to her question but it was all I could manage to say.

As I started towards the door I saw Molly's face filling the TV screen. It was a photo taken several months ago when she still had her beautiful fair hair. The news reader was saying that fifty hours had passed since she was abducted.

I felt the emotions flood through me and had to fight back the tears. I couldn't believe it had been only fifty hours. To me it felt more like fifty days. And what if I had to wait another fifty hours, or days, or years even? My stomach lurched at the thought.

In the shower, I closed my eyes and tried to imagine what it was like where Molly was being held. I'd seen photos of the sofa, the cot, the bath. But it was hardly a complete picture. Was she in a house or a flat? Was the place clean or filled with muck and germs? Was she able to go outside into a garden or onto a balcony? Was her new home close by or on the other side of the country?

Questions, questions, questions . . . They were eating away at me like piranhas trapped inside my skull.

Before stepping out of the shower, I came to a decision, and it went some way towards easing the tension in my bones. I was going to follow Adam's example and seize at least some control of the situation instead of merely reacting tearfully to events. I was no longer prepared to leave Molly's fate in the hands of other people. As much as I trusted Brennan and the rest of the team, I felt I couldn't just sit back and do nothing. I had a lot to offer, after all – experience, commitment and a willingness to do whatever was necessary to get my little girl back.

I dried myself and got dressed in front of the mirror. My eyes were red from tiredness and my skin looked like it had been bleached. I applied a little foundation and mascara, which didn't seem to make much difference, but I felt slightly better for it. I

picked up my shoulder bag and packed it with the usual stuff –
mobile, purse, tissues.

Downstairs, I walked into the kitchen where Sergeant Palmer
was pouring hot water into a coffee mug.

'I'm going to the station,' I said. 'I want to make myself useful.
You can take me or I can go myself. What's it to be?'

43

DCI Brennan

Brennan took two calls before leaving the incident room. The first was via his mobile and came from Sarah's FLO, Sergeant Palmer. She wanted to alert him to the fact that Molly's father had gone off on his own again.

'I heard him telling Detective Mason that he intends on talking to some of Bobby Knight's old mates,' she said. 'I thought you ought to know, sir.'

He thanked her and told her to leave it with him. But he had no intention of doing anything about it. If Adam Boyd was going to act like a loose cannon then so be it. They wouldn't be where they were now if he hadn't put the squeeze on Victor Rosetti. If in the process the guy got himself into bother then that was his problem. But if he got another result then it would be welcome.

The second call was received in the incident room and was sent through to his office. This one came as more of a surprise. It was from Bobby Knight's brother, Noah Carter.

'I'm sorry to bother you, Detective Chief Inspector,' he said.

'But I've been giving a lot of thought to what you told my mother and me this morning.'

'That's good to know, Mr Carter. Does it mean there's more you can tell us about your brother?'

'That's not why I'm calling. I've told you everything I can about what Bobby has been up to since he came home.'

'Then what?'

'It's to do with that little girl,' Carter said, cutting him off. 'If you're right and my brother did abduct her then maybe they were together when Tony Kemp killed him, which means Kemp is the one who has her now.'

Brennan thought about it for a moment and said, 'That's very interesting, Mr Carter, but as far as we know, Kemp doesn't have a personal score to settle with Molly's mother. So why wouldn't he have just let her go?'

'You'll need to ask him that. I don't know how his mind works. But just suppose Bobby told him before he died why he'd snatched the girl. Perhaps Kemp saw a way of making a profit by holding onto her.'

'How d'you mean?'

'Well sooner or later there's bound to be a reward offered. Or maybe he'll eventually make a ransom demand.'

It was an intriguing theory and one that Brennan hadn't considered.

'I'll be speaking to Tony Kemp shortly so I'll be sure to put it to him,' he said.

'I don't suppose the bastard will admit to it,' Carter said. 'But I wouldn't be at all surprised if that is what happened.'

'Well you can leave it to us to make the necessary inquiries, Mr Carter. Meanwhile, how is your mum holding up?'

'She's still here at my flat and as you can imagine she's pretty upset and confused.'

'Well hopefully she'll be able to return home soon. Someone will contact you when my officers have finished at her house.'

Carter had nothing more to add so Brennan ended the call. But the brief conversation left him wondering if what the man had said was at all possible. It would certainly be an unexpected development and one that would throw up a whole raft of new questions.

Over the years Brennan had met a few despicable souls who he knew would be capable of seizing such a wicked opportunity for financial gain. And Tony Kemp was one of them.

Kemp owned several properties in and around South London. He and his wife divided most of their time between a swanky apartment overlooking the Thames in Bermondsey and a large converted oast house near Sevenoaks in Kent. Both had been purchased with the proceeds of his many illicit activities, including extortion, prostitution, drugs, people trafficking and illegal gambling. But as with the likes of Victor Rosetti the money was always channelled through legit companies, in Kemp's case a chain of small cafés and a firm that imported toys from China.

DC Foster had arranged for them to meet him and his daughter Lauren at the Bermondsey apartment. She had explained what it was about over the phone and Kemp had said that it wouldn't be a problem since they were both there all day.

Foster's reward for setting it up so quickly was to go along with Brennan. She was driving the pool car and Brennan sensed that she was a little nervous. He wasn't entirely surprised. At twenty-nine she was the youngest member of his team and had never met Kemp, but had heard a lot about him, none of it good.

'Compared to the other London crime barons, Kemp comes

across as a Neanderthal. But that doesn't mean he should be under-estimated.' Brennan told her. 'He wouldn't have reigned supreme for so many years if he wasn't so clever and so cunning.'

'Do you think he had Bobby Knight killed, guv?' she asked.

He shrugged. 'I really don't know. But I do know he's always been very protective of his daughter, so I wouldn't put it past him if she was being harassed.'

'And what about the suggestion that he might be the one who has Molly Mason?'

'It's a scary thought,' Brennan said. 'And for her sake I hope it's not true.'

The apartment block had a large, sumptuous reception area. A liveried concierge sat behind the desk and a security guard stood to one side.

Brennan and Foster were expected but still had to show their warrant cards. They were then directed to a lift and told to take it to the top floor, the penthouse.

'I didn't expect Kemp to be living in a place like this,' Foster said as they were going up. 'It seems far too upmarket for a South London gangster.'

Brennan laughed. 'Then it might surprise you to learn that at least two of his neighbours are also villains. One's involved with the Russian Mafia and the other is an Albanian pimp. I know because a while ago I carried out surveillance on the block.'

She rolled her eyes. 'And there was me thinking that crime doesn't pay.'

When the lift door opened they were met by a shaven-headed man who had a frame that his suit was barely able to contain. It looked to Brennan as though he was about to start a shift as a bouncer outside a nightclub.

'My name is Ross,' he said, with a vague semblance of a smile. 'Mr Kemp is waiting for you in the lounge.'

They followed him across the carpeted corridor to the only door on the top floor. It was open and he led them along a short hallway and into a room with stunning views of London. The windows were all floor to ceiling and there was a large balcony. It had stopped raining outside and the sun was casting its warm glow over the city.

Tony Kemp was sitting cross-legged on one of two black leather sofas that faced each other across a marble coffee table. He was wearing baggy chinos and a white shirt, the sleeves rolled up to reveal beefy forearms. His hands were clasped together over an expansive stomach that strained the shirt buttons to breaking point.

'Long time no see, Mr Brennan,' he said, his voice rough and pure South London. 'And I take it this is the polite young lady I spoke to on the phone.'

Foster nodded. 'Detective Constable Foster,' she said and then cleared her throat.

Kemp grinned, lips parting to reveal custard-coloured teeth.

'Well sit down. Is there anything my man Ross can get you? Coffee, tea or maybe something stronger?'

'We're fine,' Brennan said, speaking for both of them as they sat down on the other sofa. 'I'd like to thank you for seeing us at short notice.'

He shrugged. 'Well I couldn't pass up the chance to get the inside track on all this business involving the missing little girl and that worthless cunt Bobby Knight. It's pure fucking drama and I'm hooked along with the rest of the nation.'

The old gangster hadn't changed much, Brennan realised. He was still nasty and uncouth, a hard, uncompromising villain with no soft edges. He had a drinker's bloated face and cruel eyes, the kind that enjoy seeing others suffer.

Brennan flicked his gaze around the lavishly furnished apartment. 'I thought your daughter was going to be here with you,' he said.

Kemp uncrossed his legs and spread his arms out along the back of the sofa.

'She's having a shit,' he said. 'I took her out for dinner last night, just like I always do when she stays here with me. But a combination of dodgy fish and too much wine has given her the squirts. She'll be along in a minute.'

Anyone else would have said she was getting dressed or was on the phone. But not Kemp, who was known to be a foul-mouthed tosser.

'Is your wife here as well?' Brennan asked.

'No. She's at our place near Sevenoaks. She prefers the country-side to the city. She hates noise and fumes and seeing the streets full of dossers.'

Brennan produced his notebook and took a moment to reflect on his first impression – that Kemp was more relaxed than perhaps he should have been. Was it because he had nothing to hide or because he knew that he'd taken the necessary steps to ensure he wasn't going to be caught out?

'So come on, Detective Chief Inspector,' Kemp said. 'Let's get this show on the road. What is it you want to ask me?'

Brennan pushed his shoulders back and said, 'You're obviously aware that we now believe Bobby Knight is responsible for abducting fifteen-month-old Molly Mason, who happens to be the daughter of the detectives who arrested him.'

'Yeah, of course. Like I told you I've been following it with interest. But what the fuck has it got to do with me?'

'You also know that Knight dropped out of sight two weeks ago and that his family are convinced that you had him killed because he was pestering your daughter.'

Kemp snorted dismissively. 'I've already spoken to your lot about that and I told them I didn't do anything to him.'

'But isn't it true that you threatened him?'

'Sure I did and I'll tell you this, if he'd carried on giving Lauren grief I would have broken both his legs myself. But I didn't have to because he stopped harassing her. I didn't know he'd vanished off the face of the earth until the coppers showed up telling me his old dear was blaming me.'

'So you have no idea what happened to him?'

'No I haven't and I don't give a shit anyway. The guy's a twat and if he is dead then good riddance. The world's a better place without him.'

'I'm guessing you thought differently when he worked for you.'

'He didn't actually work for me, so get your facts straight. He was involved in illegal drugs and that's not my bag. I'm a respectable businessman just like I keep telling everyone. All that stuff about me being a big player in organised crime is bollocks.'

'Of course it is,' Brennan said. 'So how come Knight ended up getting engaged to your daughter?'

'Why don't you let me answer that question?'

It was a woman who spoke, and when Brennan turned he saw Lauren Kemp standing there. She had entered through a door on their right, a thin thirty-something with long wild ringlets of hair framing an attractive face full of natural angles. She was wearing tight jeans and a V-neck sweater that showed a hint of cleavage. As she came closer, Brennan saw that she had feline-shaped eyes and a dark splutter of freckles across her nose and cheekbones.

She walked across the room and stood behind her father, resting her hands on his shoulders. She inclined her head towards Foster and her smile was white and charming. Then she looked at Brennan and said, 'I met Bobby in a nightclub that my dad part-owns. We got on really well from the off and I quickly fell in love with him. So after six months or so we got engaged. I had no idea he was dealing drugs, so when he was arrested and charged it came as a shock. While he was in prison I decided to break off the engagement. But Bobby wouldn't accept it. He bombarded me with nasty letters and when he got out he wouldn't leave me alone. He scared me, and once when he turned up at my house he even said he would rather see me dead than with someone else.'

When she finished speaking she rocked back on her heels and took a deep breath. Brennan could see tears gathering at the edges of her eyes.

'So why didn't you go to the police?' he asked.

'I was going to,' she said. 'But I still had feelings for him, believe it or not, and I didn't want to see him back in prison. So I asked Dad to have a word with him, which he did. After that he left me alone. And that's really all I can tell you. I don't know where he is now and I believe my dad when he says he had nothing to do with his disappearance.'

There was a tense silence which lasted several seconds. Then Foster said, 'How many times have you seen him since his release?'

Lauren wiped her right eye with the back of her hand.

'Four times in all,' she said. 'The first time I made the mistake of letting him into my house so I could explain to him how I felt. But he became rude and aggressive and wouldn't leave until I started screaming.'

'And during these conversations did he ever mention Molly Mason or her mother, Detective Sarah Mason?'

She shook her head. 'Never. I couldn't believe it when I saw on the news that he was linked to the girl's abduction.'

'But you must have known he had a grudge against her mother,' Foster said.

'Everyone did. He made no secret of that from the moment he was arrested because he claimed he was fitted up. But not in my wildest dreams would I have thought he'd snatch her child.'

Brennan was surprised that she was being so open and articulate and found it hard to believe that she was her father's daughter.

'It's obvious to everyone except Bobby's old dear that the prick is still alive,' Kemp said. 'Even you lot think he's the one who took the kid and is now sending those sick messages and photographs to her mum. So I'm surprised you're wasting your time talking to us.'

'We have to follow up every lead,' Brennan said. 'And that includes the suggestion that you killed Bobby and then took the child from him.'

For the first time Kemp's face lost its composure and his eyebrows shot up. 'You have got to be fucking kidding me,' he growled. 'Why would I want to do a thing like that?'

'Well the theory is that you'll eventually demand a ransom or get someone to claim a reward on your behalf, if and when one is offered.'

Kemp's temper suddenly flared and he heaved his heavy bulk up off the sofa.

'Now you're taking the piss,' he shouted, pointing a rigid finger at Brennan. 'If I'd known you were gonna start accusing me of child abduction, I would never have agreed to see you.'

'I'm not accusing you of anything,' Brennan said.

'It sounds like it to me. So you can fuck right off.'

'Look, Mr Kemp. There's no need to—'

'Don't bother saying anything else, because I'm not listening. If you want to ask me any more questions, then you can arrange it through my solicitor. But let me be clear. If you don't have any evidence to back up these absurd allegations then you can be sure I'll kick up a fucking stink.'

He told Ross to see them out and then stomped around the sofa, took his daughter by the hand and led her into another room, slamming the door behind them.

Brennan wasn't sure what to read into Kemp's reaction. Either the man was genuinely offended or he was shocked and angry at being found out.

It meant they would have to think carefully about how to proceed with this line of inquiry. One option was to pile on the pressure, which would include hauling Kemp in for more questioning and obtaining warrants to search all his properties. But that would take up a lot of time and resources, and if he was telling the truth it wouldn't lead them to Molly Mason.

It was a tough decision, especially in view of the fact that Brennan himself did not believe that Bobby Knight was dead.

44

Sarah

Even before I got to the station I started having second thoughts, although I didn't voice them to Sergeant Palmer.

She had tried to talk me out of leaving the flat, but when I told her I was going to call a taxi she agreed to drive me. I couldn't drive myself because my car had been at the station since Monday.

I'd set out determined to follow Adam's example and do something, anything, to help find Molly. But unlike him I had no idea what I was going to do.

Palmer had told me I was too emotionally strung out to be of any use to the investigation. And she was probably right, but it wasn't what I wanted to hear. I needed to be involved somehow, to know that I was playing a part.

Of course, protocol demanded that as Molly's mother I had to keep my distance. But as far as I was concerned protocol could take a flying jump.

As we arrived at the station I willed myself to think clearly, to close down my imagination and fill the cold space inside me with positive thoughts. I told myself there was reason to be optimistic because the team now had a prime suspect who was becoming more credible by the minute. Surely it wouldn't be long before his whereabouts were known.

When I walked into the incident room alongside Sergeant Palmer, I could feel the anxiety stirring in my gut.

I was immediately struck by how packed it was. There was a detective at every desk, while others stood around in small groups, immersed in animated conversations.

My appearance brought everything to an abrupt standstill for a couple of seconds. I felt I had to do something, so I gave a nervous little wave and mouthed a 'thank you' to show how much I appreciated what they were doing.

A couple of people acknowledged by waving back, but most just looked away again and got on with their jobs.

One detective came right over to me. DI Tommy Driscoll had been tasked with looking after me whilst in the office. I knew him and had a lot of respect for him. He was in his early forties with a high brow and jutting chin. He gave me a cuddle and said he was surprised to see me.

'I had to get out of the flat,' I said. 'I feel I should be helping in some way.'

From his expression I could tell that he understood. He had children of his own, after all, and one of them wasn't much older than Molly.

'I can fill you in and explain what's happening,' he said. 'And you can tell me if you have any thoughts. OK?'

I nodded. 'That's fine.'

He turned to Sergeant Palmer and said that it would be best if all three of us spoke in his office. She said something back but I didn't hear what it was because I was distracted by what was going on around us.

I only recognised about half of those in the room. They were the people I'd worked with for several years. When they looked at me their eyes were soft with concern. I offered up a small smile here and a nod there, and it hit me suddenly that I knew lots of people but had few real friends. That was because all my time was spent being a copper and a mother. And it didn't help that the friends I'd socialised with before marriage and motherhood were now wives and mums themselves and we'd all lost touch.

Driscoll touched my arm and suggested we move to his office. Halfway across the room my eyes fixed on the huge mugshot of Bobby Knight staring down from the screen over by the window. I stopped and stared as the blood began to thunder in my ears. I could not take my eyes off the face of the man who had ruined my life.

'He's an evil-looking bastard for sure,' Driscoll said. 'One of the difficulties we face is not knowing if he's still alive.'

The parameters of possibility said that he was and I refused to believe otherwise. The alternative, that some unknown person was holding Molly, made it less likely that she'd be found.

'If he is alive we'll track him down,' Driscoll said in an effort to reassure me.

It was then that I noticed the whiteboards either side of the screen. They were covered with photos, including those the kidnapper had sent to me. Most of them were of Molly but there were also screen grabs from the street camera footage showing the kidnapper walking away from my mother's house with Molly in his arms.

And then, to my horror, I spotted an image from the video clip of Molly being held upside down and smacked.

My heart jumped and my vision blurred with tears. I thought I was going to have to flee the room so as not to lose control in front of everyone. But just then I was distracted by a sudden commotion that broke out behind me. Voices were raised and there was a swell of excitement.

I immediately lost the urge to run from the room because it was startlingly obvious that there had been a significant development.

It was a call from a pub landlord named Jeremy Flynn that had got everyone excited. He had phoned the incident room in response to the televised appeal for information on Bobby Knight.

The pub he ran was in the town of Hayes, which was part of the Greater London borough of Bromley.

Mr Flynn was saying that a man who bore a striking resemblance to Knight had spent time in his pub one evening three weeks ago. He remembered it well because the man had got into an argument with one of the locals and it had almost led to a fist fight.

Mr Flynn also revealed that the incident had been recorded on a security camera and the footage was still on the system's hard drive.

Dozens of other people had so far responded to the appeal but this was the most credible and it spurred the team into action.

DCI Brennan was alerted at once. He was on his way back from interviewing Tony Kemp and was now going to make his way to Hayes to talk to Mr Flynn and check out the security footage.

Detectives at Bromley station were informed and asked to send officers to Hayes to see if there had been other sightings since that night.

I was caught up in the excitement even though nobody could be sure at this stage if the man in the pub was actually Knight or someone who just looked like him.

If it turned out that it was him, then they would need to

establish if he had any kind of connection to the town or had merely stopped at the pub while passing through.

I suddenly felt like I was in the way. I could see that DI Driscoll had things to do so I told him I'd go and wait in Brennan's office.

Sergeant Palmer said she was going to the canteen to get a sandwich and asked me if I wanted one.

'You really should eat something, ma'am,' she said. 'You can only run for so long on adrenaline alone.'

She wasn't wrong. I was leaden with exhaustion and felt weak all over. I needed sleep and sustenance in order to keep going.

'I'll have a bacon sandwich then please,' I said. 'And a strong black coffee to go with it.'

In Brennan's tiny office I sat behind his desk and took out my phone. I wanted to find out more about the town of Hayes. I wasn't sure I had ever been there and knew only that it was on the outskirts of South London.

A Google search provided more information. The town had a population of just over 16,000 and had grown up around a small ancient village. There was a railway station, post office and a range of small shops. To the east and south of the town was Hayes Common, a sprawling 225 acres of heath and woodland.

It wasn't the sort of place you would expect someone like Bobby Knight to hang out. So why had he been there and why had he got into an argument in a pub?

I was still mulling over these questions when Sergeant Palmer came in with my coffee and sandwich. She sat with me while I forced them down, but she didn't try to draw me into a conversation and I was glad of that.

We had to wait another hour for an update on the call from the pub landlord. DI Driscoll came to tell us that Brennan had visited the pub in question. He'd spoken to the landlord and viewed the security footage.

'The boss reckons there's absolutely no doubt that the man in the video is Bobby Knight,' Driscoll said. 'That's not all, though. Knight visited the pub twice before that, apparently. But he hasn't been back since.'

45

DCI Brennan

Brennan felt his chest tighten as he watched the security footage for the third time in a back room of The Queen's Head pub in Hayes.

The sequence had been recorded in the public bar by a camera fixed to the wall above the entrance. It was a high quality image and so Brennan had no trouble identifying Bobby Knight. He was wearing a dark crew-neck sweater and jeans, and he was in full view of the camera for about fifteen minutes while sitting on a stool at the bar. He got angry when another man brushed against his back while walking past. The contact was barely perceptible but it caused Knight to spill some of his pint. In response, he spun around and started yelling at the other customer, a middle-aged Asian man.

Knight then jumped off the stool and there was a heated exchange with both men jabbing fingers at each other. But the sound quality was poor so Brennan couldn't make out what they were saying.

Just when it looked like it was about to come to blows, the

landlord, Jeremy Flynn, stepped in and pulled them apart. Knight then threw his arms up in the air, swore at Flynn before storming out of the pub.

'As soon as I saw the picture on the news I knew it was the same bloke,' Flynn said, repeating what he had told Brennan and Foster earlier. 'He was an arrogant bugger and even though Thomas tried to apologise for knocking into him he just kept spewing abuse.'

Flynn was a large man with a florid complexion and a beer gut. What remained of his hair was close-cropped.

Brennan and Foster had surprised him by turning up so soon after his call to the incident room. But even though he'd been busy with the lunchtime crowd he'd been only too happy to talk to them and show them the security footage. He had already transferred the sequence to his laptop and sent it as an email attachment to the incident room. It was Brennan's intention to show it later at the press conference.

Now they moved back into the bar area where Flynn sat with them in a booth while Brennan asked him more questions and took more notes.

'Like I already told you he'd been here twice before that night,' Flynn said. 'But he kept to himself and probably had no more than three drinks each time. As far as I know he didn't engage with the other customers. He was a bit of a miserable sod if I'm honest.'

'So did you talk to him?'

'Only while pulling his pints. But it was clear to me that he wasn't looking for a conversation.'

'So what, if anything, did you learn about him?'

He shrugged. 'Second time he was here, about a month ago, I asked him if he was local and he said he'd just moved into the area. But when I asked him where exactly, he picked up his drink and went and sat in one of the booths.'

Brennan felt his stomach flip. This was hugely significant, and the wheels began turning frantically in his head. Was it possible that Knight was living close by? Was he lodging with an accomplice who owned a property here? Or was it just him and Molly in a rented house or flat a short distance from the town centre?

Before they left the pub, Brennan called the incident room to pass on what he'd been told. He spoke to DI Driscoll who confirmed that Bromley police were now involved.

'We need to throw everything at this town,' Brennan said. 'We should speak to estate agents and get a list of all the properties that have recently been sold or let out in the area. And bear in mind that Knight might not have made his own arrangements. As an ex-con he'll have problems getting finance and committing to anything. So an accomplice could be helping him out.'

Brennan then said he wanted someone to round up CCTV footage in the town.

'There's probably not much from three weeks ago,' he said. 'But we might get lucky. And at the same time let's flood the place with photos of Knight and Molly.'

Outside the pub he told Foster to hang around and help coordinate things when the troops started to arrive.

'I want to get back for the press conference,' he said. 'We need to get this out there as quickly as we can.'

He looked at his watch. It was one o'clock. Plenty of time to get things started. Above them shredded clouds streamed across the sky and there were many more hours of daylight left.

The pub was situated just outside the small town centre which was about a hundred yards off to the left. Brennan drove through it in the pool car on his way back to central London. He spotted the railway station, the post office, a Costa Coffee, a Chinese takeaway.

And then he passed a police patrol car – the first of many that would soon be pouring into the town.

46

Sarah

I didn't want to leave the incident room while things were happening. The information from the pub landlord had triggered a burst of activity. Officers were shouting into phones, tapping frantically at computer keyboards and rushing around with sheets of paper in their hands.

About a dozen detectives had already rushed out of the door to go to Hayes. They would join the local cops who were already trying to find out if Bobby Knight had taken up residence in the area.

It was an exciting development and it gave me hope that we were closer to finding Molly. Whether that hope was justified remained to be seen.

I flitted in and out of Brennan's office, feeling like a spare part and not caring.

I rang Aunt Tessa's house to speak to my parents and give them the news. But she said they had already gone home. I explained to her what was happening and a few minutes later I went through it all again when I spoke to my mother.

'I've been to Hayes,' she said. 'I used to have a friend who lived nearby in Keston. Why would he take Molly there?'

'We can't be sure he has, Mum,' I said. 'But it's a strong possibility.'

'I heard Knight's mother being interviewed on the radio this morning. She's told the police that her son is dead.'

'I know that, Mum, but she doesn't know for certain. She would rather believe that than accept that he's abducted a child.'

My dad came on the line then and asked if I would come and see them today.

'Your mother's really not coping well, Sarah. She still feels responsible for letting that man into our house, and she can't stop crying. It'd help if you were here.'

'I'll try to come by later,' I said. 'But I can't promise, Dad. There's a lot going on.'

'But she's your mum, Sarah, and I'm worried about her. She needs you.'

My thoughts danced and a weight of guilt settled in my chest. I wanted to be there for my mum but right now she wasn't my number-one priority. Molly was.

'Look, Dad, just do what you can to comfort her. And try to make her understand that I don't blame her for what's happened. There was nothing she could have done to stop it. Why not call her GP and get them to prescribe something?'

I didn't give him a chance to respond. I said a quick goodbye and hung up, hoping that he wouldn't be upset.

Next I called Adam to see if he was across what was going on. I hadn't heard from him since he'd left the flat and I had no idea where he was or what he was up to. But his answerphone kicked in so I left a message: *Ring me when you can. Bobby Knight has been sighted.* I wondered if he was still going through the NCA files or perhaps he was following up a lead of his own. I told myself not to worry and to trust that he was all right. But it wasn't easy.

I then sat back in Brennan's chair and closed my eyes. I could feel another headache beginning to drill through my frontal lobe. But was it any wonder? My nerves were frayed and the blood was tearing through my body at a rate of knots. It felt like I was on autopilot while being battered by events.

Sergeant Palmer and DI Driscoll came and sat with me to watch the three o'clock press conference live on Sky News. This time it was just DCI Brennan and a press officer fronting it.

He kicked off by repeating the appeal for information on Bobby Knight.

'There's already been a tremendous response from the public,' he said. 'Knight has been seen in Hayes, a town on the London-Kent border. We understand that he may have moved into that area some weeks before Molly Mason was abducted.'

They then showed the clip of security footage from the pub, while Brennan explained what it was and what was happening.

'The man in the sweater has been positively identified as Bobby Knight,' he said. 'He visited that same pub, The Queen's Head, on several occasions and indicated to the landlord that he was staying nearby. So I want to appeal to anyone in that area who thinks they may have seen him to contact us.'

He then opened up the floor to questions and the first came from a BBC reporter who asked, 'Bobby Knight's mother has been interviewed by phone on BBC radio. She's adamant that her son has been murdered on the orders of an underworld figure who is well known to the police. Could she be right?'

Brennan caught his bottom lip between his teeth and considered the question carefully before he answered.

'I've spoken personally to Mrs Knight and as you can imagine she's very upset,' he said. 'Her son hasn't been in contact with her for two weeks. But there is not a single piece of evidence to suggest that he's come to any harm. However, I can assure you that we are giving serious consideration to her remarks.'

The reporter persisted. 'But if he is dead then aren't you wasting time looking for him? Wouldn't it be better to keep an open mind and pursue other suspects?'

'That is exactly what we are doing,' Brennan said, irritation creeping into his voice. 'At this stage we're ruling nothing out. But all the evidence so far points to Bobby Knight being the person who abducted Molly Mason. Our objective is to reunite her as soon as possible with her mother.'

The press conference continued for another ten minutes and Brennan managed to come across as a man who had things under control.

When it was finished Sky News switched their attention to Hayes and I was surprised to see that they already had a reporter on the ground there.

She was a smart lady named Trish Scott and I'd seen her on the screen many times before. She was doing a piece to camera in front of The Queen's Head pub and saying that police teams had already begun to arrive in the town.

'A Scotland Yard source has told me that their efforts will be confined to speaking to residents, shopkeepers and local business people. At this stage there are no plans to carry out an extensive search of the heaths and woodlands around the town.'

As I watched and listened, thoughts of Molly swamped my mind. I wondered what she was doing while all this was going on. Was she awake or asleep? Was she eating or drinking or playing? Or was she suffering at the hands of that monster?

My imagination was suddenly out of control again and being colonised by disturbing images. I saw Molly being slapped around the face and on the bottom. I saw her screaming as her face reddened and the tears gushed out of her eyes. I saw her lying naked on top of a double bed while a man wearing nothing but a balaclava knelt beside her and ran his hands over her tiny body.

I didn't realise I'd started crying again until Sergeant Palmer placed an arm around me and began stroking my hair.

'I'm sorry, I just can't help it,' I sobbed.

I felt I had already cried a million tears but it was like trying to turn off a tap that was broken.

'I think I had better go home,' I said. 'I need to sort myself out.'

'I'll take you,' she said.

I shook my head. 'If you don't mind I'd rather not have company. I'll be fine on my own.'

She wasn't happy but knew she had no choice in the matter. I didn't have to have a family liaison officer with me if I didn't want it.

She offered to drive me back to the flat but I told her there was no need because my own car was still parked here at the station.

I thought about going to see my parents but decided not to. I really did want to be by myself.

DI Driscoll promised to ring me if there were any developments and Sergeant Palmer told me to call her if I wanted her to come over.

But what they said barely registered because as soon as I turned my back on them I started scolding myself for losing it. Now more than ever I needed to be strong and resilient. Not weak and emotional. And instead of just telling myself to seize at least some semblance of control over the situation, I had to actually step up to the plate and do it.

47

Adam

Adam's mobile had run out of juice and he didn't notice it until he left Barney's snooker club and got back in his car.

He plugged the phone into the charger he kept in the glove compartment and switched it on.

He had two missed calls. The first was from Helen and he was sorry he hadn't taken it because he knew it was time he stopped pretending they had a future together. What was happening had made him realise that it wasn't what he wanted. So the sooner he confronted it, the sooner he could stop thinking about it. Besides, Helen needed to know where she stood and why he felt it necessary to end the relationship. He was going to call her straight back until he saw that the other missed call was from Sarah and she'd left a message saying that Bobby Knight had been sighted.

So he rang Sarah, but there was no answer. Her message prompted him to check the BBC online news feed. And sure enough it was all there, including a clip of DCI Brennan at the press conference.

Adam considered Knight appearing in Hayes to be a solid

lead, especially in view of what Barney Nichols had just told him. For that reason he was determined to carry on doing his own thing. He knew it was a long shot, but it was better than doing fuck all.

After leaving Sarah's flat earlier he had gone to the office to download Knight's NCA file onto his computer. He had printed off several pages, all the time managing to avoid being seen by his boss and having to explain what he was up to. Then he'd spent an hour in a pub going through the printout. He'd picked out the names of some of Knight's old haunts and known associates. He was aware that the information was out of date because Knight had spent the past four years behind bars. But he didn't let that faze him.

He left the pub with the names of four individuals – all sleaze-bags that Brennan's team would probably call on eventually – plus the addresses of places where Knight used to hang out.

Barney's snooker club in Camberwell had been his first port of call and it had got him off to a promising start.

Barney was well known to the Met, and his club was frequented by a lot of South London spivs and villains.

The air in the place had been stale and heavy and he'd been sized up by punters with a world-weary suspicion in their eyes. They could spot a copper from a mile away.

Barney himself was a squat, bullish man with a square, craggy face. Adam had known him for years and more than once had drawn on his knowledge of the manor and the reprobates who did business in it. He wasn't a grass exactly, but with a few drinks inside him he could be gloriously indiscreet.

Knight was a keen snooker player and had been a regular at the club before going to prison. Fortunately for Adam, Barney had been knocking back the beers and brandies all afternoon so his tongue had been loosened up. He saw no reason not to tell Adam that Knight had popped into the club just the once and that was four days after his release.

'If the bastard has taken your kid like they're saying on the news then I hope you get to him first,' Barney had said.

'Have you any idea where he is?' Adam had asked him.

'None at all.'

'So why did he come here?'

'Well it wasn't to play a few frames of snooker. He wanted to pump me for information.'

'About what?'

'About the bloke they call The Keyholder.'

'The what?'

'He's been on the scene for a while apparently, but I only heard him mentioned for the first time about six months ago.'

'Why do they call him The Keyholder?'

Barney had grinned. 'He looks after the properties of those of our brethren who are forced to leave these shores for any length of time.'

'You mean fugitives?'

'I do. I'm sure that at least a couple of the characters who appear on the NCA's most-wanted list are among his clients.'

'So what does he do for them?'

'Well ain't it obvious? Most of the guys who go on the run have hidden assets in this country, usually houses and flats that they bought as investments. So while they're sunning themselves on the Costa Del Crime or down in South America, The Keyholder provides a unique service. He can arrange for their properties to be sold or he can rent the places out on their behalf. Word is, he even allows them to be used for clandestine gatherings. All the money goes to the owners, minus his commission.

The arrangement works well for those who've managed to avoid having their assets seized.'

'So Bobby Knight came here to see if you knew how to find this bloke. Is that it?'

'Correct. He said he had heard about him in prison but wasn't given a name.'

'And did he say why he wanted to contact him?'

'He said he was looking for a short-term let that was well below the radar. Preferably somewhere out of the way.'

'And were you able to help him?'

'Sure, why not? After he slipped me a ton I gave him the guy's name.'

'So who is he, Barney? Give me the name and I'll be in your debt.'

'I'm happy to do that on this occasion, Detective, because I don't hold with people snatching little kids. But I'm not sure it'll be of any use to you.'

'Why not?'

'Well the bloke was attacked a couple of nights ago. He was left for dead apparently but ended up in hospital with multiple knife wounds.'

The possibility of a link between The Keyholder and Hayes spun around inside Adam's head.

As he drove across town, he tried to connect the dots. Had The Keyholder fixed Knight up with a temporary property there? Was that why he'd been seen in the town? And was there a connection between any of that and the knife attack that had put The Keyholder in hospital?

Eddie Lomax. That was the name Barney had given him. The man they called The Keyholder, who was now recovering in St Thomas' Hospital.

The name rang a bell and Adam realised why after he made a couple of calls – the first to an on-duty colleague at the NCA and the second to the detective at West End Central who was investigating the stabbing.

Lomax was a lawyer who, for some time, had been linked to organised crime in London. He had represented a number of high-profile villains, including two who had fled to Spain after warrants were issued for their arrest. Both men were on the NCA's most-wanted list. The charges they faced included attempted murder and conspiracy to import and supply heroin.

Adam was familiar with both men. Indeed, he had been actively involved with the investigation into one of them, a Scot named Steve Monk. He was a principal member of a Europe-wide crime network involved in high-level international drug trafficking. Following the execution of a warrant at his home address in North London, officers discovered over £200,000 cash, a cash-counting machine and a kilo of cannabis resin.

His house and car were seized under the Proceeds of Crime Act, but it was strongly suspected that he had hidden assets that would probably never be recovered. So to someone like Monk, Eddie Lomax was a godsend.

Adam was surprised that he hadn't already heard about the service Lomax was providing. And if *he* hadn't then it was unlikely that anyone else in the agency had been tipped off about it.

According to DI Jason Hughes at West End Central, Lomax was attacked two nights ago after leaving a casino in Soho. He suffered two stab wounds to the stomach and one to the chest, and it was a miracle he was still alive.

'He's in a bad way, so he hasn't been able to provide a statement,' Hughes said. 'But the hospital reckons he should be up to speaking to us tomorrow. The thinking is he was the victim of some kind of revenge attack. We don't think it was robbery because they left his wallet in his pocket.'

'I know that Lomax is one of the go-to lawyers for villains in the capital,' Adam said. 'But it's rumoured that as well as trying to keep them out of prison he also looks after their assets if they have to flee abroad. Were you aware of that?'

'No, but it sounds interesting.'

'They call him The Keyholder apparently.'

'Where did you hear that?'

'From a snout, but I can't talk about it now. I'll let you know if I hear any more.'

By rights Adam should have called Brennan and told him what he'd found out. But he knew that would lead to a delay and get bogged down in the legal process. So he decided to press on to St Thomas' Hospital on the banks of the Thames opposite the Houses of Parliament.

When he got there he flashed his warrant card to get a prime parking spot and then showed it again at reception.

Lomax was in a room of his own having been moved out of intensive care. In the old days the Met would have stationed an officer outside, but with cutbacks biting into manpower and resources they only did that if they felt it was absolutely necessary.

Adam was waved through and even got to speak to the doctor in charge, who said, 'We've been told to alert Detective Hughes the moment the patient is in a position to speak.'

'Well it's actually become necessary for us to ask him questions as a matter of urgency in relation to another matter,' Adam said. 'Would that be possible?'

'I'm afraid not. He's drugged up to the eyeballs and I'm not prepared to induce consciousness because it might prove harmful.'

'So when is he likely to come around?'

'Not for some hours. Perhaps not even until tomorrow morning.'

'Then I'll wait if that's OK. I promise not to get in the way.'

'As you wish. You can make yourself comfortable in the waiting room. It's just at the end of the corridor.'

'Thank you. Has he had any visitors?'

The doctor nodded. 'He has a son who came in early today. But I gather Mr Lomax is divorced and his parents are no longer alive.'

'Would it be all right if I just pop in and see him?'

'Don't see why not.'

Lomax was lying on the bed hooked up to a drip and a monitor, and there was a thick bandage around his chest. But his face was uncovered and after a close look Adam realised that he had never met the guy before.

He was in his forties, with a lined forehead and a crown of curly fair hair. Adam touched his arm and asked him to wake up. But Lomax didn't move a muscle. He was out cold and breathing heavily.

Adam looked at his watch. Just after five. He decided he had no option but to stay until the guy came to. He couldn't walk away without knowing if the man they called The Keyholder held the answer to Molly's whereabouts.

48

Sarah

A handful of reporters and photographers were still hanging around in front of my block. But I managed to avoid them by parking in the road behind it and using the rear entrance.

My head was pulsing with a deep, relentless ache by the time I stepped back into my flat. So the first thing I did was dose up on paracetamol. Then I poured myself a glass of wine and puffed on a cigarette.

I was glad I'd forced down the bacon sandwich earlier because it meant I didn't have to think about food. I did not want to think about anything other than my precious daughter.

Despite the promising developments, the fear that I would never see her again was like a raging fire inside me.

I longed so much to hold her and smell her and smother her with kisses. I wanted to put her on my lap and tell her she was safe and that I would never let any more harm come to her.

I found myself in her bedroom again, clutching the wine glass and talking to her as though she could hear me.

'It won't be long, sweetheart. You'll soon be back with Mummy. I promise.'

I ran my fingers over her clothes and pillow. I breathed in the scent of her and it made me shake with emotion.

When my glass was empty, I went downstairs for a refill. I was in the kitchen when my phone rang, and as usual now my heart did a backward somersault.

It was Adam, calling to tell me that he was following up a lead.

'The guy I need to speak to has been stabbed,' he said. 'He's in hospital and I'm waiting for him to wake up. It's possible he knows where Bobby Knight is.'

Adam filled me in on Eddie Lomax and why he was known in the underworld as The Keyholder. The revelation made me feel tense but hopeful. Was it really possible that the man could lead us to Molly?

'So I can't leave without talking to him,' he said.

'Does Brennan know?'

'Not yet, and I don't want him to. He'll just make me step back from it and if I do there's no way they'll get the guy to open up.'

'Well you need to be careful.'

'I know and I will,' he said, before hanging up.

I took the fresh glass of wine into the living room and switched on the television. There was nothing else for me to do and it was encouraging to see that the story was still leading all the news bulletins. Publicity could only be a good thing, I told myself.

Most of the content was a rerun of what had gone before, but at ten o'clock the BBC carried a short clip of an interview with Bobby Knight's mother and brother. The reporter had caught them arriving outside the mother's house in Peckham.

She looked nothing like the woman I'd seen at the Old Bailey during her son's trial. She had aged considerably and her face was full of bags and wrinkles.

'I want to believe that Bobby is still alive but I'm convinced that he isn't,' she said tearfully. 'I'm also convinced that he had nothing to do with the abduction of that little girl.'

Her youngest son, named on the screen as Noah Carter, stepped between her and the camera and said, 'Can I ask you please to respect my mother's wish to be left alone. We won't be giving interviews, but I want it to be known that we're cooperating fully with the police and we do not know what's happened to my brother.'

They were filmed going into the house and when the door was closed behind them the reporter faced the camera and before signing off, he said, 'Meanwhile the search for Molly Mason and her kidnapper is now concentrated on the town of Hayes near Bromley where Bobby Knight was last sighted.'

I sat there reflecting on what I'd just seen, and it wasn't long before an uncomfortable thought began to form in the back of my mind – could the mother and brother be lying? Brennan had interviewed them both, but what if they had managed to pull the wool over his eyes?

It was a question I suddenly knew that I had to seek the answer to. And the only way to do that was to go to the house in Peckham myself.

I knew I was the last person that his mother would want to see. But that didn't stop me from going online to find Mrs Knight's address.

Five minutes later I picked up my bag and car keys and headed for the door. The time had come to act on my own initiative.

* * *

Bobby Knight's mother lived less than two miles from my flat in Dulwich.

I parked across the road from her house and didn't spot any reporters or photographers outside, which was a relief.

As I approached the house I saw a strobe light from the television dancing across a ground-floor window. I shivered when I reached the door, a knot tightening in my stomach.

Until this moment I hadn't really thought about what kind of reaction I could expect, although I knew it wouldn't be pleasant. I was, after all, the person Bobby Knight accused of stitching him up. He blamed me for ruining his life and his family probably did as well.

But I was also the mother of the little girl he had abducted, so to my mind that made it all right for me to be here.

I stiffened my spine and braced myself as I rang the doorbell.

It was Knight's mother who answered. She was wearing a dressing gown and looked exhausted, her eyes red-rimmed and bleary.

'If you're a reporter then you can bugger off,' she said. 'I've told you I'm not . . .'

The sight of my warrant card stopped her.

'My name's Sarah Mason,' I said. 'Detective Inspector Mason. I've come here to speak to you about your son, Bobby.'

A puzzled look wrinkled her features and she stared at me for at least five seconds, as though trying to place the name and the face. Then it dawned on her who I was. She drew a swift breath and her chest inflated.

'I can't believe you've got the nerve to come here after what you did to my boy,' she said.

'I have to talk to you about what he's doing to my daughter,' I said. 'I have a feeling you know where he is despite what you told the police.'

Her eyes hardened with anger. 'How dare you say that to me, you filthy, lying bitch. Now piss off and leave me alone.'

She started to slam the door in my face but I stepped over the threshold and put my shoulder firmly against it.

'You're mistaken if you think I'm just going to go away,' I said.

Before she had time to react I put my hand against her chest and pushed her into the hallway. She let out a small cry and stumbled back, but managed not to lose her balance.

The fire grew in her eyes and her body shook with rage.

'That's fucking assault,' she screamed. 'I'll have you done for that.'

I shut the front door behind me and stabbed a finger at her.

'I don't care what you do after I leave here, Mrs Knight. And I don't care what happens to me. But I do care about my little girl and your bastard son is holding her somewhere.'

I stepped forward and she backed away from me towards a doorway that I could see led into the kitchen.

'Where is your other son?' I said. 'I want to speak to him as well.'

'You can't. He's gone home.'

I knew I was overstepping the mark and I wasn't proud of myself. But I was possessed now by something I couldn't control. I didn't see the woman before me as weak and defenceless. What I saw was a ghastly creature who was protecting her vile son.

Four years ago I learned about her chequered past, about the whoring and the shoplifting, and I thought then, just as I thought now, that she had to bear responsibility for creating the monster that was Bobby Knight.

'Go into the kitchen and sit down,' I said. 'We can talk in there.'

She shook her head. 'You can't make me. You're a copper. You shouldn't be doing this.'

'I'm here as the mother of a young child,' I said. 'Not as a police officer. And as you can see, I'm desperate. So I suggest you do as you're told before I lose my bloody temper.'

There was nothing stopping me now. All the pent-up anger and frustration was coming out and it felt like I was plugged into the electricity mains. I was determined to find out if this woman was holding something back and to hell with the consequences.

'Let's just get this over with shall we?' I said. 'I don't want to stay here a second longer than I have to.'

She realised I meant business and stepped into the kitchen, which was drab and dated.

She sat down at the table and as I watched her light up a cigarette I felt myself shaking all over.

I sat down opposite her and tried to steady my breathing before I spoke.

'The police don't believe that your son Bobby is dead and neither do I,' I said. 'And if he isn't dead then he must be hiding out somewhere with my daughter. I'm certain you know where they are and I'm begging you to tell me.'

She blew smoke at the ceiling and fixed me with a hard stare. Then she said, 'Even if I thought he was alive, and even if I knew where he was, I wouldn't tell you. Not in a million fucking years.'

'As a mother you must surely know what I'm going through? Molly is just fifteen months old, for heaven's sake,' I said.

'You gave no thought to me when you lied about my son and planted the evidence to get him convicted.'

'But I didn't plant any evidence,' I said. 'I would never have done something like that.'

'Liar,' she bawled. 'Bobby swore to us that the gun and the drugs didn't belong to him and I knew from the start that he was telling the truth. I could always tell when he was or wasn't lying.'

'Your son is a vicious drug trafficker, Mrs Knight. He's not a saint. He would have ended up in prison sooner or later anyway.'

She drew on her cigarette again and glared at me.

'Not long before you arrested him, he told me and his father that he wanted to get out of the business,' she said. 'He and Lauren were going to get married and start a family. They even talked about moving away. But you ruined his life. You ruined all our lives. Lauren left him, my husband committed suicide because of all the stress and Bobby got fucked up inside because he couldn't accept the way things had turned out.'

'And that's why he stole my baby,' I said. 'So that he could get back at me. Have you seen the sick messages and photos he's been sending me? And the videos? He's even threatening to rape Molly.'

She leaned towards me across the table and I could feel her smoky breath on my face.

'And why shouldn't you be punished for what you did? I have no sympathy for you. You brought this on yourself the day you put that gun and those drugs in Bobby's bedroom.'

'So you do accept that your son is the one who's punishing me and that this stuff about him being dead is just nonsense.'

'I didn't say that. I know he's dead because if he wasn't I would have heard from him before now. And although it was Tony Kemp who must have killed him, I blame you for that as well. Everything that has happened is down to you.'

The force of her words shocked me and I felt my hands grow damp.

She suddenly threw her lighted cigarette across the room and into the sink. Then she abruptly stood up.

'So there you have it, bitch. Coming here was a waste of your time and mine. Whoever has taken your daughter has my blessing. I'm sure he'll be a better parent than you are anyway.'

I stood up slowly, my nerves shrieking.

'I still think you're lying,' I said. 'And I'm going to do everything I can to prove it.'

Her eyes drilled into mine, unblinking. 'There's nothing to prove and deep down you know it. Now fuck off and don't ever come near me again.'

We continued to stare at each other across the kitchen for what seemed an eternity. If the woman had been much younger I would have grabbed her by the shoulders and shaken her until she told me what I wanted to hear. But she must have been twice my age and she looked quite frail, so it wasn't an option.

And that was probably a good thing because I wouldn't be doing myself any favours if I ended up in a police cell.

I didn't want to go straight home but at the same time I didn't want to be with anyone. So after leaving Knight's mother, I drove around for a bit, with no sense of where I was going.

I felt I'd achieved nothing by confronting the woman, but I had discovered just how much she hated me. It was a raw, visceral hatred that went to the core of her being. And it was probably exactly how her son felt.

I saw a pub and pulled into the small customer car park. Thought I would get myself a quick drink before closing time. Only one, though, because the two glasses of wine from earlier were still sloshing around inside me.

But one large neat vodka wasn't enough to silence the screams in my head. And neither were two. When I asked for a third I slurred my words and the barman shook his head.

'It's time to go home, lady,' he said. 'We're about to close.'

But he let me buy a bottle of white wine and I took it out to the car. The plan was to drink it when I got home, but I realised suddenly that I was in no fit state to drive. I didn't even know where I was.

Shit.

I looked around and noticed that the pub was called The Bell Inn, and I wondered if that meant they had rooms. So I went back inside and got lucky. They had three rooms and only one of them was occupied tonight. I handed over my credit card and took the key.

It was a small room with absolutely no character, but I didn't care. My aim was to lie down on the bed and think about Molly while slowly drinking myself into oblivion.

But I was still awake twenty minutes later – and had only drunk half the wine – when my phone pinged with a new message.

In my haste to reach it on the bedside table I dropped the bottle on the floor and the wine went everywhere.

My head spun and it took a few moments for me to pull the screen into focus and then a few more to figure out how to open the message.

There was an attachment and I looked at that first through bleary eyes.

It was Molly and she was sitting outside on grass in what looked like a garden. She was holding a big red ball against her chest and behind her there was a small plastic slide. She wasn't smiling, but she didn't look upset either. She was wearing a yellow top and blue shorts that I'd never seen before, and her feet were bare. I could only assume that the picture had been taken earlier in the day.

I checked the message next but the words were hard to read because they swam in front of my eyes.

Molly cried today and asked for her mummy. So I told her you didn't want her anymore. She's fine now. BTW I'm not who you all think I am. You're looking for the wrong man in the wrong place. But that's cool.

I felt the room tilt and I went with it, landing with a crash on the floor.

And that was where I stayed, crying into the carpet until the darkness pulled me under.

49

DCI Brennan

Brennan called his wife to tell her that he wouldn't be home any time soon.

'I'm really sorry, love,' he said. 'But this is shaping up to be another all-nighter.'

'Don't you worry, my dear, I completely understand. Just do whatever it takes to bring that little girl home to her mum.'

It was almost midnight and there was still a lot going on in the incident room. The latest text message to Sarah's phone had thrown everyone.

I'm not who you all think I am. You're looking for the wrong man in the wrong place.

So what were they to make of it? he wondered. Was it true? Or was it a desperate ploy by Bobby Knight to deflect attention away from himself?

'It wouldn't surprise me if he's beginning to panic,' Brennan said as the team gathered around him for a briefing. 'Firstly I'm sure it would have come as a shock when he was linked to Molly's abduction. He couldn't have known that Victor Rosetti would spout his mouth off. And then evidence emerged that he might have taken up residence in Hayes. So he could be concerned that the whole thing is unravelling and we're closing in.'

'If that is the case then I think we should be even more worried about Molly,' DC Foster said. 'Who knows what he'll do to her if he is panicking? If we're lucky he'll leave her somewhere so that she can be found. But the ultimate punishment he can inflict on her mother is to kill her.'

Foster's words came as a sobering reminder of the kind of person they were dealing with and it gave everyone pause for thought.

The silence was broken by an officer who asked how Sarah had reacted to the latest text and photograph.

'I haven't spoken to her yet,' Brennan said. 'I tried ringing but she didn't answer so I'm guessing she's in bed.'

He went on to say that the IT department had already begun the process of trying to trace the phone the message was sent from but had warned him they didn't expect to succeed.

Brennan then listened to the various updates from detectives whose voices were hoarse with tiredness.

He learned that officers were still collecting and trawling through CCTV footage from Hayes, but so far there had been no further sightings of Knight.

Estate agents in and around the town had been spoken to and properties that had been sold or rented in recent months were still being checked.

'We've been given access to Knight's bank account,' DI Driscoll said. 'The balance stands at five hundred pounds, but on the day he was released from prison it was four thousand. He's withdrawn various sums of money, but three weeks ago all deposits and withdrawals stopped. And he doesn't have any credit cards. It would suggest that if he is renting a place then he's paying in cash.'

Brennan called a halt to the briefing after another ten minutes and told those officers who had been working most of the day to go home and get some rest.

His own eyes were dull and ringed with fatigue, but he himself was in no position to leave just yet. There was paperwork on his desk that he wanted to clear before the day got started. And he wanted to spend some time going over everything they had, in an effort to make sense of it.

The investigation was now the largest and most intense he had ever been in charge of. There had been times during the day when he'd felt that there was something he was missing. But he hadn't been able to put his finger on what it was.

The latest photo of Molly on the grass had reminded him that the fate of that poor child was in his hands. It was an incredible responsibility and one that scared him shitless.

Sure, they had made some significant progress, but the fact remained that they still had no idea where Molly was. And the latest message from the maniac who had her gave rise to the possibility that they were actually no closer to finding her.

Brennan was about to start wading through the pile of papers on his desk when DC Foster appeared in his office doorway. Her cheeks were flushed and she looked excited.

'There's been an anonymous call to the hotline, guv,' she said. 'A man who refused to give his name claimed that Bobby Knight was murdered two weeks ago and his body dumped in a wood in Kent. He even gave the location of the wood.'

Brennan's eyebrows peaked. 'Jesus. Where is it exactly?'

Foster stepped into the office and dropped a sheet of paper on his desk.

'It's a small wood near Sevenoaks, guv. And get this – it's situated right behind the converted oast house owned by Tony Kemp.'

The first thing Brennan did was to go online and check Google maps.

Sevenoaks was a town surrounded by countryside and huge expanses of woodland. But it was also within easy striking distance of London. It took just over half an hour to get to Waterloo by train and so it was popular with those who worked in the city.

Property prices were high and it was an expensive place to live. The affluence was apparent from the air when Brennan switched to the aerial view on his computer. The landscape was dotted with large detached houses and back garden swimming pools. Tony Kemp's house was among them, and did indeed back onto the wood that the anonymous caller had referred to. The wood was a couple of miles east of the town, close to a huge deer park. It was called Oaklands Copse and was squeezed between Kemp's house and two winding country lanes. There were a few facts and figures about it elsewhere on Google. It was spread over eighteen acres and described as an ancient coppice of beech, ash and oak.

On the face of it Oaklands Copse seemed like the perfect place to hide a body. But that was jumping the gun. For all Brennan knew the call was a hoax to propagate the rumour that Knight was dead. Or perhaps it had come from someone who just enjoyed wasting police time. And searching woodland, even a relatively small area the size of Oaklands Copse, would be an expensive and time-consuming exercise.

Before taking any action, Brennan listened to the recording of the anonymous call. The voice was distorted by an electronic changer, and it sounded like some evil villain out of a sci-fi film.

I know for a fact that Bobby Knight is dead. He was murdered a fortnight ago and his body was left in Oaklands Copse near Sevenoaks. So don't waste time searching for the bastard elsewhere.

Brennan was told the call couldn't be traced and had probably come from yet another unregistered mobile.

'Now why doesn't that surprise me?' he said to the detectives who had gathered round him to listen to the tape.

They stood waiting for him to tell them if the call was going to be taken seriously. If so then there was work to be done and tasks to be assigned.

'I'll have to refer this upstairs,' he said after a few beats. 'But I'll be recommending that we mount a search of the wood from first light. In the meantime, we need to flag this up to Kent police, but it's not to be made public. And I don't want Molly's parents to know just yet.'

'What about Tony Kemp?' DC Foster said. 'Do we bring him in for questioning?'

'Not right away. Let's wait and see if there is a body there before we launch a murder investigation.'

50

Adam

Adam woke up suddenly from a dream in which he was playing with Molly in the park. He was chasing her across the grass and she was laughing so much it was making her dizzy.

When he realised it was a dream he felt his heart crumble in his chest. He dragged his eyelids open and blinked out the crust that had formed beneath them.

He was still alone in the small hospital waiting room and the TV in the corner was still on. The time code at the top of the screen told him it was two a.m. He hadn't intended to drop off and he wished he hadn't.

He could tell from the news headlines that there hadn't been any further developments. The hunt for Bobby Knight was still under way and Molly was still missing.

He sat back against the cushioned chair and heaved a sigh. His muscles felt weak and heavy, and a dull weariness that went beyond exhaustion pervaded his body.

For a fleeting moment he wondered if he was where he should be. Pursuing Eddie Lomax – alias The Keyholder – had seemed like a good idea earlier, but now he wasn't so sure. He felt less confident, but maybe that was only because he was disoriented and his memory was blurred around the edges.

He stood up and stretched, then checked his phone. There were no missed calls but there was a text from Helen asking how he was holding up. He decided to call her because he didn't want her to hurry back to the UK in the mistaken belief that he wanted her by his side. It was six hours earlier in Chicago so it came as no surprise when she answered on the first ring and told him she was in her hotel room watching Molly's story unfold on CNN.

'I'm booked on a flight first thing in the morning,' she said. 'It was the earliest I could get.'

He didn't beat about the bush. He told her as gently as he could that he was calling time on their relationship. He blamed the stress he was under and the fact that he was still in love with his ex-wife. She took it better than he'd dared hope, perhaps because she'd been half expecting it. She told him she was sorry and that she prayed for his daughter's safe return. And then she hung up abruptly before he could say any more, and although he knew he'd done the right thing he still felt a total shit.

He decided he needed a coffee, but the vending machine would have to wait until he'd had a pee.

As he walked along the corridor he was surprised to see that there was still a lot going on. Nurses were slipping in and out of rooms, machines were humming and wheels were grinding across polished floors.

By the time he reached the toilets he'd pushed Helen from his mind. After he'd emptied his bladder, he washed his hands, and looked at himself in the mirror. His face had lost all its colour and his hair looked as though it suddenly had a mind of its own.

Sharp radial lines that he was sure he hadn't seen before creased the sides of his eyes.

The last few days had changed him inside as well, but in ways he had yet to discover.

He knew the guilt would weigh heavily on him for ever, no matter how this terrible business ended. If only he could go back in time to when he made that reckless decision to plant the gun and drugs in Knight's bedroom.

It wasn't as though he had done it before and he hadn't done anything like it since. But back then it didn't seem such a bad idea. Knight was a ruthless gangster and deserved to be taken off the streets. He'd reasoned that by fitting him up he'd be doing the world a favour and at the same time he'd ensure that Sarah got her collar.

It had been so simple. He had known where to lay his hands on the pistol and some drugs, and planting them had been a doddle. It had all worked out so perfectly and he'd felt justified when the jury passed the guilty verdict.

But now he realised it was the biggest mistake he had ever made. And bringing Molly back home was the only way to make amends.

He rinsed his face in cold water and decided to go and check on Eddie Lomax. He still couldn't be sure that it wasn't a waste of time, but there was no point bailing out before he had even talked to the guy.

He dried his face on paper towels before stepping back into the corridor.

And that was when he heard the scream.

The scream came from along the corridor to his left and sent a current searing through his body.

At first he thought it must be a female patient in terrible pain. But then he saw a nurse stumbling backwards out of a room as though in a frenzied panic.

'Help, help,' she screamed. 'Someone call security.'

Instinct propelled Adam along the corridor towards her. Just then a man in a grey suit emerged from the same room and darted off in the opposite direction.

It was then that Adam realised it was the room he'd entered earlier, the room that was occupied by Eddie Lomax.

The nurse turned towards him, her eyes wide with horror. She started shouting as she pointed at the fleeing figure.

'That man – he was trying to suffocate my patient with a pillow.'

Adam caught his breath and felt a surge of dread. Then, without a second thought, he broke into a sprint.

The suited man was about fifteen yards ahead of him. A white-coated doctor who stepped in front of him was shoved out of the way with such force that he thudded into the wall and fell to the floor.

Adam ran for all he was worth, his breath coming in gasps, his legs pumping hard.

The man went crashing through a set of swing doors and Adam raced after him. He was in police mode now and focused entirely on catching the perp.

There was another corridor on the other side of the swing doors. As Adam entered it he caught sight of the man shooting off to the left. He kept pace with him even though he was panting frantically.

Ahead of them was a bank of lifts. There were two people waiting in front of them, a man and a woman, and they were both startled by the commotion.

It looked for a moment as though the perp was going to run

into them, but then he suddenly veered to the right, hurling himself down a flight of stairs.

Adam stayed with him. He wanted to scream at the bastard to stop, to reveal that he was a copper, but he didn't have the breath.

Two flights down, the guy burst through another door into a brightly lit reception area. And there he came unstuck because a security guard was standing between him and the exit.

The man shoulder-charged the guard and the guard hit the floor like a felled tree. But the impact unbalanced the perp and he stumbled sideways, just managing to stay upright. It gave Adam time to catch up and slam into him.

They both went sprawling across the floor. But the perp recovered quickly and struggled to his feet. He turned and aimed a fist at Adam, who was still on his knees. But contact was weak and the punch slid off the side of his head.

Adam responded by throwing his own punch and it was bang on target. The guy screamed in agony and staggered back, clutching at his groin.

Adam jumped up and got his first look at the man who had apparently attacked Eddie Lomax in his hospital bed. He was aged somewhere between thirty and forty and white, with a hard face and shoulder-length brown hair. He was gritting his teeth through the pain and started mumbling in a language that Adam didn't recognise.

Adam lunged forward and grabbed his right arm, with the aim of twisting it up his back and forcing him to the floor. But the guy wasn't about to let that happen and fought back.

There was a struggle and blows were exchanged. Adam was punched on the forehead and chest, and kicked in the shin. But he thought he was getting the better of his adversary and he hoped it was game over when the security guard appeared and grabbed the guy from behind.

But in the same instant, Adam felt a sudden, sharp pain in his side that caused him to cry out. He stepped back and gulped in a huge breath.

He felt his body convulse as he pressed a hand against the point of impact.

And that was the moment he realised that he hadn't been punched. He'd been stabbed.

He touched the handle of the knife and felt the warm blood on his fingers.

'Oh fuck,' he croaked before white spots flashed in front of his eyes and he keeled over.

51

Sarah

I was forced to ask myself two questions the moment I opened my eyes: Where the hell was I? And why did I have such a stonking headache?

The bed I was in was unfamiliar and so was the room. Daylight poured in through a big gap in the heavy, dark curtains.

I blinked away the sleep and winced because the pain behind my eyes was so intense. It felt like my skull had been struck by a sledgehammer.

Gradually it all came back to me. The confrontation with Bobby Knight's mother, the vodkas, the wine, the photo of Molly with the ball, hauling myself up off the floor in the early hours and crawling into bed.

I had managed to strip down to my underclothes and switch off the TV, but I hadn't taken off my make-up and it was smeared across the pillows.

I threw off the duvet and got out of bed. According to the digital display on the bedside clock it was seven in the morning, which sparked a spasm of anxiety in my chest.

I couldn't believe I'd slept for so long. Was there any news? I wondered. Why hadn't I heard from anyone? Had Bobby Knight been found? Had I received any more messages from him?

I could see my phone on the dressing table, but I was desperate for a pee so I had to get that out of the way first.

When I did check my phone, I saw that I had one missed call from Brennan. He'd left a message telling me he had seen the latest photo and wanted to know if I was all right.

I had to scrunch up my eyes to see the digits on the phone's keyboard, but eventually succeeded in calling him back. He didn't answer, though, and it went to voicemail.

I brought up the photo to check it again in the cold light of day and my heart leapt. It seemed so fucking ordinary. Molly sitting on the grass with a ball and a child's slide behind her. It was the kind of picture I might have taken myself and then framed.

The panic was growing and the hopelessness I felt was almost paralysing.

I rummaged in my shoulder bag in the hope of finding some painkillers. And luckily there were two paracetamol left in the pack. I swallowed them with some water and then grabbed my phone and called the incident room.

I was put through to someone I didn't know and he told me that Brennan and most of the detectives were out working on the investigation. He also told me that there had been no developments overnight other than the message and photo from the kidnapper.

There was a tea and coffee-making facility in the room so I put the kettle on and spooned coffee into a mug. Then while it was boiling I thought about Adam and was surprised that he hadn't contacted me again to tell me how he'd got on at St Thomas'.

I called his number but there was no answer, so I left a message.

The water boiled and I filled the mug. My throat felt thick and sticky so the first mouthful of coffee went down a treat.

I sat on the edge of the bed to drink it and switched on the television. It was already tuned to BBC news and I was glad to see they were still devoting lots of airtime to our story.

There was no mention of the kidnapper's latest text and the coverage was centred on Hayes. Police were still making inquiries in the town to see if Knight was living there. Officers were showing photos of him to as many people as possible.

There were interviews with the pub landlord who had responded to the appeal and with several local shopkeepers. There was also some aerial footage of the town and the surrounding area which brought home to me the enormous task facing my colleagues.

Beyond the little town centre was a spider's web of roads lined with hundreds of homes and beyond those lay fields and woodlands leading into neighbouring conurbations.

The report then cut to a map of the area, showing Hayes in relation to other towns including Bromley, West Wickham, Chislehurst and Beckenham. Dulwich and Peckham also appeared on the map and it made me realise that I didn't know the location of the hotel I was in.

There was a brochure on the dressing table and it told me that The Bell Inn was situated close to Crystal Palace park.

To have ended up here I would probably have driven through Dulwich, but I hadn't paid attention last night because I'd been lost in thought.

Now I had to decide where to spend the rest of the day and how I could possibly make myself useful.

My options were limited. I could go home and sit around under the watchful eye of Sergeant Palmer, which didn't appeal. Or I could return to the incident room and help without allowing my emotions to get the better of me, which would probably be impossible.

And then it struck me that there was a third option. I could go to Hayes, which was where most of the action was taking place now anyway. I could be another set of eyes and ears on the ground. And I could speak to the reporters who were there and appeal again for people to come forward with information.

Hayes was only about six miles south of Crystal Palace so it would probably take me about half an hour to get there, traffic permitting.

By the time I'd finished the coffee, I'd convinced myself that I should go to Hayes. And by the time I'd showered, I'd decided there was no point going home first to change. The jeans and top I'd worn the previous night were a little creased but still clean enough. I made myself look presentable with what I kept in my make-up pouch.

So at precisely nine-fifteen I walked out of The Bell Inn and got in my car.

A strange feeling came over me as I started the engine. It was almost like a premonition that something bad was going to happen, and it was so strong that it made me tremble with trepidation.

Later, when I looked back on the events that unfolded that day, I would remember the feeling and know that I'd been right to be worried.

52

DCI Brennan

Brennan arrived at the Oaklands Copse at nine-thirty. Three police cars and two vans were parked up in the lane.

Officers were already searching the woods with cadaver dogs and sticks. If they didn't uncover anything, then Brennan had been given the go-ahead to bring in another team along with ground-penetrating radar equipment.

The morning was dry and mild with not a cloud in the sky, the kind of morning for long walks or just appreciating the country-side. Not for sifting through the chaos of foliage for a dead body. But at least it wasn't freezing cold or raining.

The wood was thick with trees and bushes and wild flowers. There were no paths and it was pretty much off the beaten track.

The nearest property was the one belonging to Tony Kemp. DC Foster, who had been on the scene for a couple of hours, pointed to the west and explained that the house was on the other side of the wood so they couldn't see it from where they were. That was why they'd approached the wood along this country lane and not the other one. There were no homes on this side and hopefully it would take longer for the news to get out.

'The search got started an hour ago,' Foster said. 'There are twenty-five officers in the wood and four dogs. They're working from east to west.'

The wood was about the size of nine soccer pitches so it was going to take quite some time to cover it.

Brennan had been working flat out to get things organised since the anonymous call had come in. He'd spoken to the Commissioner who in turn had liaised with Kent's Chief Constable and the wheels had been set in motion.

Brennan had stressed throughout that it might be a hoax, but everyone agreed that it could not be ignored.

Before coming to Sevenoaks, Brennan had driven to Hayes, which wasn't far away, to check in with the team there. He'd come away disappointed because nothing new had turned up. Now he was becoming anxious because if both lines of inquiry led nowhere then they were back to square one. And that did not bear thinking about.

Soon he would have to respond to Sarah's message and give her a call. He'd been putting it off in the hope that he'd have some good news for her. But that was now looking unlikely.

He wanted to shut off the fear, switch off the negative thoughts, but it was impossible to do that so long as little Molly's whereabouts remained unknown. The poor kid was so helpless and so vulnerable. Every time he thought about her his heart ached.

'It's not going to be easy to keep the press away once they get a sniff of what's going on,' DC Foster said.

Brennan took off his jacket and draped it over his forearm. Sweat had pooled on his back and under his arms.

'Are you all right, guv?' Foster asked him. 'You look shattered.'

'I feel it,' he said. 'But I know I'm not the only one. This case is taking its toll on all of us.'

He and Foster spent the next hour trudging through the wood with the search team.

The sun got stronger and the air grew heavier. He started to believe they were on a wild-goose chase and that his instincts were right about the call being a hoax. But then one of the police dogs started barking, a shout went up, and officers converged on a small glade among the trees.

When Brennan reached it a tiny patch of undergrowth was being cleared.

'The pooch has got the scent of something,' a dog handler told him. 'My guess is it's not that far below the surface.'

Two officers wearing forensic gloves removed broken twigs and leaves, then started scraping away the dry earth.

Even before they uncovered anything, the smell of rotting flesh seeped into the air.

'Jesus fucking Christ,' someone shouted, stepping back. 'That's bloody awful.'

The first thing to be revealed was a hand, followed by an arm covered in threadbare material that looked like saggy skin. Shortly after that the dirt came away to reveal a man's face. The eyes were sunken, the muscles retracted, and the flesh was in the early stages of decomposition. It was evident that insects had been feasting on the soft tissue including the lips and gums. But even so, Brennan was pretty sure that he was looking at the putrefying remains of one Bobby Knight.

53

Adam

Adam had been lucky. The knife that was used to stab him had a short, thin blade. It penetrated the flesh and muscle on his right side just above the hip bone. So there was no damage to vital organs or arteries.

The speed with which they got him into a trauma suite meant that blood loss was kept to a minimum and the shock to his system was controlled.

He'd lost consciousness for a while and spent some time on the operating table. But now, almost eight hours after the attack, the wound was stitched up and the drugs had reduced the pain to a dull ache.

He was lying on a bed in the recovery area, waiting for DI Hughes from West End Central to come and speak to him. He was still feeling light-headed and confused. But at least he was alive. If he'd been stabbed elsewhere on his torso the wound could have been fatal.

There was a lot he still didn't know, like who the guy in the suit was and why he had tried to kill Eddie Lomax by putting a pillow over his head.

What he *had* been told was that Lomax was still alive and that the perp had been brought down by the security guard. He was now in police custody.

Adam hadn't had a chance to let Sarah or Brennan know what had happened and he saw from a missed call on his phone that Sarah had tried to reach him.

He was eager now to find out if there had been any developments, but as he was about to call her back, the curtain around his bed was tugged open and a tall black guy stepped into the cubicle.

'Hello there,' he said to Adam. 'I hope you're feeling better. I'm DI Jason Hughes.'

They were the same rank so there was no need for the introduction to be any more formal. Adam held out his hand and Hughes shook it.

The DI was middle-aged and had a face that was open and welcoming. He was wearing a sharp blue suit and his dark skin stood out against the crisp whiteness of his shirt collar.

'I'll have to take a statement from you at some point,' Hughes said. 'But before we get around to that you need to tell me why you're here and if it has anything to do with your daughter, Molly.'

Hughes sat on the bed and listened to Adam explain how he had come to be at the hospital.

'It's possible that Eddie Lomax, in his guise as The Keyholder, made a property available to Bobby Knight,' Adam said. 'If so, then there's a chance that that's where he's keeping Molly.'

'So why didn't you just pass that information on to the investigating officers?' Hughes asked as a frown gathered on his brow.

'They've got enough on their plate,' Adam said. 'And besides, I don't have to fuck around with protocol so I can get things done more quickly.'

294

Hughes grinned. 'I can see where you're coming from.'

'So are you going to let me speak to Lomax?'

'I don't see why not, but it won't be for a while because the doctor has put him under again. The shock of what happened gave him a bad turn.'

'So what did actually happen?' Adam asked. 'All I saw was the guy come rushing out of the room.'

'Well it was lucky for us that you were on the scene or I'm pretty sure he would have got away.'

'If I'd known the bugger had a knife I might not have been so determined to stop him.'

'I very much doubt that,' Hughes said. 'Anyway, he's in a cell now and he'll be charged with attempted murder. If the nurse hadn't entered the room when she did it would have been murder.'

'I need to know if this has got anything to do with Bobby Knight,' Adam said.

Hughes shook his head. 'Nothing whatsoever. I managed to have a brief chat with Lomax before they put him back to sleep. The guy who tried to suffocate him is the same guy who attacked him with a knife and left him for dead. He came to the hospital to finish the job so that he couldn't be identified. He claimed he was a relative and managed to walk in without being challenged. I regret now that I didn't post an officer outside the door. It was a mistake on my part.'

'So who is this bloke and what's his problem?'

'His name is Stefan Buzek. He's a Polish national and he claims Lomax has been shagging his missus. The woman works behind the bar in the casino where Lomax is a regular. He likes to gamble, apparently, and is also a bit of a ladies' man. Well, the other night, Buzek waited for him to leave the casino and confronted him. There was a scuffle and the Pole pulled out a knife and stabbed him twice.'

Hughes went on to explain that Buzek had a criminal record and a history of violence. He'd served time for slashing another man's face with a knife during an argument in a pub.

'Thanks to you we'll now be able to lock him up for a long time,' Hughes said.

Adam shrugged. 'That's all very well, but it doesn't bring me any closer to finding my little girl.'

54

Sarah

When I got to Hayes I couldn't help but feel disappointed. It was a pleasant town for sure, with nice shops and a friendly atmosphere. But that was the problem. It didn't look or feel like a place at the centre of an horrific news story. I had expected it to be buzzing with uniformed police officers and TV satellite trucks. But it was like a normal weekday morning. There were people window-shopping, pushing prams, chatting to one another, drinking coffee at pavement tables.

I'd parked behind the railway station and had already walked up and down the main shopping street. And so far I hadn't seen a single copper or TV crew.

I wasn't sure what to make of it. I would have expected a police presence here, since there was a constant stream of people coming and going.

I popped into a newsagents and went up to the girl behind the counter. She was in her twenties and wearing too much lipstick. I asked her if she'd seen many police officers in the town.

'There were quite a few around earlier this morning,' she said.

'One of them came in here and showed me a picture of that bloke on the news.'

'Do you know where they are now?' I asked.

'I gather they've moved off into the housing areas. They're looking for that little baby that's been kidnapped. I hope to God they find her, the poor thing.'

She didn't recognise me even though my picture was on the front pages of at least three of the newspapers spread across the counter. Perhaps that was because I'd applied enough make-up to fool anyone who didn't really know me.

'What about the man in the picture you were shown?' I asked. 'Has he been in here?'

She shook her head. 'Not that I can recall. And I've never seen him in The Queen's Head either. That's where I drink. I saw the video of him on the telly. Bloody creepy.'

Before leaving the shop I bought a copy of the *Daily Mail*. Molly's picture featured on the front page alongside Bobby Knight's ugly face and it caused a shiver to pass through me.

With the paper tucked under my arm I went outside and looked up and down the street. Still no sign of any uniforms or media types.

My rational self told me I might as well go home, that I wasn't going to achieve much by staying here. Sergeant Palmer had already called my mobile to tell me she was ready to meet me there. I told her I'd let her know when I was back. But I wasn't ready to go just yet. I intended to talk to shopkeepers myself, showing them the front page in the hope that it would jolt someone's memory. After all, if Knight was staying in the area then it was likely that The Queen's Head wasn't the only place he had visited.

I started working my way back along one side of the street, dropping in at a charity shop, a butchers, an estate agents, a betting shop, a florist. I showed my ID along with the newspaper's front page.

Uniformed officers had been to all the businesses before me and none of the people could recall seeing Knight.

The woman in the florist recognised me and told me how she was praying for Molly's safe return. But rather than prayers I needed answers and leads.

By now my hangover was kicking in again and I was feeling like a flat battery. I needed some more painkillers so I bought a new box of paracetamol in the chemist and slipped into a café to take them with a strong coffee.

When I was seated at a table by the front window I took out my phone and rang Adam. I was curious to know what he had been up to since last night as he still hadn't returned my call. But this time he answered and when he told me where he was and what had happened my heart dropped to the floor.

'Oh, Adam you should have let me know. Are you all right?'

'I'm all fixed up now so don't panic,' he said, his voice remarkably calm considering. 'It could have been a lot worse, but no serious harm was done. All I'm left with is a small scar.'

I was sure that he was playing it down for my benefit. But the shock hit me hard and I began to tremble with a flood of emotions.

I hadn't forgiven Adam for what he had done to Knight, but I didn't want him to come to any harm while trying to redeem himself.

'I'll be talking to Lomax soon,' he said. 'If he knows where Knight is then you can be sure I'll get it out of him.'

He asked me where I was and I told him and then I went on to tell him about my visit to Knight's mother, the latest photo of Molly and my binge at The Bell Inn.

He was shocked that so much had happened and wanted to

know more about the photo and what Knight's mother had said. I gave him a detailed account and forwarded the photo to his phone. He then asked me if I'd spoken to Brennan.

'Not today. I've left messages but he hasn't got back to me.'

'Well maybe you should go home, Sarah. There's no point hanging around in Hayes just for the sake of it.'

We agreed to talk later and I ordered another coffee, which I needed to steady my nerves. I was feeling completely overwhelmed again, as though my body was on the verge of closing down.

In my mind was an image of Adam lying on his back with a knife sticking out of his body, blood dripping onto the floor. And on the table before me was a blazing headline that read: IS THIS MOLLY'S KIDNAPPER?

I shook my head and told myself that this nightmare had to end eventually, that it couldn't keep getting worse.

But just minutes later it did – when I answered my phone to DCI Brennan and he said he had something important to tell me.

55

DCI Brennan

He'd been dreading having to break the news to Sarah. But there was no way he could avoid it any longer. In a short time the news would be out there and he didn't want her or Adam to find out from the TV or radio. That wouldn't be fair on them.

'I've been trying to reach you, guv,' she said.

'I know and I'm sorry, Sarah. But things have been really crazy. Where are you?'

'In Hayes.'

'What the hell are you doing there?'

'Trying to make myself useful. I thought I could work alongside the team you sent here, but I haven't seen any police, at least not in the town centre.'

'That's because we've had to switch some officers to another location and the rest are checking out the residential districts.'

He heard her breath catch and before she could jump to the wrong conclusion about Molly, he said, 'There's still no sign of Molly, Sarah, but there is something you need to know.'

'What is it?'

His jawline pulsed as he spoke. 'We've found a body and we're 99 per cent sure it's Bobby Knight.'

'Oh God. Where? How?'

'We received an anonymous call late last night. Guy who distorted his voice told us Knight had been murdered and dumped in a wood near Sevenoaks. I didn't call you because I wanted to be sure it was a credible lead first. We started searching this morning and a short while ago we came across a shallow grave.'

'So how can you be so sure that it's him?'

'Most of the body has been uncovered and decomposition has been slow, thanks to the dry earth. So he's recognisable. Plus, he was still fully clothed and there was a wallet in his trouser pocket containing his probation officer's card and his old driving licence.'

'Was he murdered?'

'That will have to be established by the pathologist. But it would appear so. We've spotted an injury to the back of his head that looks bad enough to have been fatal.'

'So his mother and brother were right,' Sarah said.

'Looks that way. And the state of the body suggests he's been in the ground for a couple of weeks, which tallies with when he went missing.'

Brennan tried to keep the disappointment out of his voice. It was, after all, a development that moved them no closer to finding Molly.

'So do you think Tony Kemp did it?' Sarah asked.

'He's our number-one suspect, but not just because of what Knight's mother said. You see, Kemp owns a house that backs onto the wood. Knight was actually buried about three hundred yards from the property.'

'So this means that someone else has got Molly.'

'I realise that, Sarah. I think we're now looking for an accomplice. We've suspected all along that he probably had one. So whoever it is could still be holding Molly in or near Hayes.'

'But what if you're wrong?' Sarah said, her voice breaking. 'What if Bobby Knight had nothing to do with it?'

'We know he was plotting to punish you, Sarah. He told Victor Rosetti and then there were the photos on the phone we found under his bed. He was stalking you.'

'I know that, but none of us knows for sure if he actually went through with the abduction.'

Brennan could tell she was struggling to take it in and he understood why. Her hopes had been cruelly dashed. The discovery of the body was a serious blow to the investigation and he was reminded of what the kidnapper wrote in the message he sent the previous night.

BTW I'm not who you think I am. You're looking for the wrong man in the wrong place.

Well they now knew that to be true. Bobby Knight did not send that text or any of the others. And he wasn't the man in the balaclava who abducted Molly from her grandparents' home. But there was no doubt he was involved and must have had an accomplice.

'We need to tell Adam about this,' Brennan said. 'Do you know where he is?'

But Sarah didn't respond and Brennan immediately realised that it was because she was no longer on the line. She had either hung up on him or the signal had cut out.

56

Sarah

My phone just died on me while Brennan was talking. A flat battery. I hadn't noticed that it needed charging. I didn't have a charger with me so I'd have to wait until I got home. But right now it was the least of my worries. The discovery of Bobby Knight's body was a shattering piece of news. I knew now that it wasn't him who had taken my daughter. It was someone else. Another man who wanted to punish me.

But who? And why?

It was a further twist of the knife and it left me feeling sick and confused.

It was going to change the whole dynamic of the investigation and make finding Molly even more difficult, if not impossible.

It was also going to have a negative impact on Brennan and his team. They had made such a big thing of how they believed Knight was the kidnapper. Brennan had been at pains to suggest that Knight's mother didn't know what she was talking about when she claimed her son must be dead. Yet she had been proved right. But was she also right about Tony Kemp? Had Knight's former underworld boss killed him – or had him killed – because he was harassing his daughter, Lauren? Or was it conceivable that Kemp himself had been involved somehow with Molly's abduction?

I didn't know what to think and the questions were swamping my brain.

For a long time I just sat there staring out of the café window without really seeing anything. And as the minutes ticked by my apprehension grew.

I knew I ought to find a public phone and call Adam and also my mother. They needed to know as soon as possible about the body. But I couldn't bring myself to move, at least not until I'd decided how I was going to respond to this latest setback.

I eventually managed to motivate myself to leave the café. I came to a sudden decision, which was to stick around in Hayes, at least for a while. Bobby Knight might well be dead, but that didn't mean that Molly wasn't in the area being looked after by an accomplice. And if she was I had to do what I could to find her. The alternative was to go home and just sit there waiting for further bad news, while the fear and anxiety clawed at my insides. At least here I could keep myself distracted while I came to terms with the latest disturbing development.

I planned to visit more shops and businesses with the newspaper photos. And as soon as I came across a public phone I'd call Adam and my mother. Luckily I knew both their numbers by heart.

It worried me that I didn't have the use of my own phone because it meant that nobody could contact me, and that included the kidnapper. But at least it granted me a brief respite from the agony of knowing that at any second I might receive a message, photo or video clip that would break my heart all over again.

There were a lot of premises I hadn't yet been to, including the post office and a big pub on the corner. I knew I was clutching at straws but surely that was better than losing all hope.

And there was still a chance, albeit a slim one, that Adam would get something out of Eddie Lomax at the hospital. If the so-called Keyholder gave him the address of a property in the Hayes area then I was well placed to make my way there straight away. I told myself I could not stop believing that Molly might still be in the area. It was still the only lead I had.

So I got started. I dropped in on a shoe shop, a hairdressers, another estate agent, a bakers, an Iceland supermarket, a couple of clothes shops. But each time I got the same response. A police officer had already been there and none of the owners or assistants could remember seeing Bobby Knight. But of course it was a lot to expect since he hadn't been around for a couple of weeks.

I counted another four shops on this side of the road leading down to the big corner pub. I decided that after those I'd cross the road and work my way back up towards the station.

I noticed that one of the shops sold baby stuff. It was called Kiddies Corner and displayed in the window were children's clothes, plus a range of accessories, including toys, pushchairs, shoes and car seat covers. There was a store just like it back in Dulwich and Molly and I were frequent visitors.

The interior was bigger than I expected and stretched way back into the building, with racks of clothes and shelves full of toys.

The woman behind the counter looked to be in her fifties. Her eyes were soft and coffee-brown, and her hair was smooth and flat, like a steel-grey helmet.

She gave me a warm smile and asked me how she could help. I showed her my ID, then held up the newspaper, pointing to Knight's picture.

'You've probably been asked this question already,' I said. 'But I wondered if you might have seen this man before.'

She looked from me to the paper and shook her head.

'I'm certain that I haven't,' she said. 'Another police officer came in here earlier today and I told him the same thing.' She tilted her head to one side and frowned. 'You're that little girl's mother, aren't you? I recognise you from the television.' When I nodded, she continued: 'I saw you on the news speaking outside your flat to all those reporters. What you said made me cry. I hate to think how hard this is for you. I have children of my own.'

'That's why I came to Hayes,' I said. 'I just needed to get involved with the search.'

'Well I really hope they find your daughter soon. She looks such a sweet little mite. It's terrible what that man is doing to her and to you. And I'm truly sorry that I can't be of any help.'

I lifted my shoulders. 'I thought perhaps that man might have come in here to buy things for Molly.'

'It's quite possible that he did at some point. There are three of us working here and one of them may well have served him.'

'So what about your colleagues. Where are they?'

'Mable's at home and Brenda's on holiday. We work a shift pattern.'

I felt my heart sink for the umpteenth time and the air wheezed out of my chest.

'Well thank you for your time,' I said.

As I turned to go, my gaze snagged on a collection of larger toys on the floor towards the back of the shop. Among them was a small plastic slide that looked just like the one that appeared behind Molly in the latest photo the kidnapper had sent to me.

I turned back to the grey-haired woman and gestured towards the slide.

'Would you be able to tell me if you've sold any of those recently, say in the past couple of months?'

Another frown. 'I don't know offhand. But I could check for you. We keep a record of every sale on the computer.'

'Would you please check for me? I'd really appreciate it.'

'Of course. That's no trouble.'

The tension built inside me as I waited for her to trawl through the sales log. After two minutes she lifted her eyes from the computer screen and looked at me.

'We've only had two of those slides in stock since April,' she said. 'The other one was sold by Brenda just over a month ago.'

I shivered with excitement. 'Have you got the details?'

'Well it was part of an order that also included a cot, a high chair, three packs of nappies, some other toys and various clothes for a girl aged between one and two.'

Now it was a struggle for me even to speak.

'What about bank or credit card details? Can you give me those?'

She shook her head. 'I'm afraid not. The man who bought them gave his name as John Smith and paid in cash – a total of four hundred pounds. But he wanted us to arrange for the order to be delivered to his home. And the address happens to be quite near here.'

I bolted out of the shop and headed back towards the car behind the station. In my hand was a piece of paper with John Smith's address scrawled on it. I didn't for a second believe it to be his real name. But I was convinced that the man who'd purchased the goods from Kiddies Corner was the same man who had abducted Molly.

There was very little room in my mind for doubt. I had never been a great believer in coincidences, and this had to be more than a coincidence.

The guy had bought clothes for a girl aged between one and two. Molly was 15 months old. Then there was the slide. The one in the shop was identical to the one in the photo. And all my senses were telling me that the one in the photo was the one bought by John Smith.

The blood was burning in my veins as I ran along the street, and my pulse was beating high up in my throat. I was praying that I wasn't wrong and that this was the breakthrough we'd been waiting for. If so then Molly was possibly only a couple of miles away from where I was, and it wasn't going to take me long to get there.

When I reached my car, I wrenched open the door and got in. Then I tapped the address I'd been given into the satnav with trembling fingers.

Before I got going I took out my mobile to alert Brennan to what I'd found. It was only then that I remembered the battery was flat.

Fuck.

I had a choice to make. Go and find a phone to call Brennan or 999, and then be forced to wait for them to send a team to the house to check it out. Or I could go there by myself and be there in minutes.

It was a no-brainer. I was far too hyped-up to hold back, too driven by the prospect of finding my daughter.

So I dropped the dead phone onto the passenger seat, slipped the gearstick into first and stamped on the accelerator.

57

DCI Brennan

The patrol car raced through South London, the shrill wail of its siren piercing the air.

Brennan sat in the back, feeling flat, disconnected, miserable.

He'd left DC Foster in charge at Oaklands Copse. She would oversee the painstaking forensic examination of the grave and make sure that the integrity of the crime scene was preserved. His job now was to inform Bobby Knight's mother that her son's body had been found and that she and her other son would have to make a formal identification.

He had already broken the news to Sarah and Adam. The call with Sarah had ended abruptly and when he'd tried to ring her back her phone had been dead.

Adam had been totally shocked, but Brennan had been just as surprised to learn that he'd been stabbed, and that he was waiting at St Thomas's Hospital to speak to a man known as The Keyholder.

Brennan knew he should have warned the guy off and told him that once again he had broken all the rules in the book. And if he hadn't been so close to retirement he almost certainly would have. But now he just wanted Molly Mason to be found by whatever means. So instead he'd simply said to call him if Eddie Lomax opened up about what Knight had been after.

He found it hard not to sympathise with Adam Boyd. His actions, after all, were those of a desperate father who was prepared to do whatever he deemed necessary to get his daughter back. Brennan could see himself behaving in much the same way if his own grandson Michael had been abducted.

As they arrived in Peckham, Brennan readied himself mentally for the meeting with Mrs Knight. He'd phoned ahead to tell her that he was dropping by but hadn't said why. He was sure the news would come as a shock even though she'd been convinced all along that her son was dead.

Brennan, on the other hand, had believed with a cold, hard certainty that Bobby Knight was alive. Now he felt like a fool for being so dismissive of the alternative, particularly during the press conference. And he wasn't looking forward to facing the media again because he was going to have to answer some frigging difficult questions. Like where would the investigation go from here? Did the police have any clue as to the true identity of Molly Mason's kidnapper? Was Tony Kemp now firmly in the frame as a murder suspect?

Brennan had yet to hear back from DI Driscoll who had been tasked with bringing Kemp in for questioning. It was assumed that the old gangster was still at his flat in Bermondsey because when officers called at his house in Sevenoaks his wife said he wasn't in but he was due to arrive later that evening.

Brennan still couldn't work out why, if Kemp was indeed responsible for Knight's death, he would have dumped the body so close to his country home. Perhaps it had been down to sheer convenience and plans were in place to move the body eventually.

Another question mark hung over the anonymous caller. Was he someone who worked for Kemp? A disgruntled employee maybe? Or even an arch-rival who got tipped off about the location of the grave and thought he'd use the information to his advantage.

Brennan didn't know what to think right now, and his internal dialogue was filling his head with doubts and chilling images of dead bodies and men in black balaclavas.

Mrs Knight was alone in the house and she made it obvious that she wasn't pleased to see him.

She threw open the front door and without so much as a hello, she stormed off into the kitchen, where she struck up a fag and sat at the table, her face as hard as granite.

'I don't believe this,' she moaned as Brennan entered the room along with one of the uniforms. 'I was up half the night because that bloody woman upset me. And now it's your turn to have a go. Why the fuck can't you just leave me alone?'

'What woman are you talking about, Mrs Knight?' Brennan asked.

'That lying bitch, Sarah Mason. She came here last night and threatened me. She accused me of lying about Bobby and even hit me. But she won't get away with it. I'm gonna put in a complaint.'

'I had no idea that Detective Mason came here, Mrs Knight. I'll make it my business to have a word with her. But you have to appreciate that she's extremely stressed out as I'm sure any mother would be in her situation.'

Brennan was pretty sure that if his own wife had been in Sarah's shoes then she would have come here too.

'That's it, jump to her defence,' she snarled. 'It's exactly how I knew you'd react. She's one of your own so she can do no fucking wrong.'

Brennan sat down opposite her and tried to soften his expression. He didn't want this conversation to go off on a tangent, but that seemed inevitable considering the mood she was in.

'I came here to give you some news,' he said. 'But I was hoping your other son would be here with you.'

'He will be shortly,' she said. 'He's coming over to take me to the shops. But why does he have to be here anyway? I don't need him to look after me.'

Brennan put his fist over his mouth and cleared his throat. Then he took a deep breath through his nose and said, 'We found Bobby's body this morning, Mrs Knight.'

She stiffened and her eyes became slits.

'I told you,' she said, her voice trembling. 'I told you that Tony Kemp had killed him and you wouldn't believe me.'

She twisted her cigarette into the ashtray on the table. Then a shuddering sob erupted from her body.

Brennan reached across the table and covered her hand with his own. But she whipped it away.

'He was a good boy,' she snapped. 'He didn't deserve to die.'

'I'm truly sorry for your loss, Mrs Knight. And for what it's worth, I'm sorry I doubted you.'

Her eyes flashed at him. 'Where did you find my Bobby? I want to know.'

'In a wood in Kent,' Brennan said, and after a pause added, 'He was buried in a shallow grave and we believe he was killed soon after he disappeared. There's a lot we still don't know about the circumstances surrounding his death. As soon as we do you will be informed.'

She clenched her eyes shut and swallowed.

'How did they kill him? Tell me.'

'We're not sure yet, but he did have a serious head wound which is the likely cause of death.'

'So he wasn't shot or stabbed?'

Brennan shook his head. 'Almost certainly not.'

'Had he been tortured?'

'I don't think so.'

She opened her eyes then and shot him an angry look.

'Tell that bitch Sarah Mason that she has my boy's blood on her hands. So I hope she never sees her daughter again. I hope whoever has the little sprog rapes her until she bleeds to death.'

Brennan lowered his eyes, not trusting himself to speak. But the officer who was standing behind him said, 'I'm sure you don't really mean that, Mrs Knight.'

It was like a red rag to a bull. She leapt up out of the chair and thrust her face towards him, her eyes wild.

'I mean every fucking word of it, you stupid twat. That tart destroyed my family and my life. I pray that she never has a day's peace for as long as she lives.'

She then turned to Brennan and pointed towards the door.

'Now I want you to go,' she said. 'And don't be in a hurry to come back. I'm sick of you lot. All you ever do is bring me bad news.'

Brennan had intended to hang around, at least until her youngest son arrived, but her reaction made him change his mind.

He got up, said again how sorry he was, and headed for the door.

Back in the car the officer whose head she'd bitten off, said, 'I'm sorry I piped up in there, guv. I didn't think.'

'Not your fault, lad. That's one fucked-up woman if you ask me.'

Brennan told the driver to take him to Wandsworth and the incident room. But just as they started out his phone went. It was DI Driscoll.

'I thought you should know that we're having problems finding Tony Kemp, guv,' he said.

'Have you been to his flat?'

'We have. His daughter was there, but he wasn't. She let us look around. And she said she has no idea where he is.'

'Do you believe her?'

'Well she sounded genuine and a bit concerned actually.'

'Did you tell her why we want to speak to her father?'

'I thought it best to since she'll be hearing about it soon enough.'

'What about his phone?'

'It's switched off. Both his daughter and his wife reckon that's pretty unusual. We're now in the process of checking out his haunts and employees.'

'This is something I didn't expect,' Brennan said.

'Me neither. Maybe the guy got wind of what we've been up to in the wood and decided to make himself scarce.'

It seemed unlikely to Brennan, but the possibility dominated his thoughts on the drive to Wandsworth.

It was another unwelcome turn of events. And exactly what he didn't need at this time.

58

Sarah

The satnav guided me south out of Hayes town centre. It was more rural than residential, and much of the area was heath and woodland.

As I drove, my breathing became heavier and I trembled with anticipation. In my head a voice was warning me not to build up my hopes.

You're jumping to conclusions, Sarah. The man who bought the cot and slide and other stuff from Kiddies Corner might not be the same man who has Molly.

But I refused to listen. Instinct told me I wasn't wrong, that I had stumbled on a lead that was both strong and credible.

Each time the satnav spoke to me, my stomach jumped. I was getting closer. One mile away. Half a mile. Turn left three hundred yards ahead.

I followed the directions into a narrow country lane. On both sides were smart detached houses on spacious plots of land. Then came some fields. A bit of dense woodland. Another lane off to the right.

Finally the satnav told me I'd reached my destination: the address to which Kiddies Corner had delivered £400 worth of baby things.

The house was set back from the road. It was a two-storey, red-brick property surrounded by high hedges. There was a short driveway and an integral garage, but I couldn't see any vehicles.

I parked up on the grass verge and got out, leaving my shoulder bag inside the car.

All my police training told me that to go in without back-up would be an extreme act of recklessness. But I wasn't thinking like a police officer. I was thinking like a mother and nothing short of an earthquake was going to stop me finding out if my daughter was in this house.

I had no plan as such, and it was too late to do anything other than walk up to the front door and ring the bell. What I'd do after that would depend on whether someone answered.

Clouds had moved in overhead and the sun had all but disappeared. But it was still bright and warm and birdsong filled the air.

I walked slowly up the gravel driveway, my heart thrashing against my chest.

The house was pretty secluded. There were properties either side but with patches of woodland in between.

I paused about ten yards from the front door. Took a moment to look around and listen. There was no sign of life, and the only sound came from the birds in the trees.

The house was older than it had appeared to be from a distance, and the brickwork had been discoloured by age. If it did belong to a villain who had fled the country then my guess was he'd bought it as an investment or to launder money. He probably hadn't actually lived here.

There were four large windows facing the front, two up and two down. Curtains were pulled across them.

I stepped up to the door, which was green and made of wood. I rang the bell. Waited. There was no response so I rang it again and this time left my finger on the button for thirty seconds. I could hear it ringing inside but no one answered.

I wasn't about to let that put me off, though. I banged my fist against the door a couple of times, then stood back and shouted: 'Is someone at home? I'm a police officer. Open up.'

There was a side gate on the right of the building, which presumably led to a back garden. I crossed over to it, thinking I might have to contend with a padlock. But the gate opened when I pushed my thumb down on the latch.

A path led around the side of the house, between the wall and the hedge. There was a door with a frosted glass panel and a window to the left of it. The venetian blinds were in the open position so I stood on tiptoe and peered into a kitchen with wooden units and grey walls. The room was empty and when I tried to open the door I found it was locked.

I then carried on to the end of the path, which brought me to a paved patio, and beyond it a garden that was in need of some TLC. The flower beds had been colonised by weeds and a section of the rear fence was missing. But what really drew my attention were the two objects in the middle of the lawn – a yellow slide and a big red ball.

The last time I'd seen them had been in the photograph that was sent to my phone last night. Of that I had no doubt.

Hope swelled inside me at the thought that a short time ago Molly had been sitting in this very garden.

The blood started roaring in my ears as I turned my attention to the back of the house. There were four windows and a set of patio doors, which did not have curtains or blinds on the inside.

When I stepped up to the glass I could see into the large room.

And that was when I got another shock.

In the middle of the room was a white leather sofa which I knew must be the one that Molly had been sitting on in that first photograph from the kidnapper.

As I strained my eyes to look at the wall behind it I saw a framed print of a sailboat on water. The same one that appeared in the photo.

My legs almost gave way at that moment, and the panic rose in my throat.

This is definitely the place. This is where that bastard has been holding Molly.

There were no outside handles on the patio doors, and a quick check confirmed that all the windows were shut and locked. But I had to find a way in. There was every chance that my baby was inside, all alone and waiting for me to come and get her.

I walked back round to the front of the house, looking for a means of access. It was suddenly obvious what I had to do and that was to smash my way in through a window.

It didn't take me long to find a stone half the size of a brick in the garden. I reckoned it was big enough and heavy enough to do the trick.

I opted to go in through the patio doors, so I stood about five yards back and hurled the stone with as much force as I could muster.

It bounced off the first time, but left a jagged network of cracks across one of the doors.

The second time the glass shattered with an almighty crash and left an opening plenty big enough for me to step through.

The living room was spartan and stretched through to the front of the house. The only furniture was the sofa, a mismatched armchair, a small cabinet and a television in one corner on a stand.

I stood still for a few moments, half expecting an alarm to go off or the man in the balaclava to appear. But nothing happened and I realised then that he wasn't here.

Suddenly I feared that maybe he had done a runner and taken Molly with him.

Oh please God, no.

I stalked across the living room and into a wide hallway with a staircase. The front door was to my left, the kitchen to my right. So I checked that first. There was a part of it that I hadn't been able to see when I'd peered through the window. It contained a breakfast bar and a high chair. A dirty bib was resting on the tray and in the sink was a child's plastic food plate. The scene sucked the breath out of my lungs and my heart started to race. It was hard for me to imagine that these were items that Molly had been using, probably just a few hours ago.

There was another room on the ground floor but it was unfurnished.

So I moved slowly up the stairs, ready to defend myself if somebody leapt out at me.

On the upstairs landing there were four doors and they were all closed. I checked them all. The first two were bedrooms with double beds and wardrobes. Only one of the beds was made up with pillows and a duvet. The other contained a bare mattress. The third door led to a bathroom with a fitted shower. But as I pushed open the fourth door my chest exploded with a spasm of joyful relief.

There was a cot up against the far wall and I could see a child lying in it.

I rushed across the room on legs that suddenly felt too weak to support me. I grabbed the edge of the cot and leaned over it. And there, tucked beneath a blanket, was my baby.

She was lying on her side, her eyes closed, a thumb in her mouth. She looked different with short, dark hair. But she was still my beautiful little girl.

I was so relieved that I screamed out loud and tears welled in my eyes. But the scream didn't wake her so I lowered the side of the cot and started telling her that she was safe and Mummy was here.

She was wearing a two-piece pyjama set, and I could see a stain where her nappy had leaked while she slept.

'Wake up, sweetheart,' I said, stumbling over my words. 'I've come to take you home.'

But she didn't stir, not even when I lifted her out of the cot and pulled her tightly against me. The sweet smell of her body brought a huge lump to my throat and I could barely breathe.

'It's me, Molly. Mummy. Wake up, darling. I'm here now. We can go home.'

I held her away from me, shook her gently, willed her to open her eyes and smile at me.

And that was when I realised that something was wrong. My daughter was limp and unresponsive in my arms. And try as I might I just couldn't get her to wake up.

59

Adam

The long wait ended for Adam when DI Hughes came to tell him that Eddie Lomax – alias The Keyholder – was awake at last.

'He's still drowsy but he is able to speak,' Hughes said. 'I told him another officer wants to ask him some questions about an unrelated matter, but I didn't give him any details.'

'Thanks,' Adam said. 'I'll go and see him now if that's OK.'

'I wasn't sure if you'd still want to in view of what's happened.'

Adam had shared with Hughes the news that Knight's body had been found.

'However the evidence suggests that he was involved at the outset and must have had at least one accomplice who abducted Molly after he died,' Adam said. 'So if Lomax did rent out a property to him, then the other guy could still be there with Molly.'

'Good point. But a word of warning. The guy's pretty shrewd and tight-lipped. It's how he's managed to stay under the radar for this long. So don't be surprised if you don't get much out of him.'

Lomax was sitting up against the pillows when Adam stepped

into the cubicle, his face deathly pale. He was still attached to the monitor and his chest was bandaged, but the drip had been removed.

'I'm Detective Inspector Boyd,' Adam said. 'I'm the one who chased the guy who tried to kill you.'

Lomax ran his tongue over dry, cracked lips and said, 'The other detective told me that Buzek stabbed you as well.'

'That's right. But he didn't do as good a job on me as he did on you, Eddie. Or would you rather I address you as Mr Keyholder?'

Lomax's face darkened. 'What is this? I don't know what the fuck you're on about.'

Adam moved closer to the bed and stood over him.

'I haven't got time for lies, Eddie. My fifteen-month-old daughter has been abducted and I want your help.'

Confusion twisted Lomax's features.

'What's it got to do with me?'

'Well I'm hoping you're going to tell me where she is.'

'Is this some kind of sick joke?'

'I wish it was,' Adam said. 'But I'm deadly serious.'

Lomax shook his head. 'I don't know what you're trying to pin on me but I'm not prepared to listen to whatever it is.'

Adam rested his hands on the edge of the bed and leaned over, invading Lomax's space. Then he delivered his words in an angry whisper.

'You haven't got a fucking choice, mate. And if you dick me around, your life won't be worth living when you finally get out of here.'

Lomax pushed himself back against the pillows and he grimaced as it caused him some pain.

'So don't try lying to me or denying that they call you The

Keyholder,' Adam continued. 'I know all about the services you provide to villains with assets.'

Lomax started to speak, but then stopped himself and began panting heavily instead.

'One of the villains who came to you recently was Bobby Knight. I gather he wanted you to fix him up with a property somewhere. A safe house in other words.'

'I don't know anyone—'

Adam grabbed his arm and squeezed it. 'I warned you not to lie, Eddie, and now I don't want you to say anything until you know the story in full. A lot's been happening while you've been struggling to survive in here, including the demise of dear old Bobby. So just relax and let me put you in the picture. Afterwards I'm hoping that for your own sake you'll tell me what I want to know.'

60

Sarah

It was some moments before I realised that Molly was breathing. In the panic that had engulfed me I'd failed to notice that her chest was moving up and down.

Thank God, thank God, thank God.

I checked her quickly to see if she had any serious injuries. But there weren't any visible cuts or bruises, although she did stink of urine.

So what was wrong with her? Why wouldn't she wake up?

'Molly, sweetheart,' I said, tapping my fingers against her cheek. 'Please open your eyes for me. It's Mummy. I'm here.'

But she didn't respond, didn't move.

Had she suffered some kind of head injury? Or had the bastard pumped her full of drugs?

I needed to call an ambulance. Or failing that get her to a hospital as quickly as possible.

A phone. I needed a phone and it suddenly struck me that there might be a landline downstairs.

I wrapped the blanket around Molly and lifted her up again. My heart was beating so fiercely that I thought it might tear my body apart.

I clung to my baby as I rushed out of the room, blubbering and crying as I did so. I had never seen Molly like this before and I was scared witless. She felt lighter than usual in my arms and I wondered if she had lost weight. There were so many more questions swirling around inside my head. Where was the kidnapper? Had he left Molly here to starve? What would have happened if I hadn't found the house?

I carried her down the stairs and straight towards the living room, intending to go out the way I'd come in. Then I would rush to one of the neighbouring properties in the hope that someone was at home. I needed to phone for an ambulance or get directions to the nearest hospital. But as I entered the living room my eyes were drawn to the front window – what I saw came as a gut-wrenching shock.

The window afforded a view of the driveway and there was a car parked on it. It was a red Ford Fiesta and it must have arrived while I was upstairs and I'd been in too much of a state to hear it. But I did hear the creak of the floorboards behind me while I was staring through the window.

I spun round and came face to face with a man I had never met but who I vaguely recognised from the TV news. He was standing barely five feet from me.

'How the hell did you find this place?' he bellowed.

I was so stunned I couldn't speak. And he didn't wait for me to recover before he lunged forward. He grabbed Molly's arm with one hand and yanked her from me with brute force. Then he used his other hand to throw a fist at my face. The punch struck me on the left cheekbone and sent my head into a buzzing frenzy. The blow was so hard I fell to the floor, as if every muscle in my body had stopped working.

61

Adam

It didn't take Adam long to tell Eddie Lomax what he'd missed while he'd been unconscious in hospital. He started with Molly's abduction and described how the kidnapper had been sending her mother photographs and videos to punish her for a perceived wrongdoing.

'We think that Bobby Knight had planned it while in prison,' Adam said. 'He accused my wife of planting the evidence that got him convicted, but of course that was total rubbish.'

Adam then explained that Knight needed a place to hold Molly and it was believed he had moved to a property in Hayes because he'd been spotted there several times.

'But you just told me he was killed two weeks ago,' Lomax said. 'If that's so, then how can he be holding your daughter?'

'We're assuming there was an accomplice who put the plan into action after Knight disappeared.'

By now Lomax's face was glazed with rank-smelling sweat and his breath was even more laboured.

Adam knew he didn't have much more time to get the

information out of him. Any second a doctor was likely to appear and call a halt to the questioning. And he wasn't sure he had done enough to get the man to open up.

'You need to see this,' Adam said, taking the phone from his pocket.

He scrolled through the image gallery until he came to the clip of Molly being held upside down and smacked. And then he played it for Lomax.

'That's my daughter,' Adam said. 'The man who's taken her has threatened to rape her.'

The revulsion was evident in Lomax's expression. Adam capitalised on this by saying, 'This is not about you, Eddie. I give you my word that you won't face any comebacks if you rented out a property to Knight. This is about the life of my little girl, and I promise you it will work in your favour if you help me on this.'

Lomax closed his eyes and thought about it.

Adam stood back and rubbed a hand over the stubble on his face.

After about a minute, Lomax snapped his eyes open and gave a sharp nod.

'Bobby did come to me asking if I had any houses he could rent for up to two months,' he said. 'He wanted it in the countryside and fairly secluded. It so happened I had three on the books and he chose the one nearest to his mum's place in Peckham, then paid up front in cash.'

'Where is the house, Eddie?'

Lomax blew out a breath and said, 'In Hayes, not far from the town centre.'

A minute later Adam called Brennan and gave him the address.

'Please get officers over there as fast as you can,' he said. 'I think Molly might be there.'

62

Sarah

I remained conscious despite the force of the punch from my attacker. But my face was hot with pain and my head was spinning wildly.

'I never thought I would get a chance to do that,' he said, his voice pure ice. 'Bobby would be proud of me.'

I heaved myself into a sitting position and relief surged through me when I saw that he'd placed Molly on the sofa, where she remained unconscious but appeared to me unharmed. Then I stared up at him and he stared right back at me. There was something unsettling in his eyes, something unbalanced.

'I asked you a question,' he said. 'How did you find this place?'

He was wearing a plain white T-shirt and his legs were wrapped in tight denim. A pair of aviator-style glasses dangled from around his neck.

I ignored his question and said, 'My daughter isn't well. You need to get her to a hospital.'

'She's fine. I had to give her a sedative to keep her quiet while I went into town. It'll soon wear off.'

I was confused now, unsure whether to believe him or not.

'It's true,' he said, as if reading my mind. 'How else do you think I've been able to leave her for long spells on her own?'

'You bastard,' I said. 'What else have you done to her?'

He smiled, cocky and confident. 'I haven't touched her, apart from that little hiding I gave her to teach you a lesson. And there's no way I would have molested her. It's not what I'm into despite the threat.'

I could feel an explosion of violence stirring inside me, but I knew I wasn't yet in a position to get the jump on him.

'Do you know who I am?' he said and the question took me by surprise.

I nodded. 'You're Bobby Knight's brother. Noah Carter.'

I'd never met him before. He had stayed very much in the background when we arrested his brother four years ago. All I knew about him was what I'd gleaned from the news. He was younger than Bobby, worked as some kind of consultant, and hadn't been a career criminal like his brother. I'd been told that Brennan had spoken to him and his flat had been searched, but he'd not been considered a credible suspect, which as it turned out was a big bloody mistake.

'You're correct,' he said. 'So now that we've established you're able to answer questions I'll ask you again. How did you find this place?'

'I went to the baby shop in Hayes,' I said. 'I saw a slide – the same one I've just seen out back. It was also in the last photo you sent to me.'

He gave a small, humourless smile. 'And they told you it was delivered to this address along with some other stuff.'

'That's right.'

He sighed. 'One of the many mistakes my big brother made. He should never have told the staff to deliver it.'

331

I looked beyond him to Molly. She hadn't moved and I was becoming increasingly worried.

'Look, please let me get my daughter to the hospital. If you did give her a sedative then you might have given her too much.'

Anger flashed in his eyes. 'I told you she'll be fine. Now stand up.'

'She doesn't look fine to me,' I said. 'She looks—'

He stepped forward, grabbed a handful of my hair and wrenched me to my feet. 'I said stand up, you bitch.'

I yelped in pain and clung to his arm as he dragged me out of the living room and into the hall. There he let go of my hair and shoved me towards the kitchen.

'Go in there and sit down,' he snarled. 'I need something to drink while I decide what to do with you.'

I turned to face him.

'My colleagues know I'm here,' I said. 'They're on their way.'

He shook his head. 'If I thought that, I wouldn't be hanging around. But I'm gambling on the fact that you came here without knowing what to expect so you didn't tell anyone. But if you did and they turn up they'll find you grieving over your dead child. I'll cut her throat the moment I hear someone outside. And then I'll slit my own wrists just like my father did after you fitted Bobby up and got him sent to prison.'

A red mist blurred my vision suddenly and in a frenzied panic I threw myself at him. I stabbed fists at his head and body, but most of the blows landed on his arms and chest. One struck him on the bridge of his nose and he roared with pain.

In response, he rammed his fist into my stomach and I staggered backwards, dazed and winded.

I was still doubled over, gasping and wheezing, when he came at me again. And I didn't have the strength to defend myself.

332

This time his fist connected with my mouth and it sent me flying backwards through the doorway into the kitchen.

I fought to stay on my feet and tried to grab the worktop to stop myself falling. But it was to no avail and I crashed into a chair and ended up on my back.

I must have blacked out for a few seconds because the next thing I knew he was standing over me. He was holding a kitchen knife in one hand and a can of beer in the other.

My head felt like it was about to burst open and my mouth was filled with the bitter taste of blood.

'You made a mistake coming here,' he said. 'The plan was always to let the kid go eventually, after we had decided you'd suffered enough.'

'There's no reason you shouldn't stick to the plan,' I said. 'Please let Molly go. She's just a baby.'

'Well I suppose I could still do that. But you must know that you're going to have to die. The only thing I can't decide is whether to keep you alive long enough for my mother to come and see you. I'm sure she'd like to ensure that your final hours are as miserable as possible. She told me you went to see her last night and it really pissed her off. And I spoke to her a short time ago after your colleague told her they'd found Bobby's body. She said, and I quote, "*I'd like to murder that bitch with my own hands.*"'

I pushed myself up so that my back was resting against the wall.

'Are you telling me that your mum is involved in this?' I said.

He shrugged. 'She wasn't to start with, but after Bobby disappeared she was happy to join forces with me so that we could see his plan through.'

I stared at him, horrified. Then my eyes shifted to the knife in his hand and I realised that the only thing I could do was stall for time and pray for an opportunity that would allow me to seize the initiative.

'I can't believe you went to all this trouble to punish me for something I didn't do,' I said.

'Don't waste your breath with that shit, lady. Bobby didn't lie to us. We know you stitched him up by planting the evidence.'

'And he then spent the best part of four years planning his revenge. So tell me how come you got involved. I thought Bobby was the criminal, not you.'

He swigged some of his beer and gnawed on his bottom lip. Then, after glancing at his watch, he appeared to come to a decision. He pulled out one of the chairs and positioned it so that it was facing me across the kitchen floor.

'I suppose it won't do any harm to tell you,' he said. 'At least it'll make you realise why we hate you so much.'

63

Sarah

As Noah Carter spoke, two things became obvious. The first was just how much he had revered and idolised his dead brother. I got the impression that he'd probably lived for much of his younger life in Bobby's shadow, and to an extent had become dependent on him. The second thing was how much seething anger there was lurking beneath the surface. He may have presented himself to the world as a smart business consultant who was nothing like his ruthless, villainous brother. But it was my guess that there was a darkness in both of them that had been passed down by their dodgy parents.

'Bobby was all set to make a fresh start in life when you came along and arrested him,' Carter said. 'He was happier than ever, but then you went and shafted him just to make yourself look good.'

I thought about telling him what really happened four years ago but realised there was no point because he would never believe me. It might even make him angrier and cause him to take it out on Molly. At least while she was sleeping off the sedative in the other room she was out of harm's way.

'It wasn't just the time he spent in prison,' he went on. 'It was the knock-on effect. Lauren left him and he was completely devastated. Then our dad took his own life and our mum fell to bits. And Bobby blamed you for everything and swore that he'd make you suffer.'

Some of what he went on to say I already knew or suspected. Bobby had thought about many ways to get revenge on me, but after being told by Victor Rosetti that I had a child he'd decided to target Molly.

'All those times I visited my brother in jail he only ever spoke about hurting you and getting Lauren back,' Carter said. 'He persuaded me to help him sort you out and I did because I hated you almost as much as he did. His plan was just to take your daughter and hold her for a few months. It was my idea to send the messages and images. It struck me as a good way to make you suffer.'

I wanted to hit him then, to shove my hand into his mouth and pull out his tongue. I had never hated someone so much in my entire life.

'After we talked about it and settled on a plan I set to work getting all the information on you,' he said. 'I got your phone number, address and email. I then set up anonymous accounts so the emails and messages couldn't be traced. I'm a business consultant specialising in websites and IT so for me it was easy. When Bobby got out he arranged to rent this house from some guy he'd heard about and he stalked you for a bit. I didn't know he'd got himself another phone to take pictures, so when that copper found it under his bed it came as a surprise.'

Carter said they hadn't expected Bobby to be linked to the kidnapping and it probably wouldn't have happened if Rosetti hadn't opened his mouth.

'That was another of my brother's mistakes,' he said. 'He revealed too much to that Romanian scumbag.'

'But things must have been falling apart long before Rosetti spoke to the police,' I said.

He nodded. 'Bobby died before he could see it through. But it was his own fault. He was obsessed with Lauren and he ignored the threats from her father. It got to the point where he decided he was going to kidnap her as well and keep her here with your daughter.'

'So her father had him killed?'

Something happened to his eyes, and for the first time his face showed a flicker of emotion.

'It wasn't Tony Kemp who killed my brother,' he said. 'It was me.'

He wanted to get it off his chest. I could tell that much. And by confessing to me he could make sure it wouldn't go any further.

He described how they had a massive row over what he called his brother's stupid plan to abduct Lauren as well as Molly.

'We were here getting the place ready,' he said. 'It was the first time in years we'd argued like that. When he stormed out to the car I went after him. He punched me, so I punched him back. But he fell and struck his head on the front step. He died instantly. Just like that.'

There were tears in his eyes and his cheeks had coloured.

'So how come he ended up being buried close to Tony Kemp's house near Sevenoaks?' I said.

'I took him there after telling my mother that Kemp must have killed him. I couldn't tell her what really happened because she'd never forgive me. So it suited me that Kemp was under suspicion because of the threats he'd made.'

It was a shocking revelation, but even so I was only half listening to what he was saying. Part of my mind was still on Molly and I was desperate to return to the living room to pick her up. Another part was trying to judge whether there was any way I could turn the tables on Carter.

'I know I was the one who killed Bobby,' he said. 'It was an accident, but I'll never forgive myself. At the same time I'll never forgive you because you're to blame for creating this whole fucking situation in the first place.'

The anger was building up in him again and it blazed in his eyes.

'What happened afterwards?' I said. 'After he died, I mean.'

He pursed his lips and studied the blade of the knife as he spoke.

'That was when I told my mother what we'd been planning and that I'd decided to step into my brother's shoes to see through what he'd started. I thought she ought to know. And she surprised me by offering to help. She said it was what Bobby would have wanted.'

'So she was the one holding the camera when you were smacking Molly.'

He nodded. 'Everything went so well from the start. This house was all set up and ready, I'd obtained a phial of chloroform online, you turned up at your mother's house exactly on cue, and then your father drove off in his car. Taking Molly was so easy. When we saw how desperate you were it made it all worthwhile. We realised it had been the right decision to see Bobby's plan through. But then his name was linked to it, and suddenly it started going wrong. The video of Bobby in the pub turned up and your lot found the photos on the camera. That's why I phoned in the tip about the body. It was clear you were closing in so I wanted to move attention away from Bobby and away from us.'

He stopped talking and after a few moments he got to his feet.

'I've changed my mind about waiting for my mother,' he said. 'I can't let her see you now that you know what really happened to Bobby. Believe me this was never part of the plan, but I promise you it won't give me any sleepless nights.'

Two things happened suddenly to stop him from attacking me with the knife.

A muted cry came from the living room and I realised with a burst of relief that Molly was awake at last. And then came the high-pitched wail of a police siren outside.

64

Sarah

Time seemed to shudder to a halt and a rush of heat burned in my chest.

Carter let out an angry roar and I thought he was going to lunge at me with the knife. But instead he threw the can of beer to the floor and was out of the room in a flash. The knife was still in his hand.

I choked out a scream and struggled to my feet. My mind was a maelstrom as I ran after him, his words from earlier ringing in my ears.

I'll cut her throat the moment I hear someone outside.

He rushed into the living room and I raced after him. I thought he would go straight to Molly, who was sitting up on the sofa crying. But he went to the front window to look out. I saw what he saw – a police car pulling onto the driveway, its blue light flashing.

Carter cursed out loud and then whirled round to face me, a fierce rage contorting his features.

I switched my stricken gaze back to Molly and was astonished to see that she had suddenly stopped crying. Now she was holding out her arms towards me and the word that came out of her mouth set my heart on fire.

'Mummy, Mummy.'

Carter and I were about the same distance from her and he made the first move. But some deep, primal instinct propelled me forward like a stone from a catapult. I pummelled into him just before he reached the sofa.

We both went crashing across the room into the cabinet, which stopped us from tumbling onto the floor.

He managed to hold onto the knife as we both fought to regain our balance. Then he twisted his body and lashed out with it.

It was more luck than judgement on my part that I arched my back just in time to deny the blade a target. The tip missed me by a whisker and wedged itself in the front of the cabinet. Before Carter could pull it out, I shifted my weight into him and forced him sideways so that he lost his grip on the knife. I then drove my forehead into his face and he howled in pain as blood spurted from his nose.

'You fucking bitch,' he yelled, and grabbed me by the throat with both hands, digging his fingers into the soft flesh.

The sudden pain was excruciating, sharp, deep, intense.

I responded instinctively by stabbing my fingers into his right eye. He jerked his head back so I pressed harder, pushing the eyeball further back into the socket.

He was forced to let go of my throat in order to seize my arm. But before he could grasp it I dropped my hand away from his face and headbutted him again, this time cracking my skull against his chin.

His body pivoted backwards into the wall and I pressed my

advantage by going at him like a wild woman, kicking and flailing and cursing until all he could do was try to defend himself.

I didn't let up even as he slid down the wall onto the floor. I kicked him in the chest, punched the back of his head, stamped on his hands.

And I would have carried on until I'd killed the bastard if they hadn't pulled me off him.

It took two police officers to pull me away from Carter. They were the first of a whole bunch of uniforms who came storming in through the opening I'd created in the patio door.

'Calm down now, miss,' one of them said. 'We've got you.'

His voice snapped me out of my trance, but it was several seconds before I was able to control my rage and stop shaking.

'We know who you are, Detective Mason,' the other officer said. 'You're safe now and that man is no longer a threat.'

He edged me away from Carter who was cowering on the floor as a string of expletives flew out of his swollen mouth.

'I think your daughter needs you,' the same officer said.

Oh my God, Molly.

I heard her before I saw her. She was crying hysterically while being held by another officer. I rushed over to her and took her in my arms and then cried with her. Our bodies trembled in unison and our tears fell onto the blanket she was wrapped in.

'It's over, sweetheart,' I sobbed and then kept repeating it because I just couldn't believe it was true.

As we were ushered out of the living room, I saw Carter being hauled to his feet. Our eyes met and his were burning like mercury. There was blood on his face and he was saying something to me that I couldn't hear.

I clung to my baby as we were led outside and I covered her

head with the blanket to shield her from what was going on around us. She had already seen enough and I could only imagine how terrified she'd been as she watched me struggling with Carter.

'I need to get my daughter to a hospital,' I shouted out. 'She's been drugged and I want her to see a doctor.'

I was told that an ambulance had been summoned and would be here soon, and while I waited I sat in the back of a police car with Molly on my lap. I held her close, breathed her in, and I couldn't believe it was happening. My prayers had been answered. My baby was back. And the nightmare was finally over.

She eventually stopped crying and her distress turned to curiosity as she stared out the window at all the uniforms milling about on the driveway.

'Mummy's friends got here just in time, my love,' I whispered to her. 'Those nice police officers saved us.'

She turned to look at me, a frown on her little face. And then she smiled and it was the most beautiful thing I had ever seen.

65

Sarah

A lot happened during the following hour. An officer made notes as I told him what had taken place in the house and what Carter had revealed to me. I also explained how I had come to be there. I then had to go through it all again, this time over the police radio to DCI Brennan at the incident room in Wandsworth.

He asked some questions, and as he spoke I could hear the relief in his voice.

'So Carter admitted killing his brother?' he said.

'That's right. And he buried the body in the woods so that suspicion would fall on Tony Kemp.'

Brennan told me that Kemp had been missing for much of the day, giving rise to speculation that he had panicked after Knight's body was found.

'But the old bugger just surfaced,' he said. 'Turns out he was shacked up in a hotel room with his Russian mistress and didn't want anyone to know about it.'

Brennan said that I had Adam to thank for the fact that the cavalry had arrived in the nick of time.

'He managed to get Lomax to reveal the address of the house and he phoned it through to me.'

He then said he would go out himself to arrest Knight's mother based on what her son had disclosed.

His final words to me were: 'I'm so pleased that you've got Molly back, Sarah. It's really terrific.'

I borrowed a phone from one of the officers to call Adam. I gave him the good news and thanked him for getting Lomax to open up.

'I don't even want to think about what would have happened if those cars hadn't arrived when they did,' I said. 'Carter had armed himself with a knife and was going to use it.'

'Is our little girl OK?' he said.

'I think so. She's obviously been distressed but she just smiled at me and now she keeps pointing at people and seems to like being the centre of attention.'

'I'm on my way,' he said. 'If you leave before I get there then have someone let me know where they've taken you.'

I then watched as Noah Carter was brought out of the house in handcuffs. He was bundled into a car and carted off.

A single paramedic responder turned up on the scene before the ambulance and checked Molly over. He said she looked fine and didn't believe the drugs she'd been given had caused her any harm.

A forensic team then turned up, along with several detectives I knew from Wandsworth. I asked one of them to go inside the house and bring me out some clothes and a nappy for Molly.

I'd just finished dressing her when an ambulance pulled up on the road at the bottom of the driveway.

I gave one of the detectives the key to my car and asked him to take care of it for me. Then before the ambulance doors closed behind us I looked up at the house one last time and said aloud to myself, 'Please God let my baby forget what happened in there.'

66

DCI Brennan

Brennan left the incident room at nine o'clock to go to Dulwich. There was still a lot to be done but he decided it would have to wait. He wanted to see Sarah with Molly before the evening was over.

The last few hours had been hectic. He had briefly questioned both Noah Carter and his mother. Carter hadn't bothered to deny any of the accusations that were put to him. He admitted everything and said he wasn't sorry for what he'd done.

Brennan told him that he was going to be formally charged with child abduction, the attempted murder of Sarah Mason and the murder of his own brother Bobby. Brennan wasn't sure whether a jury would believe that Bobby's death had been an accident. But even if they did, the man would still be going inside for a very long time.

His mother had denied everything until Brennan told her that it was Noah who had killed Bobby. The revelation came as such a shock that she passed out on the floor of the interview room. After she came to and was seen by a doctor, she finally admitted that she did assist in the abduction of Molly Mason. And just like her son she was totally unrepentant.

'I'm glad I did it,' she'd said defiantly. 'And whatever happens to me now it was worth seeing that fucking bitch suffer, if only for a few days.'

The news had got out, of course, and a large crowd of reporters, photographers and TV crews had gathered outside Sarah's flat in Dulwich. Some had been there since she'd arrived back from the hospital with Adam and Molly, and the pictures taken of her going inside had already been sent around the world.

There'd been a brief statement from the Yard saying that Molly had been found and two people had been arrested in connection with her abduction.

Brennan was mobbed as he got out of his car and headed into Sarah's block. He stopped and answered a few of their questions, and as he did so he found it hard to keep from smiling.

'At this stage I can't go into details about what actually happened today,' he said. 'But I can confirm that Molly was saved by her mother who managed to trace her daughter's kidnapper to a house near Hayes. I can also tell you that Molly has been to hospital and doctors have said she's in good health physically. We must now hope that the awful experience she's been through won't have caused any lasting psychological damage.'

Brennan dashed upstairs to Sarah's flat. It felt cramped inside because Sarah, Adam and Molly had been joined by Sarah's parents and Sergeant Palmer.

The atmosphere was one of joyous relief, and when Brennan saw little Molly he couldn't believe his eyes. She was running around excitedly like it was Christmas, relishing being the main attraction. Her grandfather couldn't stop laughing and teasing her, while her gran sat on the sofa shedding tears of happiness.

Adam stood next to Sarah with a drink in his hand, staring at his daughter with wide, grateful eyes. Brennan couldn't begin to imagine what thoughts were going through his mind.

There was lots to talk about, and Brennan had a list of questions for both Sarah and Adam. But all that stuff could be dealt with in the days ahead. Tonight was for rejoicing in Molly's return.

'We'll probably never know what he did and didn't do to her,' Sarah said to Brennan after he had given her a huge hug.

'He's told me that the worst he did was to smack her,' Brennan said. 'And for what it's worth, I think he's telling the truth.'

'I really hope so. I just hate the thought that she might be scarred for life.'

Sarah's face was a mixture of relief and anxiety and Brennan noticed creases around her eyes that hadn't been there before.

'She's going to be fine,' he said. 'And so are you.'

She smiled at him and they both watched Molly jump up onto the sofa and give her grandfather a kiss. He pulled her onto his lap and tickled her, which started a giggling fit.

'That's the thing about young children, Sarah,' Brennan said, 'they live in the moment. Because of Molly's age it's likely she'll soon forget about what happened.'

It wouldn't be so easy for her parents to forget, though, Brennan thought. Their ordeal had almost certainly changed them forever – from their outlook on life to the way they would care for their daughter in the future.

He wondered if it would also change how they felt about one another.

When Brennan got home later that evening his wife was watching the news on the TV. Before he joined her on the sofa he went into the kitchen and opened the bottle of champagne that they'd been saving for a special occasion.

'I feel we ought to celebrate,' he said, handing her a half-filled glass.

She smiled and choked back a sob. 'When I heard the news I cried,' she said. 'I'd been dreading a different outcome.'

The story was getting wall-to-wall coverage on the news. Sarah and Adam were being hailed as hero parents, while Noah Carter and his mother were being vilified. An MP who was interviewed described the pair as callous monsters, and one of Emily's neighbours said the whole family should have been locked up years ago. There was footage of the house in Hayes, Sarah's flat and sound bites from a number of other people, including the Met Commissioner who was full of praise for what Sarah had done.

'Molly's mother acted without thought for her own safety,' he said. 'Thanks to her, this ghastly episode is at last over. It truly is a happy ending. But I can't claim credit for it. Molly's parents are the real heroes of the hour.'

Grace turned to him and raised her glass. 'But you're my hero, detective,' she said. 'You always have been. And we both know that this is probably your last case and that you're giving up the career you love to look after me.'

'It's no contest, Grace,' he said. 'I love you much more than I love the job.'

He clinked his glass against hers.

'So here's to the future, my darling. It's up to us to squeeze a whole lifetime into however many years we have left. And the way to do that is for us to always live in the present from now on.'

She laughed. 'I'll drink to that.'

67

Sarah

I kept Molly up until everyone except Adam had gone home. I insisted that he stay overnight in the spare room because the stab wound to his side was still giving him grief and he looked pale and weak. But there was also a part of me that wanted him to be here for our daughter's first night back.

I took Molly to bed with me and lay there stroking her hair and listening to her breathe. I still couldn't believe that our ordeal was over. My prayers had been answered and my daughter was safely back where she belonged.

I tried not to think about Noah Carter and how close he had come to killing us. Instead I focused on the positives and on how lucky we were. Carter and his vile mother would soon be going to prison for a very long time. They were no longer a threat to us and I refused to believe that even when they were eventually released we would have any cause for concern.

I didn't sleep, but I did dream about a future in which I saw my daughter going to school, getting married and having children of her own one day. It was a future that I'd feared had been taken away from me. But now, thank God, it gave me so much to look forward to.

EPILOGUE

Five weeks later
Sarah

We were in the park and Molly was feeding the ducks. It was just me, her and Adam and because it was quite early in the morning there were very few other people around.

To look at us you would never have guessed what we had been through. Molly was having the time of her life and behaving like any other sixteen-month-old child. In the weeks since I had brought her out of that house she'd been clingy and tearful, but not as traumatised as I'd expected her to be. It was as though for her it had been a bad dream that had come and gone.

But it wasn't so easy for Adam and me to put it behind us. We'd had to contend with all the questions, the publicity, the soul-searching.

I'd been given time off while I tried to decide whether to return to work or become a full-time mother to Molly. I still couldn't bring myself to leave her with anyone else yet, not even her grandparents.

Adam had told me that he had ended his relationship with

Helen because 'he didn't think it was going anywhere', and I had tried not to show that I was pleased about that.

He had also decided to put his own career on the line by confessing to Brennan that he had planted the evidence that got Bobby Knight convicted and sent down. He did it without telling me, but I'd seen it coming because the guilt had been eating away at him.

Brennan's reaction had been one of outrage and disappointment. He even came to the flat to ask me if I'd known all along that Knight had been set up. I wasn't sure he believed me when I told him that I hadn't.

Brennan had referred the matter upstairs to the Met Commissioner, who had seemed more concerned with the political fallout than the crime itself.

Adam had been hauled into his office and subjected to a bad-tempered lecture. He'd been suspended from duty and told not to speak to anyone else about it. He had also been warned that his actions were going to have serious consequences. But it was obvious that the powers-that-be were keen to avoid a storm of negative publicity. This was something I'd exploited when I made a plea on his behalf, which I felt compelled to do having found it in my heart to forgive him for what he did four years ago.

I reminded the Commissioner that there was a lot of public sympathy for Adam and that since Knight was dead there was little to be gained by charging him with a serious offence. I also told him that if it wasn't for Adam then our daughter might still be at the mercy of Knight's brother.

The feedback since then was that serious consideration was being given to a compromise deal whereby Adam would get away with a caution so long as he resigned quietly from the force. It was the outcome we were both hoping for – the least-worst scenario.

Despite what Adam had done I did not believe he deserved to go to prison. It was time to put the nightmare behind us and get on with our lives. We now had a future to look forward to – a future in which both Adam and I could see our daughter grow up.

'It's like we're a proper family again,' Adam said, as we watched Molly throw the last of the breadcrumbs into the pond. 'And it feels really good.'

I wasn't sure how to react so I didn't, but there was no denying that the dreadful experience had brought us closer together again, and that I had come to see Adam in a new light. He'd regained my trust and the more I saw of him the more I wanted to see of him.

I sensed him looking at me and guessed he wanted me to respond to what he had just said. But I kept my eyes firmly fixed on Molly and felt a rush of heat to my cheeks.

He reached out and took my hand. And I surprised myself by not snatching it away.

'Why don't we go and treat our lovely daughter to an ice cream?' he said. 'I think she deserves it.'

Before I knew it all three of us were heading back to the path. Adam continued to hold my right hand while Molly gripped my left. And I suddenly realised that Adam was right – we were like a proper family again.

ACKNOWLEDGEMENTS

This book has been a team effort in many ways, starting with members of my family who took the time to read the early drafts and made so many helpful suggestions.

And I would like to thank the team at Avon, particularly Rachel Faulkner-Willcocks, Helena Sheffield, Louis Patel, Sabah Khan and Helen Huthwaite, who have been so terrific to work with. I'm deeply grateful for their support and encouragement, and their attention to detail.

And finally, a special thank you to my dear departed Mum and Dad, who bought me a typewriter for Christmas when I was fourteen. If it hadn't been for them I might not have become an author.

Women always
uncover the truth...

The
MADAM

JAIME RAVEN

Murder, loyalty and vengeance collide in a gritty read perfect
for fans of Martina Cole and Kimberley Chambers.

Where were *you* last night?

The ALIBI

JAIME RAVEN

A perfect crime needs a perfect alibi . . .